Three's a Crowd

by

Geoffrey Allan

ISBN: 978-1-8380929-6-2

Published By: -

i2i

PUBLISHING

i2i Publishing. Manchester.

www.i2ipublishing.co.uk

To Christopher, Clare and Rebecca and
the six who've followed.

Acknowledgements

I am particularly indebted in the first instance to Sean Richards who a considerable time ago, looked over some tentative opening pages of a book I had in mind. Rightly, but helpfully, he pointed out their deficiencies. His comments ended any complacency I might have had, and they consistently echoed with me, when I later returned to the task of refining and completing my writing. I began with a review of my initial ideas, but one which, nevertheless, did not entirely sacrifice the essential storyline I'd had in mind from the outset.

Also, I have to thank former colleagues whose opinions I value and whose varying backgrounds and qualifications were certain to yield valuable insights.

I am, therefore, grateful to the poet and writer John Idris Jones, sadly, recently deceased, for many useful points of approval and criticism, perhaps, most particularly, that contrary to my opinion, the book was anything but finished. It needed an additional concluding chapter which I duly wrote.

Thanks too, are due to Sam and Elaine for reading through my efforts and for their comments.

Of course, above all, I am thankful to Lionel Ross at i2i Publishing, Mark Cripps, his senior editor and Dino Caruana, his cover designer, for their help and support in the eventual final stages of this project.

Preface

The idea for this book entered my head quite some time ago and that's where it's stayed until now, except for various preliminary scribblings.

I have set it in the nineteen-seventies, although the narrative and its context are not especially time-dependent. It would not be difficult to give it a present-day setting, but I felt this unnecessary.

The fact that the main character features in the first person, rather than the third, does not imply any considerable autobiographical element with respect to the writer, even though one element of the story, in part, reflects my own life experience. However, this is not the situation of being involved simultaneously with three women! Each of these female characters is a composite of personal characteristics and behaviours, all of which I know to have been exhibited somewhere within a greater number of other people.

Therefore, I hope that no reader might question the credibility of the individualistic attitudes and actions exhibited by one or all of them. What I hope to have done successfully, is to have brought the three women together at the same point in time. The central thrust of the story is entirely my own invention.

Geoffrey Allan. September 2020.

Chapter 1

The Wednesday-Nighters

The thought suddenly occurs to me, I'm a blue man, about to enter *The Green Man*. Actually, I'm not always blue; just recently, at work.

It's *The Green Man's* anniversary, his bicentennial in fact. Although, this is only modestly declared. You have to be observant, and willing to make the necessary calculation. '1771' is boldly chiselled into the heavy oak lintel above the entrance door.

As for me, it's not so much that I'm unobservant, more a case of being forgetful. I stupidly neglect my own considerable height. I should know about this. I buy my own clothes and have a more than vague idea of my inside-leg measurement! What's more, it's far from being my inaugural visit. So, it's hugely absurd, to thump my head into the lintel. Worse still, I quickly realise that this is a doubly unnecessary mishap. I've also forgotten that the usual drinking circle isn't happening this week. Somewhere inside me, I actually *know* that tonight, almost all the regular participants have other commitments. Immediately, I make for the Gents.

*

I'm engaged in an orgy of self-pity. I gaze forlornly into a shallow but wide mirror, which serves to emphasize, through duplication, the squalid nature of the cracked and grubby tiles adorning the other three walls. I look, in dismay, at the blue-red lump in the centre of my forehead. Its throbbing is intensifying by the second. I dab at it, yet again, with a moistened paper towel, which leaves purple remnants stuck to my skin and adds to my discomfort as I pull them clear. I start dowsing my wound in a bowlful of cold water, alternately diving like a penguin, and then shaking my head in dog-like fashion. This latter tactic is thoughtlessly dictated by my earlier profligacy with the towel supply and serves only to exaggerate the pain. By this time, the mirror belies my more normal appearance. On a better day – and I'm trying to be both flattering and honest here - it would reflect a strong, slightly square-set face, dominated by penetrating hazel eyes, vaguely freckled in summer, and topped by a shiny but tousled mass of medium-length, dark-blond hair. Sounds okay if I say it quickly enough to avoid verification. A floor-to-ceiling mirror would take in the taller horizons of broad shoulders astride a potentially athletic frame, but tonight, I have the self-pitying stoop of the injured.

Gradually, I focus on an image other than my own. It's Bill, performing at the trough, his back to the rest of the room, but immediately recognizable. Bald - I guess prematurely for someone in his early thirties - with monk-like peripheral growth shrouding his ears. He's fat and dressed as always. For purposes of identification, there's no need for him to turn around and reveal the jolly face whose crimson glow is partly the reflected glare from the massive red sweater that swoops down in folds towards his knees, and at the top, rolls over some half way up his chin. The strange thing is, that Bill's face often maintains this appearance on the odd occasion when he wears something else, like some crazy time-lapse mechanism, I had once jokingly and unconvincingly suggested. At other times, I imagine lines of wool, permeating his chest and threading through his lungs out to the rear, as if the sweater were actually alive, with head and legs appended above and below, sharing the same blood-flow as its wearer.

Suddenly, there's a Niagara-like cascade from the flush of an old cast-iron cistern hovering high above the porcelain and which, via a green-stained labyrinth of copper, partly pours out over him.

"Sod it!" He's sandal-clad and sockless.

"Tell you what. I'll swap my head for your feet."

"Heh? Oh Bernard. Bloody hell!" He looks exasperated rather than annoyed. "Your head…? Oh yes, a beauty! No deal. I'll stick with my own problem."

"I'd willingly swap!"

"Look, can you manage a drink?"

"Can I afford not to? I mean booze does have some analgesic property, doesn't it?" I'm desperate for some sort of relief.

"Search me! Mind-numbing but is that the same thing? Never was very hot on these physiological matters."

"Well, I'll give it a try."

"It'll be just you and me, Bernard, by the looks of it," he says, as if in unflattering disappointment.

"What?... oh yes, of course." An irritating realisation. For although Bill is likeable at best, tolerable at worst, he is nevertheless preferably experienced when diluted by the presence of others, and not only because he never has the money to pay his way at the bar. His head is full of empty sentiments, of vague and all-embracing good-will, and a never-ending fund of lines which hopelessly, aspire to be funny. Most Wednesdays, he's the first to dive in to break the ice of frozen conversation. Holding together the group, playing down its internal skirmishes, is invaluable practice for the greater stage outside. Bill sees himself as brimming with reconciling talent, but rarely puts it to any rigorous test. He is fashionably active, but personally timid. The causes to which he lends his skills are local in scale and uncontentious in character. With scant respect for the accuracy of the acronym, he was the founding father of C.R.O.A.K., the 'Council for the Rehabilitation of Oak and Ash Copses', a slothful body whose rural ideals have never escaped the cosy embrace of a sympathetic home region. At the world scale, however, he looks to others. An opinion often voiced, is that educated Westerners should flock overseas and lend their proven expertise to the tropical under-privileged.

"That's doubtful talk from you, Bill. You of all people!" I smile, as each week, I fail to yield to his promptings.

"What do you mean?"

"Well, persuade us all and you'll depopulate this table. That'll put your drink in jeopardy."

"Look, I'd buy my own, yours and everybody else's too for that bloody matter, if I could. It's lack of means, Bernard! Not lack of intent." He smiles back.

Bill's claim to impecunity is a just one. Although he occasionally dips his hand into the public purse, he usually baulks at seeking state assistance. This is not because he has any strongly held principles of self-reliance, but because he hates both queuing and its alternative, knowing when he will be available for a non-queuing appointment with the guardians of the public purse. Flexibility is what matters. He can't commit himself more than a day or two ahead which is something to do with personal disorganisation, not with deliberateness of lifestyle. During the summer months, he supplements his income by painting coastal scenes to sell to the local tourist influx. He works in frenzied bursts, confident in the knowledge that when necessary, he can produce three pictures a day. They are always the same three: One with the seagulls airborne; one with them nestling on the cliff face; and one with them in both poses. All three will have a ruddy hue which is further testimony to the colonizing powers of his sweater. This is worn throughout the year, Bill being seemingly insensitive to the passing of the seasons.

His monumental individuality renders him different in type to the remaining Wednesday-Nighters, though no more likely as someone I'd enthusiastically seek out for individual company, than certain other of the regulars. This perception isn't mine alone. If you ask me, this lack of consensus will either hasten the once-and-for-all dissolution of our little group or will one day effect a dramatic alteration in its component membership. The most attractive option, to me at least, would be the replacement of Clive. A bit ironic this, in that it was Clive who first set rolling this unlikely social ball.

Actually, I'd known him once before. We'd met at London University. Student lodging unit 1064, a third storey living room, serving four, with communal kitchen, two single bedrooms, one double bedroom, one bathroom, its occupants thrown together willy-nilly by the University Accommodation Bureau. This was the sort of hazardous arrangement prone to complete disintegration as soon as genuine friendships replaced those imposed by tidy officialdom. In this case, the arrangement was made hopeless from the outset by Clive's insistence that life be almost constantly accompanied by the schmaltzy emotion of Marlene Dietrich. It was a battle of record collections and being on the losing side was never to Clive's taste. A light shade wrenched from the ceiling, a tone arm pressed hard into and across the black vinyl of my choice, an angry, red-faced, and hurried exit.

Sometime later, we met again when I took up my first and, by now, my four-year-old job, in the West Country town of Steynmouth, an urban chameleon whose change from summer holiday resort to winter graveyard, I find profoundly disturbing. I have to say that I prefer the predictability of my mid-Wales hometown.

Also, I should admit that predictability is something of which I'm generally fond. When I took up permanent employment, I wanted to forecast my monthly salary cheque with computer-like accuracy, and I asked some awkward questions of the counter staff at the local tax office. To the rescue, from behind a loosely hinged wooden door, came Clive. As unimposing as always, only marginally shorter than me, but almost skeletal in build, his gaunt bespectacled face was unsmiling, still! Also, his face was still speckled with stubble which bore witness to the twice daily inefficiency of the electric razor he had inherited from his father. His work-day tie was thrust up tightly against a still-crumpled collar and cut knife-like into a still protruding and misshapen Adam's apple.

It turned out he had been unwillingly dispatched to Steynmouth. Part of the Government drive to decentralize office activity away from London. He found my enquiries silly and naive, but refreshingly challenging through being spoken at all and somehow, it all led to a drink. We met that evening at *The Green Man*, reminisced over student days that had held little in common for us, and unwisely arranged a further reunion for one week later. For reasons other than our fragile companionship, the venue established itself, and Wednesdays became the day, a ritual event whose continuation lay in the fortuitous widening of the circle of participants. This meant that from my perspective at least, Clive's sourness ceased to matter. His selfishness could be compensated for by the presence of others, well some of the others. An interesting tactic of his is to avoid volunteering the first and third rounds of the evening, those with the maximum uptake and the greatest cost to the buyer. He times his contribution carefully, ensuring that most glasses on the table are not yet ready for replenishment when he rises to his feet. This is such a liberally interpreted manoeuvre that even a semblance of moisture in a glass will deny its guardian a drink at Clive's expense. This lack of largesse is equally apparent when Clive is at work. He seems unable to distinguish between giving away personal and public money. So jealously does he guard the official coffers that I have suggested to him that the greatest mistake ever made by the Inland Revenue was to transfer him away from London. He should have stayed there, promoted to mastermind the whole miserly operation, or now be sent back, in recognition of his talent. I hope it might yet happen.

Failing Clive's exclusion from Wednesday's soirees, possibly even preferable to it, as a more personally satisfying restructuring, would be the demolition job whereby I would extricate Elizabeth and have her to myself. But this major ambition can't be furthered tonight and one-to-one with Bill isn't a good swap. I'll now have to wait to suggest France, possibly, until I return from my visit home. This is occupying my mind far more fully than Bill's gallant attempt at conversation. My fat friend, who survives via the ears of others, who depends on having a role to play, begins to feel unappreciated. No opportunity for a smiling patriarch to work his usual Wednesday magic and impossible to exercise diplomatic talents in the absence of warring factions. Instead, Bill gazes down at his sandals, suspicious that the heat of the room is acting upon wet leather in the same torturous way as did the desert sun upon the wrist and ankle bindings of those white men who fell victim to the indignation of North American Indians. Bill is a Western movie buff.

My own physical plight is no better than Bill's. At nine-thirty, after just one drink, I excuse myself and my head.

*

The streetlight is no help. The basic trouble is that I have two keys for two doors: an outer porch and then an inner door only two paces beyond. I fumble through them both. I feel my head to be physically occupying space, pulsating slowly, reminding me of its presence. I take off my woollen zip-up jacket and throw it on the sofa as a pillow. Sleep is unlikely, yet activity impossible. I choose my music accordingly. Something quiet, and with the volume set low. Dory Previn, her recent album, words partly matching my mood.

> "He lives alone
> In his great big house
> With collages on the walls
> And cathedral halls
> ....
> He calls in a voice
> That can't be heard
> To a room down a hall
> Where no woman stirred
> And he thinks of her
> And he wishes her there
> And he cannot share
> He cannot share
> Oh, he cannot share."

Nice, in a way, to live alone. I've not always been accorded the luxury of picking my own music without fear of repercussion from listeners of dissimilar taste.

*

Clive's liking for Marlene Dietrich has, perhaps, derived from an accident of birth, for which he is not personally responsible.

I've long regarded him as a misplaced person, a Germanic intrusion into a Kentish shore. I once met Monika, his German mother, a person so lightly built that I supposed a meek cross-channel breeze to have inadvertently carried her to England and into the arms of Mr Lyon, now deceased but then a robust and welcoming Man of the Weald. Clive, the product of an international liaison, a quickly fatherless childhood, an acned and friendless adolescence.

*

I prod lightly at my forehead. It's a full ten minutes before I can bring myself to switch Dory Previn from side one, to side two. I then reverse towards the sofa, as if attached by elastic and reoccupy the mould. I close my eyes, a gesture against tiredness and pain, both increasingly insistent. I eliminate the room, the Reverend and Mrs Keith's room.

Their two-bedroomed bungalow had been donated with an eye to their retirement, a tangible reward from a grateful congregationer now with his maker. It is cluttered with a lifetime of possessions with no consistency of theme, the visual mayhem against which I wisely lower my eyelids. Battered paperbacks are sandwiched between leather-bound Dostoyevsky. An old, glass-fronted, wooden bookcase in curious juxtaposition with a modern counterpart, open shelves and peeling white melamine. A large, uncomfortable, chintzy sofa flanked by sterile side-chairs in hard monotone mustard. Multi-coloured, woven woollen rugs, overlapping, with flowered carpet lurking beneath and somewhere, my invasive presence, a rented T.V. and hi-fi equipment.

The battle between resident and visiting artefacts also rages outside the lounge. In the bathroom, a dangerous electrical improvisation allows me a modern shave where only soap, water and blade had been intended. In the kitchen, my recipe books, stacked horizontally, like a corner pillar from worktop towards ceiling; my spice jars on irregular parade along the window-sill; my home-brew beer fermenting in its bloated, polythene cube at the rear of the breakfast table. Browns, yellows, reds, greens amid an overwhelming sea of indigenous blue that eagerly awaits the eventual arrival of the Reverend and his wife from the nearby Manse, to which they are unwillingly confined by expectation of the church Elders. Hexagonal, willow-pattern plates, some adorning dresser shelves, others piled clumsily in cupboard after cupboard. Blue and white striped cups, saucers, cereal bowls. Dark blue enamelled spoons and ladles hanging criss-cross from hooks screwed beneath shelves weighed down with storage pots in blue helter-skelter spirals.

My earlier - and only other - encounter with the Steynmouth accommodation market had seen me take up a bed, breakfast and evening meal arrangement with Eva Brasse, a po-faced Austrian widow whose rule-book was a collection of regulations picked up from the discarded harshness of centuries of illiberal prison regimes. Nine months of this, priced out of alternative havens by tourism, allowing no room for workaday man.

Anyway, as always in a crisis, up had stepped my mum. I don't know exactly what she wrote, but it's a pretty good guess it went something like this …

"Dear Reverend Keith,

I have obtained your name from the Free Church Yearbook. I am a practicing Christian. I write about my son Bernard, who recently took up a teaching post at Steynmouth High School. He has had great difficulty in obtaining accommodation at a price he can afford, and it is my fear that in desperation, he may resort to living somewhere unsuitable. Like all young men of independent mind, he might object to my interceding on his behalf. But I must risk this and ask whether you could help in finding him somewhere more satisfactory and at a price in keeping with his income as a new entrant to the teaching profession. Perhaps one of your congregation would welcome the opportunity to take him into his or her home,

Yours in Christ,
Mrs Elspeth Davies."

There was a kindly and unexpected response, and quickly, I said yes.

*

It just isn't sensible to stay awake any longer. Thursday, as always, will be the busiest of my working days.

I make a laboured excursion from lounge to bathroom to bedroom. A final dab at my damaged brow. A grunt-ridden removal of socks. A confused and unsatisfactory descent into sleep ... punctuated by various random and misty thoughts ... visit bank tomorrow... cancel the milk for all next week ... oh Christ, the parents' evening tomorrow! ... maybe it's time for a new ambition ... on my *own* terms ... just like that former manager of a British motor company who, unappreciated at home, had moved on to mastermind a successful concern in the Far East ... 'A CAREER IN KOREA' ... why not become a slogan writer? ... must phone Liz about the possibility of France! ...

*

The Wednesday-Nighters: Me, Bill, Clive, Liz, Amy, Warren, and Sarah.

Chapter 2

Croeso i Gymru

"Hello, Liz? ... "It's Bernard. Look I'm calling from work. Are you free for a drink tonight? ... Say about nine-thirty when I'm through with this open evening I've got on ... Sorry? ... What? ... No, no, of course you can't alter it now... Well, what if ... No, you're right, it wasn't just a drink for drink's sake ... I... I did have something to suggest ... No, it can wait till I get back from Wales ... Heh? ... No, honestly ... live on the mystery till then! Anything planned for the holiday weekend? ... What! You're both going? ... How come Amy can drag herself away from the shop? ... Oh, I see ... Look, yes, we'll leave it at that then ... Fine, okay ... See you again ... Have a good time... Yeh, you too! ... My forehead? How'd you know about that? ... Well, it's mended more or less. No long-term damage. See you when I get back. Bye Liz."

*

When Clive had arrived at work, he'd parked himself at the desk next to Liz and, with undisguised delight, had passed on the news of my bruise, acquired via Bill whom he'd met when out for an early walk. It seems she laughed, which I find surprising, but ought not to do, for she's a consistently surprising person. Not a typical tax inspector.

She is tall and unconventionally attractive. Her appeal is incongruous and curiously primeval. Her face eschews the attention of twentieth century cosmetics. Her cheekbones are so high as to frame the lower edge of her eyes and to emphasize their strange combination of a mysterious darkness and an open sparkle. Her whole face lives within a swarm of honey-coloured, loosely curled and shoulder-length hair, which at the front cascades down to, and seemingly merges with, her bold eyebrows. Her mouth, slightly large beneath a perhaps, less than straight nose, knows when to move. She smiles when others don't. She speaks when silence reigns. She demands attention without having to seek it out. On Wednesday nights, she maintains a detached presence from the rest of the group but lives off its esteem. She is scornful of its corporate frivolity, though her contributions are often the most deliberately trivial.

She fascinates me. I don't want to understand her. I enjoy her self-confidence. Others are frightened by it, but I see it as liberating my own behaviour. She seems beyond the reach of petty deception.

*

"Hello Mrs Davies."

"Mrs Parry."

"Are you expecting Bernard home for Whit week, as usual?"

"Yes, he's driving up this afternoon. It's a break for him and we're always pleased to see him!"

"And relieved too I expect. After all, he's no friends left here now to attract him back."

"You're forgetting Philip, but anyway, I'm sure he doesn't regard Harold and I as a chore."

"No, no. Of course not. There are few sons more loyal than Bernard. I'm sure you're both very proud of him. Just like Emrys and I with David. He's just been offered a junior consultancy you know, at one of Toronto's largest hospitals and our second grandchild's due next month."

"That's very good news. Send him our congratulations next time you write."

"I will do. And your turn will soon come. Bernard's certain to make his mark. He was always a hard-working boy and he's a good-looking young man. He's bound to settle down someday soon, and you'll be telling me about *your* grandchildren."

"Yes, yes. No doubt. I really must rush now, Mrs Parry. I've a lot of preparing to do."

"Roast lamb? I always remember Bernard boasting about your roast lamb. Six or seven, that's all he was. He told us how you always had it crusty around the edges. Funny, but David always wanted it like that afterwards. I had to explain to him about burning. There's nothing worse than dry lamb after all."

"Well, it's all a matter of taste. Even so, I'm not sure what time he's arriving, so it won't be a full meal before tomorrow anyway."

"Of course, yes. Something quick and simple. It'll suit him too. Bachelors and easy food go together somehow."

"I think you'll find him looking pretty well fed, Mrs Parry!"

"Yes, I'd forgotten about school meals being provided for him, of course. Even so, you must worry sometimes. I know I would if my David didn't have Susan to look after him properly."

"I don't worry, Mrs Parry. There's nothing to worry about. Things take care of themselves in the end."

As had happened with the letter to the Reverend Keith.

*

"Okay, Bernard. Five Crosses Garage you say? I'll be there in about twenty minutes. Just hang around outside."

"Cheers, Dad. See you in due course."

I return to the forecourt and look around for the fat proprietor.

"Thanks for the use of the phone."

"Mmm … you're definitely leaving the car here then?"

"Well, I can't move it."

"Listen, you can help me push the damn thing over there. Put down some sand and sawdust in all this oil. Pity you didn't think to draw into the side of the road and leave the mess there."

"Yeh, sorry, only your garage happened to coincide exactly with the first smell of burning, and a warning light. I just turned in without thinking."

"Yes!"

"Look," I'm hesitant, "will you repair it? I mean, I'll need it next weekend. It'll just be a gasket, won't it? It's all happened before."

"Gasket? Who knows? So much mess in there, I can't tell until I've had a proper look. You just call me mid-week and I'll tell you then."

"Okay, so long as it isn't going to cost too much."

"Listen. You leave it here for me to repair, or you take it away, okay?"

"Well … Umm … well, yes. You … Er … get on with it as soon as you can."

"You'll be able to pay then? I mean, you're not a face I recognize. People I know, well, that's different. You have to be careful these days. A small business like mine can't afford too many mistakes. Don't get me wrong, but none of my regulars would have driven in here with oil flowing out all over the place."

"You want me to apologize?"

"They'd have shown respect."

"Okay, I'll be more deferential if you'll just …"

"Deferential! Listen, let me tell you something. There're people round here, hill farmers mainly, don't talk half so superior, but they've a damn sight more about them. They wouldn't be quibbling about paying."

"Look, the money will be there, okay."

*

I'm hot. Hot in the head at the garage owner. Hot in the seat following four hours of man-made fibre pushing against vinyl upholstery. A hot, sweaty, victim of sunlight, exaggerated by its passage through a fly-speckled windscreen. I hang my legs loosely from the low brick-built wall which fronts the Five Crosses Garage. I tilt my body forward, straighten and then repeat this six, or seven times, in an attempt to instil some personal breeze into the heavy and sullen air.

A small group of displaced flies, moves fitfully but noisily towards me, taking one loop back for every two forwards. I wonder whether insects move in family formation. Was this mum, dad and the kids out for the weekend? They skirt my left ear, make a tentative foray into the world of decrepit automobiles behind me, and then circle around to confirm their rural allegiance, disappearing towards hedges and fields across the narrow road. Presumably shocked by the pungency of petrochemicals. Actually, do flies have a sense of smell? Yes, surely, otherwise what would draw the urban variety to gather around domestic refuse? Their noses - do they have noses as such? - lead them to the discarded remnants of human diet. Yet it must be a very unselective sense, soggy cornflakes, chicken carcasses, empty tin cans lined with clinging tomato juice, all having equal appeal. If I were a fly, I would spend some time on a preliminary survey of the neighbourhood. Searching for that household which threw out bits of pizza, surplus chilli con carne, skeletons of trout with persistent flesh stuck to the bone. Patronage has to be deserved, after all. Not like this odious garage owner. He deserves the oblivion of commercial failure, the disgrace of the bankrupt, possibly merciless physical torture. Any residual affection that I still feel for my car has been rapidly extinguished by the way in which this latest in a long line of mechanical mishaps has left me at the mercy of this man.

My anger towards DFF 542H intensifies. I turn and look at it, immobile metal stood amid its own volatile excreta. I bear it a whole battery of grudges: its plain ordinariness; the financial embarrassment of the two years it had taken me to meet its four hundred and fifty pound second hand price-tag; now on its third failure to complete the Steynmouth-Byschurch journey; and even its idiosyncratic design, whereby its rear engine had once caused me to glance backwards in needless alarm, as smoke drifted over my left shoulder. A passenger was sat behind me with a cigarette. Another car was sat in front of me. Foolishly, I had the damage repaired. A motoring enthusiast once tried to convince me that the Hillman Imp was a better buy than the Mini, its sales performance blighted only by its later arrival on the small car scene. Well, I know little or nothing about the Mini, but I know that my particular Imp is cruelly appropriate in its badge name. It delights in teasing me. Perhaps, I deserve it? I've always shown negligible interest in its inner workings. I can hardly expect reciprocal respect.

I've been humming to myself for fifteen minutes by now, an odd medley incorporating snatches of Beethoven intertwined with bits of rock, thumping along from one imaginary guitar riff to another. Then, a droning duet as the engine rumble gets nearer and nearer, gradually taking over the lead voice, rhythmically slowing down through the gears.

Harold Davies stretches across the car and opens the passenger door. "You've sorted it out about the Imp? … Here, jump in, before I turn."

I look down at my watch. I left Steynmouth Friday lunchtime, straight after morning school. "Look, it's evening opening. Pull in at *The White Hart*, eh?"

*

I peer at the alarm clock. It's ten thirty. I prop myself up against the wooden bedhead whose knurled design soon penetrates the thin pillow through to my back. At two-minute intervals, I pivot forward to ease the discomfort. For some considerable time, I hover on the brink of decision. Get up, wash and shave? Or float downstairs, have breakfast, then wash and shave? I finally opt for throwing back the curtains as a token welcome to the day. The right hand one is stiffer than the left, and the asymmetry of effort poses me considerable difficulty so early in my wakefulness. I look out to see two dogs tearing through the vegetable patch, an unfamiliar Cairn terrier harmlessly pursued by the black Labrador from next door. The chase comes to a temporary halt as the Labrador stops in mid onion-bed, raises a leg, and donates what Great Uncle Idwal had once told me was actually of benefit to this gullible crop. The Cairn looks back in disapproval at this interruption to the game and lets out a plaintive bark. My mum, her attention aroused, looks up from the washing line and dispatches both animals through the rear hedge. She has already hung out half the laundry which I'd brought back the previous day, the loving gesture of a son whose certain belief is that not to hoard dirty clothes pending his return home would be to deny Elspeth Davies a real and colourful display of maternal affection.

It is clear that she will need to spend a further minute or two outside. So, I thunder downstairs intent on a quick pick-up of the morning paper and a lightning pyjama-clad return to bed. *The Western Herald* is not on the kitchen table where expected, nor on the arm of the living room sofa where dad might have left it before setting off for work. A slight quickening of the pulse, as I hear the latch lift on the door to the rear porch and then a rapid snatch of the paper's protruding corner from its orderly but premature resting place in the brass-sided magazine rack. A kangaroo-like ascent to the bedroom, now awash with light from the Sun which has sidled past the shadowy deodar to the far-left extremity of Davies territory. For a full half-hour, I absorb, with varying dedication, the peculiar hotchpotch of world, national and parochial news which unfolds before me; the exaggerated posturing to obtain a 'Welsh angle' on things; the elevation of rugby football to a status above that accorded it by sportswriters elsewhere; the lack of those humorous undertones found beneath even the heavy Fleet Street dailies. I toss the paper to the floor, inexplicably refreshed, and accept the imminent necessity of a splash of water to the face.

The bathroom is coldly uninviting. Even on a warm May morning, it induces a shiver in the visitor. An excess of white, six-by-six tiles fringed at their top edge by a narrow line of black. A linoleum floor which by some quirk or other never aspires to body temperature, and which shocks the soles of bare feet. An array of glistening metal rails, racks and hooks which seemed constantly below zero to the touch. A blindless, curtainless window which neither keeps in bogus warmth nor keeps out genuine cold. I sing my way in, spend a forgetful second, waving an arm in a vain attempt to locate the cord to my electric razor in a socket I know isn't there, then quickly wash my stubbled face and dab my hair into place. I return to the bedroom, find the two-pin adaptor and shave, an exercise made clumsier and more difficult by the newly acquired dampness of my chin and cheeks.

Breakfast is already laid. Nothing chic here: no freshly cooled orange juice; no cereals throbbing with health-giving raisins, oats, and nuts; no choice between butter and low-cholesterol margarine; no marmalade free of artificial colouring; no aroma of filtered coffee. Cornflakes eaten, *Mother's Pride* toasted and spread with Marmite, I say yes, tea would be fine. It's delivered menacingly hot, threatening to find its own way out of a dark brown earthenware pot reputedly older than its carrier. This makes the pot difficult to date precisely, for my mum has a somewhat ageless appearance. Like most sons with their mothers, I know her birthday, but how old she is springs less readily to mind. Her hair is in that state of transition that might occur anywhere between the fortieth and sixtieth years, more fragile, patchily grey, less able to look after itself. Her face is that of 'mother' with its enduring sameness. Her manner is one that she's shown from the cradle, abrasive yet understanding, resourceful, organised, dismissive of personal silliness. She is, in fact, fifty-five, less straight and slightly heavier than ten years previously, but few people notice. Her adherence to Christ and his teachings have led her to deny the passage of time; she knows that eternity is for real. The departures from a truly heavenly posture that characterize the day-to-day behaviour of both her husband and son sometimes cause her concern. Yet, she never seeks the impossible. Beneath our temporary aberrations, she knows us to be decent.

*

I've arranged to meet Philip around eight-thirty at *The Raglan Arms*. It is now nine. Half an hour late is just about right. How he ever manages to keep a meaningful appointments diary is a mystery to me. His fellow partners in *Hughes, Jones and Meadowcroft, Solicitors*, must have a masterful contingency plan to mask Philip's tardiness, to present a facade of tidy efficiency to trusting clients.

There is some half an inch of beer left in my glass. I swallow it quickly. It's becoming increasingly difficult to maintain sovereignty over the wooden-backed corner seat. The pub is now crowded with Saturday-Nighters, many pleased to stand, but others hovering threateningly above me, lowering themselves down and inching slowly my way, along the curved bench which had once been the rear choir stall of the old Byschurch Baptist Chapel. I squeeze myself to my feet, mutter excuse-me several times, and wind my way to the exit door. I can see Philip about fifty yards away, sauntering diffidently along the opposite pavement, punctuating his progress with scarcely urgent stares into shop windows whose offerings must be peripheral to his own consumer tastes or needs; agricultural supplies, pet foods, millinery.

"Two pints of Starbright please!" I shout across the shoulders of a giant farm labourer whose belly is pressed hard against the slatted oak of the bar front. Over they come, the pride of the family owned Byschurch Brewery, golden, creamy headed, not still yet not lively, warm of taste.

"I've got yours in!" I yell to the casual Philip, wandering in, eyes vaguely searching. A raised eyebrow of recognition. A meandering path towards the welcoming brew. "Looks like we'll have to stand." I'm inwardly resentful of having lost our seat.

"Yes, well, not to worry. How are you then, Bernard? You look *remarkably* well."

"Why remarkably? We're all moving along life's path you know, you included, if you care to study the mirror."

"Heh, come on now. Nothing personal. It's all to do with parenthood really. I've got this theory that those who become parents too early on are doomed to premature senility. Hell, there are former classmates of ours, married at sixteen, with kids approaching secondary school age. Boy, they look worried. Me, married but only recently a father. You, unmarried and presumably childless. Both still in the pink."

"Okay, okay, then why *remarkably* well, if I fit in with your list of likely exceptions? I'll ignore the childless bait for the minute."

"Oh, I don't know really. No no, it's good to see you looking vibrant or whatever."

"Fine. Compliment, I think! Anyway, how's Deborah?"

"Well, she's still a very fortunate woman of course, married to me and all that. Lucky for her that teenage sortie into your arms came to nothing! No, she's very well. Actually, wants you to call around for dinner one evening before you return. Says she'd prefer to miss out on the preliminary bout of nostalgic banter tonight. Added to which, she'd never keep pace. Ready for another?"

I'm not. I've always reckoned that half of what Philip drinks is twice as much as I can reasonably manage and he's already leading the charge. "No, not yet thanks. You go ahead. We'll drink according to capacity."

Philip makes the bar with ease, the fray before him opening up in subconscious deference to his over-cultivated distinction. Greying blue-black hair, gold-framed spectacles, solidly sculpted and scented face, and a well-tailored suit decorating a frame of reassuringly medium to large build.

"That's one for me … Oh, and another for Bernard please … "

*

Byschurch is a small bossy town, the sort that insists on your approval. Ten times winner of the 'Wales in

Bloom' contest, it heralds each Spring with a mass of riverside daffodils, and enriches each summer with window boxes of geraniums slung densely across the half-timbered facades of its weathered but dignified High Street, a road curiously named in that it leads nowhere, a cul-de-sac to the livestock market. Through traffic is siphoned off half-way along its length and escorted out of town via roads whose appearance reflects a caretakership as conscientious as that in the centre. Only away from these deceptive arteries does the boring and unambitious hold sway; residential Byschurch, buildings of smoke darkened local gritstone or of monotonous heavy red brick, notable for its durability and lavatorial sheen.

I spent the first eighteen years of my life in this town, an existence neither truly urban nor truly rural. The place elicits great loyalty among its sons and daughters. I return at least twice a year. Others, like Philip, had looked at what else the world had to offer and then came back for good. An allegiance easy to account for, I think. I've long come to hold in contempt his bored adolescent bleating at 'there being nothing to do around here'. This, I now see, as a universal dissatisfaction among the young, irrespective of the differing social endowments of their hometowns. As a recent taxpayer, I see no reason why my indirect support should be summoned to help build an expensive leisure centre on every supposedly deprived street corner across the country.

My own childhood and teenage years were the normal mixture of euphoria and discontent, something that I now recognize as being divorced from milieu. Byschurch had merely loaned it its flavour: the animal aroma on market days, of fermenting hops most days. My friends and I had operated in a reassuring cocoon, feeling our existence to be not worthy of the damning scrutiny of the U.K. at large. These were our streets, our river, our overshadowing hills, on which to be as silly or as enquiring as we liked. We were ourselves; an age-group denied proper tribal rivalries through lack of numbers, a primitive unit of small-town self-sufficiency offering close but constantly shifting friendships. As for early sexual encounters, there'd been Diane Atherstone, an impressionable fourteen-year-old whose breasts were the first ever to lie beneath my hands, albeit through an optimistic and rigid bra and a thick dress in brown cotton gingham. "Come on, what did you do?" Philip had asked. "More than she did," was my disappointed reply. There was Harold George, a heavy and podgy lad who had sat inanely across my chest for a whole three hours one summer's evening, pinning me to the ground in petty revenge for some childish insult. There was Karl Wotzek, revered among his peers as the only one of us ever to have needed the ministrations of a child psychologist, following a month-long orgy, meticulously reported in the local press, which had left most of Byschurch's cats minus their tails.

Plus, there'd been Deborah Evans, now wife of Philip and soon, hostess at dinner. For a whole spring and summer, she and I had laughed, frolicked, experimented, and then parted. We had cut ourselves off from the rest, walked our own walks, flattened our own grass, explored each other's physical warmth; for each of us an early excursion into man and woman, clumsily attained, but joyous, exhilarating. In the many moments of deprivation which my bachelor self is currently experiencing in Steynmouth, my fantasising sometimes spirals uncontrollably towards the, by now, embellished memory of her smooth teenage hands, unfastening my clothes, exposing my skin to the lush Byschurch meadow grass, and then meandering slowly downwards.

*

"There's a lot more to life than fantasising, Clive!"

Lecturer three of the day had been taken ill, and I'd arrived back unexpectedly early. Nobody would join me for coffee and Clive was embarrassed to be caught gazing at the centrefold.

"If you're feeling frustrated, get out there and do something about it. Most people do."

He looked at me contemptuously, pushed the magazine aside and found a self-righteous reply.

"Unlike the majority of the student population of this university, I have interests in more worthy pursuits. Apart from which, what's it to do with you?"

"Well nothing. Look, it was just a light-hearted remark."

"From a person of light intelligence whose priorities are always south of his navel!"

This baseless vilification of me was being used by Clive to compensate for his own inability to relate to the real and breathing female form. He sought refuge in women courtesy of Kodacolor.

That evening, as I was reading, I turned and glanced inquisitively towards a staccato noise behind me.

Through the barely open door of Clive's bedroom I could see the magazine again, held out in front of its reclining reader, only this time, a long penknife was scything through its erotic gloss, with slivers of flesh-toned paper falling haphazardly onto the quilt.

*

"Detached house of character, recently renovated to the highest standard by architect owner. Exposed interior stonework and beams. Generous living accommodation on two floors. Recreational attic space. Earth-floored cellar. Extensive and well-tended grounds, with outbuildings. Offers invited."

Philip and Deborah have lived in Elm Court for eighteen months now, the material consequence of an early partnership in a prestigious solicitors' firm with a rich farming clientele. I turn into the driveway and draw dad's car to a slow and careful halt, but the deep gravel beneath its tyres announces my arrival. The front door is opened before I reach it, a sturdy, brass-knobbed mahogany barricade set centrally amid a warm brick frontage and stone-mullioned windows.

"Come in, Deborah's just putting the kids to bed."

I follow Philip the length of the pale green rectangular hall and through into the oak-fitted kitchen where I am immediately thrown a can of Younger's Tartan.

"Take a stool. I'm supposed to keep an eye on things while Deborah reads 'Mrs Nibble Moves House'."

"Well, I doubt she's moved to anything as grand as this," I say, in open hearted flattery. This is a domestic retreat of which I am illogically jealous. It's large, way beyond the needs of a single man, or for that matter a single man and any woman of the moment. It is well out of town, a poor base for the routine social excursions necessary for a sane bachelorhood. But it has style without ostentation. Owning it must be a satisfying experience.

"How's the beer?" inquires Philip. As if it could be anything other than the expected, canned certainty. As a question, it betrays the conversational difficulties that often, beset old friends long deprived of shared daily experience. For years, our paths had followed such identical courses that our talking to each other was then always spontaneous, vital. But now speech needs creation. It's no longer the reflex product of persons thinking along similar lines.

"The beer? … oh, fine."

"Well look, things seem to be under control here. Grab another and we'll go through to the lounge."

I follow obediently, only to be deserted in response to a call from upstairs. I walk to the window facing the side-garden, and gaze unappreciatively at the garland of full-bloomed perennials around the dark green, striped lawn, all bathed in a filtered orange light from the warm ball of sun, descending beyond the boundary elms. I turn slowly, and look more critically at the room, admiring it in its entirety: the coffee pastel walls delicately watering down the dark chocolate beams above; the long and shallow hearth of local slate with sympathetic iron staining, the fulsome carpet in dark beige; the deep tan chairs and sofa in buttoned hide. A thematic home for matching ornamentation; autumn tinged, limited-edition prints, copper engravings, sepia toned family photographs from yesteryear. Twenty minutes elapse while parental goodnights are whispered. A lonely but comfortable prelude to the dining room next door.

I sit in mid-table, with Philip and Deb opposite, a gathering somehow too small for its stage. The paraphernalia of mealtime seems scant and insignificant, perched tidily on felt-bottomed placemats between which are acres of polished walnut veneer. The vacant side-armed chair at table head gazes on proceedings, as if harsh condemnation of some social non-event, a convener used to greater things. The meal itself is one on which a lot of money but little time has been spent, an allocation which confirms its standing as something which for old times' sake, needs to be good, but which, set amid current priorities, need not aspire to be special.

Avocado sliced in half, filled with prawns, tossed in yoghurt. An expansive gesture this. Since there are just three of us, even I, ill-developed in mathematical skills, can speculate quietly on the fate of the superfluous segment. I imagine Philip sitting down to breakfast the following day, pouring cereal into the browned flesh of the remaining fruit, fending off the kids as they inquisitively poke marmalade smeared fingers into his organic basin.

"Oh Bernard. Before it slips my mind. You know the wooden salad bowl. The one with the four small counterparts. You got them for us from your friend in Steynmouth. The one who runs the craft shop. What was her name again?"

"Amy."

"Yes Amy, that's it. Well if she's any more to match, perhaps you could bring a further six next time you're here. The small ones that is. If you take one back with you then you can compare colour and size etc."

"Done! That doesn't sound too arduous a task." It is still in me, to please Deb. Our adolescent parting of the ways had been over something so trivial as to be beyond recollection. The rise-and-fall pendant light slung low over the tabletop, marginally off-centre, casts a half-mist across her face, denying me the full detail of her present image, and thereby rekindling more sharply focused memories by way of compensation. These prompt no aches of regret, no thoughts of thwarted ambition, no desire to take up from where time had let go. Just a preposterous wish to again envelope yesterday's girl. Even through the relative gloom there is no mistaking that today's woman looks different, now a solicitor's wife not dressed for falling laughingly off wooden country stiles, too dignified to volunteer her uncle's garden shed as a fun-filled shelter from the rain, too responsible to repeat former irresponsibility.

"Good!" She smiles back, genuinely, pure white teeth a flashing highlight within the shadowy face, then disappearing, replaced by a silhouette turned sideways towards Philip, collecting his plate. She rises, stretches forward towards me. "Shall I take yours too?" Barely a minute later, and identically posed, she lowers a large white dish whose scallop-edged lid hurls a reflective brightness towards her, emphasizing her smooth breasts, deeply exposed at centre, within a delicate black dress. Tactfully, I look up, and I catch her looking at me; large dark eyes whose strength of colour is consistent with their home, a Mediterranean face, long black hair, only lightly waved. Almost a disturbing stare, wistful, longing, accusing, even neutral. I can't decide. I have no further opportunity to do so within the movement of the evening.

Thick pieces of pork, randomly shaped, conscientiously lean, tenderised by three hot hours in the white casserole dish, kept company there by celery, still slightly crisp, mushrooms, still button-like, peppers, still highly coloured in spite of the staining brown sauce, onions, with rings still intact. Wrinkled-skinned baked potatoes. Dark green peas, perfectly round, absent of wrinkles, topped by melting butter.

"Just harking back to Deb's mention of your friend at Steynmouth, you certainly keep us in the dark about your to-ings and fro-ings down there." Philip is smiling, making light of his serious enquiry. "I mean, Amy, is she, well, a close friend? Or is there nothing worthy of reporting?"

"Why?"

"Well. We were both wondering ..."

Philip is anxious that his own married status, outside of which, he has no intention of straying, has not relegated his existence to something less exciting than that being enjoyed by me. He's asked about Amy, but really, he also wants to learn about any other women with whom I am currently unsuccessful. Deborah, he thinks, would be gratified to discover that she had avoided marrying a drifter: likeable, but still a drifter.

Oh! Then if you're *both* wondering, I must lay my heart bare." My quick mocking reply, delivered in what I'd intended as friendly jest, drowns Deborah's protest. "Steynmouth's provided me with no grand amour. Amy is, well, just a friend, as they say. Equally Elizabeth, the only other woman I know on more than either professional or nodding terms. I don't…"

Deb anxiously breaks in, not wanting to associate herself with Philip's enquiry, or at least not with its ill-concealed smugness. "No question of marriage then Bernard? Not even on the distant horizon?"

"Yes, surely, Bernard. Deb and I often wonder why you've made no move in that direction." Philip continues to lay claim to his wife's thought processes, as he often does, denying her the chance of contradiction, as if the daily trials of advocacy are such that home-life must be completely without controversy, a haven for his unchallenged ideas.

"Are you afraid I'm batting for the other side or something?" My smile again fails to impress upon Philip the flippancy of my remark. The murky half-light is no place for words from scarcely visible lips.

"Why should I be afraid? I'm as open-minded as ever, Bernard. But don't tell me you're losing your famous tolerance."

"Tolerance of gays? … Mmm … I never had any as a knee-jerk teenager of course. Who did? I acquired some later, needless to say. Part of a liberal education and all that. I'm sure I've still got it, for those with the relevant biological programming."

"What other sort is there?" ventures Deb.

"Oh, I don't know I'm no expert, though it seems *a few* observers speculate that it's possible for some socially timid men to get drawn into the circle only to find out what no one cared to tell them before. That at the end of the day, it's literally a 'right of passage'! That's 'r i g h t', not 'r i t e', so-to-speak. Sorry, a bit coarse. There's nothing like a crazy minority viewpoint, eh! Not mine I should add."

But the embarrassment is Philip's and his alone. Deborah says nothing. Is given no time. Her husband blushes vicariously and needlessly, since the object of his protective reflex is if anything pleased to hear implicit confirmation that my knowledge of same-sex relationships continues to be based on hearsay rather than any alteration in personal inclination. At least, that's how I read it.

"Look, let's ... uhm ... leave it at that then. I think we're ready to clear away for the next course. Here, I'll give you a hand to take these to the kitchen Deb."

She gets up and follows, looking back towards me, smiling widely, and pointing her fingers at him in mock pistol fashion.

I refill my glass. A sweet-smelling rosé. I half empty it in two swallows and then add more to the brim. Across the table, Philip's earlier beer lies lifeless, only one third finished and his wine much the same. A mellowing of instinct to preserve control more effectively over the pattern of events.

I take another sip. I hold it in my mouth, twirl it round using my tongue as a slow-moving paddle and reflect on my hosts' behaviour. At the weekend, Philip, on his own, had been pleasant company. Here he is edgy, with Deborah the polite victim of his anxiety. Perhaps consciously the victim, tolerantly and thereby difficult to appraise. Her last gesture has displayed independence but exhibited only behind Philip's back. Not the devil-may-care flamboyance of her youth.

The next course, less a course, more an afterthought. Proprietary biscuits and crackers. Unadventurous cheeses. A quarter of an hour of bland nibbling.

"I should have asked you before. How are the kids?" I looked for a topic potentially prolific and hopefully uncontentious.

"John has started nursery school and Emily is beginning to walk. It's tiring but … "

"Enjoyable?"

"Yes, most of the time." An almost weary smile crosses Deborah's face, now more closely seen. The dimmer control to the pendant light has been turned up, as if choosing cheese were something that demands properly illuminated scrutiny.

"Deborah is of the opinion that I get away lightly, that because I'm here far less than she is, I merely role-play. I take on the mantle of father as an end-of-day gesture. She lives her part."

I move uncomfortably in my chair. "Well that's the nature of it, I suppose. Someone has to look after them." I feel immediately that this is the wrong thing to have said, that somehow or other it sleights Deb.

"Of course, and I don't mind it being me. They're my children. One day, they'll be more than that. But I was someone else before I was their mother and still am. I have this forgotten status."

"Deborah feels ignored, though God knows why!" Philip is, for the first time, in danger of slipping off the beam. All evening, he's looked straight ahead, placing one foot carefully in front of the other.

"Because I am ignored, Philip. Not as a mother, nor I suppose as your wife, but as me."

I'm witness for the first time to a real outpouring of resentment from the married version of her, a resentment more obviously genuine for its being stated in company. I feel engulfed by the eruption. Philip looks accusingly at me, as if it were my presence that has encouraged this embarrassing behaviour.

Deborah simmers, and in the absence of an immediate response, relaxes tenuously.

I laugh nervously, grasping for an effective let-out for all three of us. Though what I find is way below unspectacular. "This isn't a topic for group discussion! Let's perhaps adjourn for a coffee."

So, invited by their guest, the hosts abandon their cheese, lead the way, and move back towards the lounge. En route, Philip turns into the kitchen. "I'll make the coffee." His fear of Deborah making further revelations is less than his fear of being witness to me hearing it all. Yet he needn't worry. In his absence, a silent and spontaneous treaty is struck. To be seen discussing something else when he re-joins us.

"Ah, I see Deb's boring you with the latest photographs." Philip is visibly relieved. His stomach instantly feels more comfortable. He pours the coffee and announces its serving.

I look interestedly at a family album made more curious by recent conversation. I hang mental labels around necks, husband, wife, father, mother, kids. Anonymous functionaries. Fuel for disputes. Way back in an earlier compilation would be people I knew, Philip and Deborah. Later, as I drive home, I wonder to what extent my own living and breathing might have contributed to hitherto unsuspected crises between my mum and dad. If so, then it would perhaps have been Philip and Deb in reverse, with my father as the aggrieved party. Not Elspeth, assured and confident. It was Harold whose personal identity would have been at greater risk. Yet it all seems so unlikely, even allowing for filial ignorance. Life at home had always been orderly, too orderly to hide frustrations and discontent. I hold my parents in considerable affection: mum for her honesty; dad for his generosity, most especially for the constant giving of his time to an appreciative son. Only once, did he ever disappoint me. When I was nine years old, he took me to a Midlands stadium for my first taste of live football league action. Some thirty minutes or so into the game, a coarse and ill-shaven, but well-meaning spectator, anxious that I be afforded a better view, had lifted me to sit astride a nearby crush barrier. This act of charity made less impression on me than the simultaneous and playful whisker rub against my left cheek, which tingled sorely for the next quarter of an hour. My dad made no protest, and I felt cheated of the protection that it was mine to expect. But this was a momentary disillusionment and years later, I would prefer to await my eighteenth birthday and his approving company, rather than that, my initiation into the world of pubs, be achieved via some furtive and premature advance party of spotty peers. This was no small sacrifice, for I had usually been quick to accept any invitation to youthful gang adventure. Normally, the recklessness had been most vociferously promoted by Philip.

*

The same Philip who now plays out the dinner party like an emasculated conductor, afraid to offend his orchestra, demanding nothing, content merely to avoid discord. Dispensing coffee, brandy, safe reminiscences, and finally a thankful au revoir.

I start up the car engine. Philip and Deborah stand on the doorstep. As I accelerate away, he jumps sideways, avoiding the shower of gravel which spatters against her shins.

Chapter 3

Independence Day

"Look, could you hold the line a minute? Or ring back if you like. I've a customer."

"It's okay, I'll hold on. It's the school's phone bill and I could be tied up later …"

"Bernard …? Good. You're still there. Where were we?"

"You were asking me about my trip home."

"So, it was alright then?"

"Yeh. Unspectacular, but alright. Which reminds me, Amy. Remember those wooden bowls I bought off you as a belated wedding present for my friends in Byschurch? … Oh, quite a while back now… Well, Deborah wants another. Do you still stock them?"

"I doubt I've got any, I'm afraid."

"Oh well, never mind. Umm, there's one other favour by the way."

"Go ahead."

"You know those over-sized kitchen tools you've got on display in your window?"

"The comic touch!"

"Precisely. Well, could I borrow the wooden pestle?"

"Whatever for?"

"Ah, ha! No, I need it for Warren and Sarah's party. Just leave it at that eh. I mean, I'm not asking you what you're going as."

"Okay, okay. Are you going to pick it up?"

"Well, I was wondering whether you might bring it along to *The Green Man* on Wednesday night."

"Bernard, you've a bloody cheek!"

"Oh, go on. Be a sport."

"I'll hide it in my tennis bag."

*

Not that Amy needs odd and attractive window displays to bring in the customers. My opinion is that she owes her commercial success entirely to her smile. Her warm, dark green eyes, a bonus to any other woman, fight a losing battle against the happy curves of her parted lips. Only she could sell Bill's sub-standard seascapes. Yet the smile, though inviting, is innocent. Friendly, but to everyone. A defence against involvement. Similarly, her hair, dark auburn and with a fringe tending to the left, quite closely cropped. Interesting, but denying the speculative passage of any unwanted male fingers aroused by the slim flawlessness of her straight-backed body. Her beauty is somewhat academic I think whereas I find Liz's is exciting.

*

I pull a red sweatshirt over my head. Its elasticated top squeezes gently at my forehead and nose. Emblazoned across the chest is a large figure nine. I'm not sure whether such prominent identification is actually displayed by a baseball player. "Sod it!" Authenticity isn't that important. After all, I do have a cap with a large green visor. Not to mention the crucial item begged from Amy. All in all, it will do. I've accepted the invitation purely out of selfish necessity, to maintain recent momentum with Liz. Sarah and Warren have asked me along only because it's impossible not to do so. Request the presence of one Wednesday-Nighter and you request them all, me included. Yet both host and hostess aren't properly aware of how shaky their own mid-week credentials at *The Green Man* are currently. They are not the sort of people to doubt their own worth. But I'd resented their intrusion from the start. One Wednesday evening, their cooker had failed, and they'd looked in at the pub for something to eat. Warren had recognized a fellow face from the staffroom of Steynmouth High School. I'd tried to hide. But Bill had made them needlessly welcome, and at the end of the evening, had issued an even more needless invitation that they come again. I was both surprised and disappointed at the acceptance, having long supposed that nothing merely social would ever lure out Warren on a regular basis.

It was enough, I thought, to have to suffer Warren at work, without adding to the misery by having to suffer him at play. Not that play comes easily to him. Life has more important calls to answer. He's a man of openly pronounced zeal, a believer in the ability of state-provided nine to four education to do anything it sets out to do. Sympathetically administered, it can free the shackles which confines many among its pupil population. Home background, dismal I.Q. ratings, lack of sociability, even plain disinterest will all count for nought. On Monday evenings, he attends a curriculum study group, from which he gleans the jargon of the week. His latest passion is for 'distributing the life chance', a phrase which makes me feel vaguely nauseous. Me, I'm not really into do-gooding, and feel that this is sometimes why I do some good. Warren and I rarely see eye-to-eye on educational matters. He's taken upon himself the mantle of the extended professional, whose mind never strays too far from the job but whose pay per hour, I've remarked, is thereby considerably less than mine. He is an arch-exponent of overkill, an evangelist who never thinks hard on diminishing returns. By contrast, I am sort-of satisfied with my own contribution and relatively free of self-doubt. I have always found it hard to respond to the promptings of the education industry. I regard Warren, unhappy and conscience-ridden, as the unsuspecting victim of the pamphleteers, a man seeking an impossible goal. He looks the part, Woody-Allenish, but without the man's capacity to laugh at himself.

His barely tolerable presence at the pub is, if anything, made even worse by the equally boring presence of his china-doll wife, whose contributions to conversation are a feeble echo of her husband's, advocating the importance of occupation, of career. At work, she's a small, finely drawn creature, perched behind and below the massive mahogany counter of the local public library, of little greater physical significance than the date-stamp. Her delicacy is what probably attracted Warren. He collects objets d'art, and her help in finding a work on eighteenth century porcelain had been the first episode in a courtship which was to be conducted almost entirely between rows of steel shelving labelled A to Z. Though they did once visit the cinema, to see the first night's showing of a three-hour epic set in Tsarist Russia. This, however, was occasioned by Warren's anxiety not to miss some unlikely insight into a subject which then comprised the academic diet of his sixth-form history group: unlikely because in class, he waged a constant crusade against glib picture story images of the past. The following day, he had denied everything to an alert seventeen-year-old who had seen them scurrying towards the ill-lit seats at the left-hand rear of the stalls.

*

I start the three-mile walk. Sarah and Warren have chosen a house located off a bus route, and a car won't be a sensible asset after the party. It's a pleasant summer evening, tempting to many a Steynmouth resident; people walking with people, and with dogs. They turn their heads in obvious curiosity at the peak-capped man with a modest club beneath one arm, and a bottle of wine beneath the other.

"Hey mister! Don't walk so quick!" yells the spokesman for a group of four small boys, who two hundred yards back, have adopted me as their own Pied Piper.

"Look. What's up with you lot? Past your bedtime, isn't it?"

"What's your name, mister?"

"Goronwy." I hope that Welsh obscurity will disenchant them. But it merely induces laughter.

"What? Are you Japanese?"

"Do I look bloody Japanese?" I'm irritated at schoolkids intruding into my post-four 'o'clock existence.

"Don't know mister. Can't see your eyes for your cap." More laughs. "One, two, quick march, left-right!"

After twenty or so strides at the head of this procession, I spin around. "Yes, Japanese: like in your war comics."

"Don't read comics mister. Seen Japs on T.V. though."

"Well then, you'll know what they do when people annoy them. Horrible it is. Now push off."

"What's the matter, mister? We're only marching with you."

"Yeh, but I don't want you to, okay?"

"Okay." They back off slightly, finally sensing that I'm not up for games.

I revert to my original direction, and start walking on. From behind me, a safe distance now dispelling fear, the noisy one shouts "Aaah soh, Goblonwee!"

"Yeh, arse'oles," voices a hitherto more-timid accomplice. They turn and run.

I maintain a steady but unspectacular pace. Twenty minutes later, I consult my mental map and confirm to my satisfaction that I'm pressing on the right doorbell.

Sarah and Warren's new place is the end unit in one of a series of tall Victorian terraces built in mushrooming response to the arrival of the railway, at a previously sleepy fishing port. With Steynmouth's seaside status, many of these four storey 'villas', as Warren likes to call them, have subsequently degenerated into holiday accommodation, self-catering flatlets, down-market boarding houses and finally, into dilapidated nothingness, as post nineteen-fifties Britishers discovered mainland Europe. It's into this blighted zone that the likes of Sarah and Warren have brought their restorative skills. Ignoring the nearby railway station and sidings, they focussed instead on the scenic attributes of the river and on the spaciousness of the houses: semi-basements below, attic above, two further floors sandwiched in between. Small builders, roofing specialists, installers of central heating, have flitted from one satisfied customer to another, spotting their next port-of-call by the hired rubbish skip dominating the diminutive front garden or blocking the footpath outside. And so, the process of refurbishment has continued with new window frames and new polished hardwood doors as the external display. Interior comforts by mail-order *Habitat* and an unprecedented demand for chic radicalism via the local newsagent.

Warren's decided that if he really has to have a house-warming party, then one held on the fourth of July should have an American theme. He knows about such things. He's an historian.

Fancy dress preferred. Sarah had protested. "Don't be silly, Warren. People won't want to be bothered."

But they have bothered. Bothered so much, that when I enter the fray, I find myself surrounded by feather-headed Red Indians, racoon-capped pioneers, gun-toting cowboys, check-shirted lumberjacks, saloon girls in daring décolletage, bare-thighed majorettes, just as I've done, imitating the archetype. Others, lacking in imagination or perhaps more imaginative, have aped individuals. There's a sequined Liberace, a uniformed Sgt Bilko, a platinum Marilyn Monroe in white pleated dress awaiting a billowing breeze.

God, this is desperate stuff, I think. Sons of the colonial masters dressing up in subject garb for Independence Day. The air is alive with pathetically appropriate comments. "Shucks. Howdy. Say you guys." Induced by alcohol, of which I decide to get my share, I make my home run through to the kitchen, where I find Bill happily in charge of the drinks supply.

"Ah, Bernard! Nothing handed out until something handed in."

I pass over my contribution of cheap Romanian wine, and immediately begin recouping the cost with something more palatable. Grabbing a can, I toss the ring-pull towards the jumble of empties already piled high on a nearby cupboard top, and down a mouthful of brown ale.

"How's it going, Bill?"

"What, me or the party?"

"As you wish."

"We're both fleeing from reality," says Bill loudly, then laughing.

"Ask a silly question." I take my leave and push my way through to the lounge. An inebriated sheriff looks me up and down. "What are you meant to be, stranger? Haven't I seen your face on a wanted poster?"

"Don't be a dumbo," giggles Marilyn Monroe. He's Babe Ruth. Isn't that right, honey?" She puts a varnished fingernail to my chest and starts tracing the outline of the figure nine. "What does this stand for?"

I raise my eyebrows.

"Wow! It doesn't? Really? ... Hey Wyatt!" She turns to the sheriff. "Are you that big?"

*

This is a pretty indulgent and undisciplined gathering. If this alcohol-fuelled behaviour reflects the everyday exuberance of Warren and Sarah's new neighbours, then I expect my hosts might soon regret having moved to so frivolous a locality. After all, Warren's immutable seriousness is even tonight betrayed by his translation into a dark-suited Abraham Lincoln.

I look around in vain for John Wilkes Booth. Suddenly I'm poked in the kidneys. "Okay, freeze!" says the artificially gruff voice. I disobediently turn around to confront my assailant. Not one, but two. Amy and Elizabeth in large felt-brimmed hats, wide-shouldered, double-breasted suits, refugees from the gangster era.

"God. You two look decidedly butch."

"Yeh, we've decided to come out. Only we can't agree on roles," laughs Elizabeth.

"Not funny," I reply.

"Why not?" quizzes Amy, "You worried about your prospects with Liz here?"

"Too right!"

Once the pursued yields to the chase, then the worries become real: practicalities as well as dreams. It had all been unbelievably easy. No, of course she'd nothing else planned for the summer. There'd been a mention of something with Amy, but in the final analysis, the shop couldn't spare her. Where did I have in mind? Fine. She hadn't been to that part of France. As long as I understood that her acceptance wasn't unconditional, didn't embrace everything I might have had in mind. Which was okay. At least I'd acquired the opportunity to consolidate and a platform for progress.

"Ladies and gentlemen! Take your partners for the hoe-down!" A shrill piercing shriek from Sarah, the pig-tailed farm girl, an unconvincingly precocious hillbilly. Abraham Lincoln switches on the music and acts as caller. Marilyn Monroe forms an arch with her lawman friend and beneath their sweaty palms pass the obedient party goers. Liberace is arm-in-arm with a lumberjack, cowboys in happy accord with Indians, and a baseball player dragged along by a feminine Capone. Two circuits and I pull Amy aside.

"Do we have to?"

"Hey! This might be the highlight of the evening and you're opting out." Her sarcasm has to be shouted above the noise of screeching violins and loud yells. She moves up to me, leaning closer to reduce the strain on her voice, pressing against me with no hint of embarrassment. "Boy it's hot in here." She waves her arms at her hat and suit.

"Well, you can take off the headgear, if nothing else."

She puts both hands to the rim, lifts the hat vertically, and tosses it in frisbee fashion over the top of the dancers and towards a pile of similarly discarded items lying on the floor beneath the half open French windows. "Oops." She laughs as it floats out onto the lawn. Her smile is more enchanting for being part of a head now on open display. Whereas Liz's hat served merely to top her flowing golden hair, Amy's had secreted away everything above forehead and earlobes. She tosses her head in recognition of its freedom, a gesture partly superfluous, her short hair denied any movement independent of the scalp.

"You're suddenly all out of proportion," I observe

"What do you mean?"

"Well, the hat was essential. It balanced the shoulder pads. Now you're all torso."

"Charming! But if I take the jacket off too, I might as well abandon any thoughts of an alternative identity."

"Yes. But you're not the gangster type anyway."

"I'm as convincing a gangster as he is an Indian! Here, let's get a drink." We weave our way through the merrymakers, and she points a discreet finger at a fat man slumped in an armchair up against the wall. His feather has bent, his Max Factor warpaint has smudged, and his heavy belly hangs limply over his leather-skin pants. No marauding horseman this.

"How!" I shout.

"Hey, don't," protests Amy.

"How!" grunts Sitting Bull, only too happy to oblige. I've accurately sensed the corporate submission to occasion, the general courting of personal humiliation.

Yet within the concord, there's an inevitable dissident presence. A disapproving Clive, leaning lazily against the kitchen door frame, forces Amy and me to turn sideways as we squeeze our way into Bill's saloon bar.

"Excuse us. Clive isn't it? Cunning disguise."

"Funny … Bernard! You can doll yourself up in Barbarian garb if you like but count me out."

If circumstances were conducive to serious thinking, then via some sharp retrospective insight, I might recognize his remark as being plucked out of a long held anti-American bag. Instead, I yield to instant observation. "Well, I suppose it's something you've slackened your office tie. Nice one Clive."

*

The student of Russian literature, a Chekov specialist, was a cultivated Ivy Leaguer, the product of an East coast private school and Princeton. Now, following a year in Moscow, he was a diligent visitor to various London reading rooms. Often at lunchtime, he would wrest himself from his work to take up with a Montrealer friend from McGill and snatch a sandwich and coffee at a favourite university refectory. His misfortune, as it came briefly to prove, was that both the timing of this visit and the shifting pattern of emptying tables in a crowded hall had frequently forced him to sit next to Clive.

For weeks, I'd paid little or no attention to Clive's crusade against the two North Americans with their supposedly sloppy table manners, loud conversation, intellectual arrogance - all wrongly observed - and their depravity, moral shallowness, idiocy - all carefully presumed. Indeed, it was not until Clive had shown signs of channelling his paranoia into a plan of action that I showed much interest at all.

"You're going to what?"

"I'm going to confront them with their own inanity. Show them up as the roughnecks they are."

"You're serious? You mean you're actually going to hire cowboy costume and challenge them. Like some demented outlaw? When for heaven's sake?"

"Next week. I can't lay my hands on the stuff until then."

"You realise you'll make a complete bloody fool of yourself. And that they'll escape unscathed, of course."

"Not so, my dear Bernard. You shall see!"

"Not me mate. I don't want to be there when you're carted off."

But I was there, for enquiry in the meantime had identified the Canadian as someone I knew from the Maple Leaf Club. This was a student society I'd joined to avail myself of cheap transatlantic air fares. I did have certain credentials, a great uncle of sorts, somewhere in Saskatchewan.

I arrived in plenty of time, first in the lunch queue. I wanted to excuse any insult that Clive might convey, to point out that this was just a harmless joke, even perhaps one worthy of taking in good part.

"Yes. What is it, dear?" asked the counter assistant, impatient at my searching gaze which peered everywhere but at her and the food on offer.

"Sorry. What? … Oh yes, uhm … nothing much thanks. Just say a sausage roll, a glass of milk, and … uhm … an apple."

"*How do you want the sausage roll, dearie, hot or cold?*"

"*Eh? ... Oh, cold will do. It'll match the milk better.*"

"*You can have hot milk if you like!*"

"*Yeh, but not a hot apple.*"

"*Well, there's apple pie.*"

"*Look, I'll take it all cold, huh.*"

"*One sausage roll, one milk, one apple. Move along and pay at the end, dear.*" *She recognized a strange face in need of instruction as to procedure. My lunches were usually taken in the outside world, an escape to better food at sometimes, surprisingly keener prices.*

I paid at the till, and moved towards a windowsill, leaning there, biting into the apple, anxiety heightening. I reckoned to move easily from a standing position, in the hope of capturing a seat next to the intended victims. Ten minutes on, they showed and only some yards behind, was Clive.

"*Hell, he's chickened out,*" *I thought. There was no sign of the promised outrage. Clive had on his long black coat, shiny through too much dry-cleaning; thoroughly unremarkable, very much his everyday winter wear. I had a tactical re-think. If cowardice had prevailed, then my own presence might be seen as a challenge that needed meeting, might arouse some other unplanned onslaught. Yes, obviously. The need now was not to be seen. I shifted sideways, taking half-refuge behind a green gloss-painted pillar, and ate the sausage roll and drank the milk, both of which I'd left untouched as a passport to a ringside seat. I then made gingerly for the door. Reaching it, I turned to confirm the wisdom of my departure. From here, I saw the confrontation, and from too great a distance to intervene.*

Clive had followed his prey to their table, had sat opposite them, had pulled out a large Stetson from the innocuous bag which I'd presumed to carry books - if I'd thought about it at all - and had removed his overcoat to reveal a torn neckerchief, a fringed buckskin jerkin, with a less than glistening star pinned on its left side, and a wide leather gun belt hanging low from the waist. He sat down with a swagger, tapped his six-guns on the table, pointing one at each of the astonished victims.

"You, buster. Pass the salt! And you, the pepper. Real slow. And keep yer hands where I can see 'em!"

"Hey man! Have you flipped?" begged the student of Chekov.

"Is this some crazy rag stunt, or what?" inquired the man from McGill, looking uncertain, not knowing whether to react with a smile or with annoyance.

"Just cut the back-talk and do as I say! Where are you guys from anyway? Coming over here, goddam upstarts, pushing your way into our seats of learning. Come on, come on, just where do you rednecks hail from? Broken Bow College of Knowledge?"

The hushed attention of the surrounding tables, the glint of ecstatic triumph in Clive's eyes, the absence of any obvious accomplice in the make-believe, all combined to quickly convince the besmirched North Americans of their predicament.

The Ivy Leaguer stretched across the table. His left hand grabbed the neckerchief and dragged Clive towards him over scattering plates of sandwiches and spilling coffee. His right hand pressed firmly against Clive's rough shaven chin. "Look here you fucking moron! Beat it. And don't bother me or my friend again." He flung him back towards the empty chair, which toppled over in protest, leaving Clive a resentful, murmuring mass on the vinyl-tiled floor.

*

"What's it to be this time, folks?" Bill has been completely taken over by barman Bill. He's cleared a bottle-lined avenue down the centre of the table and is now despatching each order in sliding fashion towards the customer end.

"Why, that'll be a beer for me, whatever Amy wants, and something for the horse." My request would have sounded better coming from one of the many kitchen cowboys drawling their way loudly through B movie conversations.

"What's the horse gonna drink out of?" inquired Bill, volunteering a brandy glass in his left hand.

"Have you got a pitcher?" A question whose potential I failed to recognize.

"He fancies a game," said Amy sharply, laughing and taking up an exaggerated baseball stance.

"Funny … funny … " Bill feigns amusement, but suddenly loses control and is swamped by the genuine thing. He leans against the larder unit, lips widening from ear to ear, waist vibrating helplessly up and down.

"My God. Somebody should take over. The barman's disappeared up his own mirth." I help myself to a drink and then, one handed, serve Amy with the dry Martini she doesn't want.

From now on, Bill is a ruler without an Empire. Others follow my example, grabbing their chosen bottles, pouring their own drinks. Bill can make only vain attempts to heal the breach in the dyke. For every set of impertinent arms he repels, others break through and enter his lost kingdom. He has made the mistake, as I point out to him, of letting a customer dictate the ambiance.

"Sorry. I don't follow you."

"Well, look at it this way, Bill. Jack and Maureen down at *The Green Man*. They tell the jokes and expect you to laugh. They see their role as dispensing more than booze. After all, a pub isn't a supermarket liquor shelf. However, you tell them a joke, and they'll not respond beyond a polite smile. They need control. It's their premises."

"Come off it! You're having me on."

"Well maybe," I say dishonestly, for I strongly believe pub landlords to be purveyors of only token friendships. For some considerable time, Roy, at the *Cross Foxes*, Byschurch, had welcomed me with a smile, a story, and at the end of an evening, a generous half that soared to within an inch of the rim of my pint glass, after which I was banned, for life.

"But Christ Roy, it was an accident. What do you want? That I crawl nose down from door to bar in penitence?" It had been an accident. A Scottish friend, sampling Byschurch by night, had inadvertently spilled beer over Frank Evans, affluent and arrogant farmer, time-honoured patron of the *Cross Foxes*. "Look Bernard, I can't have prize customers subjected to this sort of thing. Your pal here, he might indulge in all sorts in the Gorbals, but not down here he doesn't … Well maybe, but you and Philip brought him here, and all of you have had too much, if you ask me."

"Served by you with no hesitation, Roy!"

"Your attitude's come as a shock to me, Bernard. You had your first drink here, with Harold. God knows what he'd say to this. You'd best not show your face here again. Come on now, drink up and go!"

"Oh, leave off Roy, you're joking."

"Like as hell I am."

*

"Shall we seek pastures new?"

"Yes, good idea."

Amy is happy to agree to my suggestion. We both feel, without saying so, that to stay in the kitchen will see us conscripted as allies of Bill, leading the counterattack to regain ground lost to the thirsty enemy. Besides, I have another motive, a mild curiosity as to Elizabeth's whereabouts. I've not seen her since I joined Amy on the dance floor. She isn't in the hall, nor in the kitchen. Of course, there are other rooms I've not yet visited, all part of the party, I guess. Then a sinking feeling; the fear of a lustful overspill upstairs. I quickly reassure myself. Firstly, nothing untoward would dare take place chez Sarah and Warren and secondly, Elizabeth, deliberately attractive but defiantly proud, would *never* do it with a party drunk.

*

"Do you find it hot, Bernard?"

I don't answer immediately. She removes her jacket and lowers it carefully to the floor. "Bernard! I'm talking to you."

"Oh … yes, sorry. Yes, it is hot. High summer. Lots of sweaty bodies!"

"How about some fresh air? I thought we might kill two birds with one stone and look for my hat."

"Can you remember its flight path?"

"Not really, but there can't be many like it on Sarah's back lawn."

"True. Lead on. I'll follow."

We zig-zag our way through the party goers, smile politely to cries of "hi y'all", ignore Abraham Lincoln's invitation to the next organised game, and retrace the hat's journey to the grassy outdoors.

"There it is!" I cry, amazingly triumphant at spotting the grey felt. Even in the advancing twilight, the hat stands out as an obvious intruder on a lawn meticulously manicured for the benefit of visitors, accurately striped, perfectly trimmed at the edges. "Allow me."

"No, leave it there, Bernard. We can point to it as our reason for being here."

"Now, you've lost me. What do you mean?"

"Nothing … no … uhm … look, I'm really hot. Let's sit down for a few minutes." She points to a white painted bench with wooden slats and elaborate cast iron arms and legs. "When we're caught out here together, we can excuse our presence via the hat." She laughs. Both of us know our excursion to be only what it claimed to be at the start, a flight from a disconsolate Bill and oven-like temperatures, a needed change in both social and physical atmosphere.

No one else has yet ventured outside and we walk unimpeded to the empty bench.

"This really is rather nice." Amy looks around her. "A sort of brick-walled womb. Cosy, if you can use that word for a garden."

The lawn is small and intimate, a kidney-shaped centre to a circumference of herbaceous perennials whose scent is entrapped by the eight-foot-high brickwork beyond. The wall has that eternal look, a late nineteenth century construction whose weathered pointing and mossy face suggest an even greater age. It encloses the garden on the three sides away from the house, and at the rear is broken in the centre by a green wooden door leading to a riverside walk beyond, a watery setting that has enhanced the appeal of the neighbourhood and accelerated the renovation of its housing stock.

Amy then mentions the unmentionable. "Elizabeth tells me you and she are going abroad together next month."

"Yes." I seek to belittle the issue by pretending that tactically, there's been no alternative. "Well it seemed sensible."

"Sensible?"

"Yes, well … I've got my usual six, or seven-week break, and Liz has somehow, accumulated time owing to her. Neither of us fancy holidaying alone. It's just a question of company."

"Of course. What else could it be? Two is company."

"Yes."

"Close company."

"Well who knows? Churchill and Stalin probably shared the same taxi at Yalta."

"But didn't hold hands!"

"Precisely."

Amy remains persistent, not convinced by my tenuous smile. "Are you hoping for something beyond what you already have?"

"With Liz?"

"Yes, of course, with Liz. Stop beating about the bush, Bernard. It's only a friendly enquiry."

"But an audacious one."

"This is a party, Bernard. Normal convention doesn't apply."

"Honestly, no conceit on my part, but are you jealous?"

"I don't know. I might be, but of what, I'm not sure. It's probably just not being part of it all. Nothing more."

"Look, there is nothing more, as yet. You know it, I know it. But Liz is even more suspicious. She's accepted on plainly stated terms, as I'm sure you'll guess."

"No bed games?"

"That wasn't how she put it, but yes."

"You're hoping that yours is the stronger will then."

"Amy! Let's be friends. No sour conversation, okay?"

"Hell, I am your friend, and a good one." She slides sideways along the bench towards me. As I turn my head, she places two slightly open lips on mine, leaves them there for five or six seconds, and then moves gently away. Her arms never leave her sides. It's an affectionate gesture, but a safe one.

"Mmm … that's a new experience! Pleasant, but embarrassingly unexpected."

"Don't be embarrassed. It's not like you." Her elbow digs me playfully in the ribs, signalling that it's time to blow the whistle on our chat, or at least on its recent theme. Later, in the quiet of that same night, my head on the pillow is little troubled by the event in the garden. It leaves in me no conflict of emotion. My ambitions are too strongly with Liz to be diluted by a sudden party kiss from another quarter. But I dreamingly speculate about Amy's perspective.

I get up from the bench and fetch the hat. Spinning it round on my right forefinger, I walk back towards her.

"Thanks." Her gratitude is less a consequence of its retrieval than of my transparent determination that the fun of our evening together should not be sullied by her foolish inquisition.

"I wonder how Bill's coping?" We both grin at her query. "He looked so hurt."

"I shouldn't worry. Bill could never get really hurt. He's basically insensitive."

"Bill, insensitive? But he's Steynmouth's leading altruist!"

"Yes, but not its leading bleeding heart. If the plight of the starving millions really got to him, he'd not be the jovial nit we know him to be."

"You're not suggesting he's a charlatan?"

"No, no. But he's a realist. I'm the only person he's admitted this to."

"Perhaps your sense of hopelessness has contaminated him". She laughs.

"Come off it, Amy! I can do compassion as well as the next man."

"Steady! You don't have to convince me of your personal merits. I just kissed you, remember?" She smiles again. "Come on, let's go back inside."

But as we get to our feet, the party comes outdoors to join us. It's barbecue time.

*

At least that had been the intention.

"Sarah! Sarah, what the… Sarah! Where the hell is she?"

Abraham Lincoln has lost his political cool. Or rather, has found coolness where none ought to be. In the barbecue pit, which he'd lovingly constructed out of stone and brick. It had been a rush job, embarked upon only some eight days before. He now hoped to see grey, dusty, expectant charcoal. But instead, nothing.

"Sarah!"

"Yes, what is it?" She comes skipping through onto the narrow patio between house and lawn, the projected scene of the great campfire.

"What the hell's happened to the barbecue?"

"Sorry love, what was that?"

"Don't sorry me! You were supposed to have lit it hours ago. These things take an eternity to heat up. Look at it. Just look at it!"

Sarah stops skipping, fidgets nervously, conscious of the perplexed audience.

"I … I don't recall you asking me to do it."

"Don't recall! Of course, I asked you, dammit. What am I supposed to do? Slice rolls and light fires at one and the same time."

Well intentioned interventions abound. "Don't worry, Warren … obviously a misunderstanding … happens to us all … use your kitchen cooker and pass the hot stuff out through the window … "

Flippant interventions are fewer, but more readily seized upon by an angry Warren who feels himself increasingly displayed as an inefficient host. "It's early yet. Light it up … we can all blow, like human bellows."

"Shit!" He rips off his beard and flings it into the lifeless charcoal. His next move is awaited with interest by everyone except Sarah, who tearfully retreats into the house.

"Bernard, I think I'd better go after her."

"As you wish."

Amy fights her way through the crowd. With calculated deceit, she might just convince Sarah that it's all a storm in a teacup. She finds her in the hallway, sitting on the bottom stair, brow against her knees.

Sarah's head lifts at the sound of approaching feet, and she wipes at her reddened eyes with the rear of her left hand. Her face looks even more fragile than normal, its delicate features somehow exaggerated by her own yielding behaviour.

"Blast it, Amy! I shouldn't let him do that to me." She tears off the blond, pig-tailed wig and loosens the grips in her own dark hair which falls down the short distance towards the base of her neck. "Do you have a comb?"

"Sorry, no. It's in my bag upstairs."

"Never mind." She shakes her head instead.

"Are you coming back out? It'll be harder, the longer you leave it."

"Yes of course. In a second or so. I wish he wouldn't do this sort of thing. There's no middle way with Warren. He's either suffocatingly protective or just plain boorish. On balance, I prefer suffocation to humiliation."

"Hey, cheer up. You'll be sorry to have maligned your husband, even to a friend. Or perhaps, especially to a friend. Come on, I'm sure the crisis will be over by now." She puts her arm around Sarah's shoulders and coaxes her back outdoors.

The removal of Warren's beard and of Sarah's wig proves a gestural watershed between carefree fantasy before and self-conscious uncertainty afterwards. Mock American accents subside. Voice boxes are taken over by the undistinguished sameness, typical of the educated beings Warren feels to be worthy of his company. Just occasionally, there's the conspicuous intrusion of Steynmouth patois, the West Country tones of the milkman and his like. After all, serious educationalists must associate with the people. Warren places great store on his pet working folk but keeps their numbers limited.

Amy and Sarah return to a suddenly languid occasion. A sense of defeatism fills the air. Volunteer ferrying of beef burgers and frankfurter sausage between kitchen and patio can't disguise that this is not how it had been intended. There are no cowboy songs around dying embers. None of the pioneer camaraderie that Warren had planned. Clive, whose melancholy had hitherto set him apart, is now almost one of the boys, his mood less off-centre than before.

His sullen stare is only slightly more intense than that of others around him, though theirs are the lowered lips of new-found disappointment, his, the gaze of established disgust. His integration need not, in fact, have been so belated. Given the will, he could have been a convincing participant in the earlier masquerade. Whereas other products of Twentieth Century Britain have looked ill at ease as men of the Wild Frontier, Clive's lean and threatening presence suggests a bit-part player from a Spaghetti Western. As always, his poorly shaven chin seems the product of four days in the saddle.

His skulking misery has one fortuitous spin-off. It helps rehabilitate Sarah. She looks around for Warren, largely so as to avoid him, a search ironically made more difficult by his skulking at the back of the crowd. He now needs anonymity, to weigh the balance against his conspicuous ill-temper over the unlit charcoal. But if she is to ignore Warren, and at the same time, not become a burden to Amy, she has to establish fresh contact somewhere. The assembled guests either turn away in hushed embarrassment at her return from self-imposed exile or appear as if their welcoming-back ceremony will be exaggerated and claustrophobic. She escapes this latter danger by pointing Amy back towards me and then strides deliberately across to Clive.

"Hello. Sorry not to have had the chance to talk before now. Are you enjoying yourself, by any amazing chance?"

"I think I know what you mean, Sarah, but I can't believe your tactlessness."

"To understand is to help."

"Help?"

"Yes, to cheer you up."

"You don't do that by telling someone who feels his normal self how cheerless he looks."

"But that's just it. You don't look your normal self."

"Careful! Any minute now you're going to say that I'm particularly morose tonight or something."

"Aren't you?"

"No. Not morose. Just unwilling to regress into childhood."

"Is that what you think the rest of us are up to?"

"Well, were up to, before the party spirit went the way same way as the barbecue. Not that you'll rekindle either now."

"Not the barbecue I admit, but attitudes are more easily shaped."

"Only if you're the pacesetter, especially as Warren's opted out." Clive points at him. "Look. You'd hardly think it was his party. It's going to run itself from now on. Fizzle out, leaderless."

"What makes you think that I won't rescue it?"

"Because, of the two of you, only he could ever show initiative."

"You really are disgustingly condescending."

"No. I'm just pointing out your role as victim."

"Of what?"

"Of the inevitable inequality of status within a male-female liaison."

"Don't be wordy. You mean within a marriage?"

"You don't need legal standing for the rules to apply."

"Then what do you know of it, apart from your silly preconceptions? Seems to me, you're short on experience."

"You're really upping the insults now Sarah. Like I care!"

"Look, I have to assert myself for the rest of the evening. Nobody wants to be put down twice. Anyway, why do you come along to events like this if they're so obviously to your distaste."

"Oh, I don't dislike them completely. Somebody else's food and drink are always welcome."

"Good grief Clive! You really are one of nature's disasters at times."

"Only at times?"

"Well, no one can be nasty to the last."

"And I'm no exception?"

"Well, let's say that you've never given me real cause for hating you. We've hardly the same open hostility as that displayed for example between you and Bernard."

"What makes you think that I've something against Bernard?"

"The same thing that tells me Big Ben is a clock."

"It isn't. It's a bell. So, you're wrong on both scores. Bernard arouses in me nothing other than underwhelming indifference."

"Come off it. He's your bête noir."

"Don't be silly. I'd have to feel that he was somehow treading on my toes to accord him such status."

"Well, he may not be directly. But on an aspirational level, you envy his manner."

"His manner is coarse. Hardly likely to elicit jealously."

"No, he can be coarse, but that's different. He's at least able to vary his behaviour, whereas you are increasingly, Mister Morbid, day in and day out. Look. You've no family down here. Yet, you know people, drink with them every week. Don't be so disparaging. Make a bit of effort and you could slap loneliness in the face."

"Lonely I'm not! Thank you for your concern, Sarah. Now run along and organize your little games."

"Stay as long as you like, Clive!"

*

She leaves him leaning against the frame of the French window. She feels renewed and is confidently busy for the rest of the evening. He feels no different. It is just one more confrontation to write off as having nothing to say about him.

Despite Sarah's efforts, the party never regains its earlier jollity. It struggles up out of the trough into which its irate host has consigned it, but never again does it return to the heady delights of the square dance. In fact, it becomes less a party, more a conference centre. With the declared theme now discarded, groups of delegates seek their own points of discussion including the nature of humour (as in the telling of crude and third-rate jokes), art appreciation (as in the cheap disparagement of room decor a la Sarah and Warren), and the mechanical world (as in the inevitable boyish enthusiasms of grown men for their four-wheeled delights). Dismayed by base vocabulary and talk of twin-bore exhausts, some wives and girlfriends slowly disengage themselves from their partners, further raid the vodka and vermouth, and try to manufacture their own fun. Group forays into the outer circle of the male scrum see the willing and unwilling alike, picked off. To invitingly soft sounds, the raiders drape their arms around unfamiliar necks, and sway provocatively against bodies which tomorrow's sobriety will tell them were not as alluring as those to which they are normally accustomed. Not that this will be mine or Amy's recollection, as we join unspectacularly, cheek by cheek, in what for others becomes a mass smooch. Neither of us has a regular bed mate from whom we need to escape, and, in any event, we are merely continuing our being together. This may well be a by-product of Elizabeth's unexplained disappearance, but it troubles Amy little. Nor, as the evening has worn on, has it worried me. Indeed, I've convinced myself that Amy is the better party option tonight. With Liz now an assured holiday companion, the less I have to do with her in the meantime, the more unlikely I am to irritate her and cause a last-minute change of mind.

"Have you ever thought of buying a place of your own, Bernard?" With her mouth so close to my ear, Amy's enquiry is no more than a necessary whisper.

"Not if its initiation ceremony were to ape this one!"

"No seriously."

"Seriously then, no. You need at least a medium-term plan to contemplate something like that, and I really do feel that I've outlasted my job here already."

"In what way?"

"Well, the conventional wisdom is that a first teaching post should be a short-lived one."

"You're looking for promotion?"

"I don't know. That might mean subscribing to Warren's philosophies. Making the right noises. I'm not that concerned about education."

"Then why teach?"

"Umm … you've no choice in the matter of your birth, right? Well, that's how I ended up at the chalk face. I can't really ever remember deciding it was something I wanted to do. I only ever made passionate decisions about things I didn't want to do."

"Such as?"

"Oh, civil servant, lion tamer. You know the sorts of thing."

"But now you're disenchanted with the product of your non-choice!"

"Well I guess so. In fact, I have to make a conscious effort not to hate it. Any workday despair would carry through to other areas, and who the hell would knowingly enslave themselves like that? Actually, teaching's okay. In a quiet place like this, the kids don't back-bite like their big city equivalents. It's all the peripheral nonsense that gets up your nose."

"Like what?"

"Oh … pastoral overkill, impossible ambitions. Stuff to make the foolish feel inadequate."

"You think you know better then? Mightn't your viewpoint be a rather narrow one?"

"Why yes. I suppose so, but not because I think I know better. In fact, I admit to not knowing much. I'm happy for others to be the High Priests."

"You'd like to pack it in?"

"Perhaps. But for what? I could never do without a salary cheque. I've no *Easy Rider* fantasies."

"Coward."

"Hey, listen to the shopkeeper."

"Do you mind? I wish Napoleon had never opened his mouth."

"I don't know. He may have had a point."

"Really?"

"Yes. You're a parasitic breed, Amy. Buying cheap, selling dear. It's a rip-off, and you know it."

She brings up her knee. It lands off-target and catches me in mid-thigh. Not for the first time in the evening, we laugh in unison. I pull away slightly and rub my left leg.

"Oh, come, come. I'm sure I didn't hurt that much."

"Well, not as much as you'd hoped, that's for certain."

We laugh again and with no signals of intent, make a combined move to the kitchen. This has become a well-worn track, though by now, the pot of gold at the end is decidedly tarnished. All that is left is flat beer at the bottom of opened cans, and one or two cloudy, home-made wines of which people have wisely steered clear.

"Bernard, I suddenly don't feel thirsty."

"Lemonade?"

"Okay, yes, if there is any."

"Here's some. About as effervescent as tap water."

"Aw, leave it then. What happened to Bill, by the way?"

"Good point. Haven't seen him since he switched roles from barman to short-order cook."

"Good thing he did too. Warren was more than upset at the thought of electricity rather than charcoal. The goodies would have stayed raw but for our Bill."

"Yes, but where is he now? There must be some man trap here, floorboards that suddenly open. The same ones that swallowed up Liz, wherever she got to."

"You've missed her then?" Amy's question hints at her own lack of curiosity about Elizabeth.

"Amy! I'll bring my knee up next."

"Hey. That would be unbecoming for a gentleman and painful for me."

"Always assuming my aim is better than yours."

"Mmm … change of subject, please. What do we do now? No booze left, time pressing on, few people either of us know."

"You're right. It could be time to call it a day. I suppose we'd best thank our hosts."

We find Warren and Sarah back out on the patio. It's an unfortunate intrusion into their first words since the barbecue incident. I quietly pull Amy away, and we hover just inside the door, looking for a facial expression that would suggest it is safe to approach. Eventually, the heart-to-heart subsides into what seems more harmless conversation, and I move purposefully forward.

"Umm … excuse us, but Amy and I are just leaving. Thanks a lot. It's been a pleasant evening."

"You have to go so soon?" Sarah seems less than ready to have Warren all to herself.

"Well, I don't think we're the first to leave."

"No, no, you're not. Well, you know when you have to go, of course."

"Yeh. We've all got to make a move sometime. It's not that we've not enjoyed ourselves. By the way, while we're on the subject, did either of you see Bill or Liz leave?"

"No. Did you, Warren?"

"I'm just surprised that we had anybody stay on after the shambles mid-way through."

This time, the taunts have little effect. "It proved to be a shambles in your eyes only, dear. There's hardly an ounce of food left in the place. I don't suppose people minded too much how or where it was cooked."

"True. Very true. But once again, what happened to the stand-in cook?" I'm still interested in Bill's whereabouts.

Warren has the answer. "He took the few remaining bread rolls down to the river. Said he was going to feed the ducks. Wondered if I had any objection."

Amy and I again laugh together. "Perhaps, if we walk back that way, Amy, we might stumble across him."

Warren has more information. "Maybe him, but not Liz. She left … oh hours ago. Seems like Clive was pestering her. Even Liz is too polite to fight in someone else's house."

Neither of us say anything in reply. We neglect to point out that Warren has been Public Squabbler Number One. More so, we are both seized by the reflex guilt of having abandoned Liz to Clive in a setting where her rebuffs would need to be diplomatically repressed. Can't have been much fun for her.

"Okay. Have a pleasant walk back. Warren and I are glad you could come."

"Yes, and as Bernard said, we have enjoyed it. You can be confident of that Sarah." Amy looks coolly at Warren, wanting him to know that he ought not to exact reparations from his wife over the next few days.

"See you both soon. You on Monday, Warren." I place my hand on Amy's left shoulder, that next to me and we go back inside to collect our belongings. I twirl the gangster hat on the baseball bat. The party is in its death-throes. The joke-sack has been emptied; political arguments and ideological sparring are on the verge of ugly confrontation; adulterous couples are groping away on sofa and armchairs; and a wide-eyed, drunken Geronimo is sitting cross-legged on the hearth, plucking feathers out of his drooping headgear.

Amy and I walk back out into the garden. The midnight air is chilly, promising a heavy morning dew. Amy drapes her now creased jacket loosely over her shoulders. It slips off to the right. I replace it, and leaving my arm there pull her tightly to my side. She puts her left arm around my waist, and we make for the door in the wall. It's too narrow for us to pass through head on. We swivel around, keeping hold of each other, and sidle through like clumsy conjoined crabs. The salty smell of the river, now at high tide, cleans out our nostrils, dispelling smoke and sweat.

"God, what an evening," sighs Amy.

"And what a coup de grace,".

"Sorry? what do you mean?"

"Didn't you see it?

"See what?"

"As we left."

"No. What?"

"Marilyn Monroe throwing up over Sgt Bilko."

Chapter 4

A French Road Trip

Whatever else it might be, it will be different from any holiday I've ever known before. Whatever the outcome is, it is something which will affect me greatly after we return. All previous holidays have finished on the day they've ended, they've been simply enjoyable breaks, but never significant nor portentous. This one has Liz along. The two of us in a hire car, hurrying down to Burgundy, staying there, moving on to Lyon and then to the splendour of Haute Savoie.

And offering plenty of time 'en route' for holiday reminiscences from the era before 'us'.

*

"Are you ready yet Bernard? Your father's been sitting in the car for ten minutes."

"I can't find my fishing net, Mum. The one we bought last year."

"Oh c'mon. Never mind. We can get another." Mrs Davies ushered the excited eight-year-old me out to the shining black Austin, freshly valeted for the holiday fortnight.

"Hurry him along, Elspeth. We were meant to meet up with Dick and Sybil half an hour ago."

It was a short trip of some one and a half hours to the Cardigan Bay Caravan Camp. This was the fifth such excursion. An annual pilgrimage and the third in the company of my Uncle Dick and Aunt Sybil. There was no debate as to possible alternatives. 'Seaside Wanderer' was an inappropriately named static caravan owned by a Byschurch butcher who made only a token charge for its hire, a generous recompense for the mile lengths of sausage sold each year to the Davies household.

"Hurry along to the shop, Bernard. You know, over by the camp entrance. Just a pint of milk, that's all. Your father will be back with the fish and chips any second, and I've still to unpack the suitcases."

"But Mum, I want to see the sea."

"There'll be plenty of time for that later."

The truth was that there was great difficulty in not seeing the sea. The dining end of 'Seaside Wanderer' gazed out through a large seagull-soiled window to a shingle beach only some ten yards distant. At mealtimes, the shaking of the salt cellar was almost superfluous. At night, with the table folded away, frustrated sleepers would find their slumber interrupted by noisy spray against the glass pane, a hazard made more likely in our case by the fact the Byschurch butcher's generosity was limited to the period of low-season tariffs with its blustery westerly winds.

"Why can't we come in August, Mum? I always miss the school sports, first week in May."

"You hardly need worry about sports, Bernard. Your father and Uncle Dick will keep you occupied."

And they did. Beach cricket made farcical by the improvised wicket with its pebble-induced bounces; chasing after kite strings amid the uncertain footing of sand dunes; long evening walks along concrete topped sea defences.

"Bernard! I do wish you'd stop singing that blessed song."

"Why, Dad?"

"Well, it's bad enough having to listen to it every morning as it is."

My rendition of 'Last Train to San Fernando' was not helped by the circumstances of my learning it, at times, an indistinguishable noise blurted out each breakfast time over the wind-rocked public address system.

*

"Why that song all the time?"

"Search me, Liz. I shudder to think it was by popular request."

"Did you enjoy it there, year after year?"

"Yes. Seems strange now, but yes."

"Mmm ... it's adults who are difficult to please."

"True. Let's just hope we end up feeling all this has been worthwhile."

"Well, we've no cause for regret, yet." Liz's remark sounds uncomfortably pessimistic. It would be surprising if there were already any reason for disquiet. It is ten o'clock in the morning on day one, and we are only two hours out of Calais. My reminiscences have been but part of happy road-going conversation. Like most touring British motorists, we've made deliberate haste through the distant horizons of northern France, whose multicoloured open fields are unencumbered by the dispersed farmsteads and the more confining hedgerows of the English landscape. At each small town, we obey the Toutes Directions sign, at each linear roadside village, we laugh at their umpteenth siting of Monsieur Meuble and his dilapidated outline, a flaking advertisement adorning a prominent wall or gable end.

It's a hot blistering day, the sort which a Frenchman would regard as exceptional, but a Summer visitor, as typical. All four windows of the car are fully wound down, and the breezy turbulence inside flings our hair wildly back from our foreheads, and then suddenly forwards, jeopardizing our view ahead. Every now and then, I take my hands from the hot plastic ring of the steering wheel and wipe my sticky palms against the red cotton of my shirt. That apart, the heat seems to be sinking into my legs, necessarily immobile, poised for peddle pushing. Whereas Liz, sat in the passenger seat, moves about more freely in her quest for comfort. Some distance into the journey, she hoists up her yellow skirt, sets the soles of her bare feet on the parcel shelf, and displays a pair of sun-tanned thighs that figure strongly in my hopes for the holiday.

We've decided in advance on a masochistic run for Reims with no stop until we get a glimpse of its cathedral. We park close to the city centre and flop exhaustedly into its streets. Our ears are assailed by noises which are unremarkably urban - traffic, pavement conversations - but which are different in detail of expression, prominent sounding of car horns, foreign vocabulary. Liz tosses a large brown leather bag over her shoulder and takes off, leaving me to check on whether there is some expectation that I display a ticket on the car windscreen, or that I obtain evidence of the time of parking, or that I insert a coin somewhere. With no obvious direction as to procedure, I move away and catch up with her in mid-alley between road and cathedral square, where after a cursory and preliminary glance at

Ecclesiastica, we make quickly for the only cafe with immediately visible sitting room. Despite the hours of bent legs in the car, we still fight shy of standing to drink. I order a coffee and lemonade for myself, quietly pondering in which order to consume them. Liz, sweating less or admitting it less, makes do with coffee alone. She sits opposite me across a wobbly, round metal table. The yellow and orange of the canvas sunshade gives her an Oriental colour cast, converting her sleeveless white top into a pastel offshoot of her skirt. Her face suddenly seems discordant with her loose and long Scandinavian curls. Over my left shoulder, she can see the cathedral facade, alive with Medieval intricacy aside and above its deep and elaborately carved centre arch. Each remark of appreciation from her lips causes me an annoying need to twist around in confirmation. We sit here for twenty minutes, postponing the tiring look inside the cathedral, an inspection motivated partly by curiosity, but mainly by the thought that it is an inescapable duty. Not to stand beneath its towering nave would be indefensible for someone who has drunk coffee on the edge of its precinct. We get up and spend half an hour partaking of our cultural diet before slowly sauntering back towards the car.

"Care for a peach?" invites Liz, delving into her cavernous shoulder sack.

"Mmm … yes. When did you get them?"

"Oh, while you were faffing around in the car park."

"Ah, resourceful to the end! Thanks."

I bite into the furry skin. It sends a mild shudder down my back. Peaches belong to a category of food which, though basically attractive, have certain flaws of effect, like rhubarb and its distasteful lacquering of one's teeth. With rhubarb, it is the after effect, with a peach, the effect before consumption. Its eating is on this occasion, a self-righteous and almost penitential exercise, the fresh juicy interior ultimately cleansing out the indulgence of caffeine and sugary fizz.

*

It is twilight when we reach St. Aillant. We've spent all day on the E2 route, at a more leisurely pace after Reims. Just north of Chaumont, we ate at a small roadside brasserie, after which we ascended the plateau towards the hilltop town of Langres, a divide not only topographic between the Paris Basin and the Saône valley, but also spiritually, between Europe North West and Europe South. From Dijon on, the river is the route to a more truly foreign experience. Through Beaune and on to Chagny, the sun sets slowly over the tiered vineyards of the Cote de Nuits and the Cote d'Or, a sight so enthralling in its empathy between man and nature that we two travel-weary Britons feel our first day to be at a beginning rather than at an end. At Chagny, we'd left the main riverside artery of the Route Nationale and followed a minor road, hugging the foot of the limestone escarpment of the Cote Chalonnaise, here more discontinuously clothed with the vine, as if in open admission of its lesser repute in the gastronomic world outside. At the small village of Givry, our underlying but suppressed weariness sees us confused by the simplest of one-way systems, delaying by five annoying minutes, our imminent arrival at our final destination.

Ferrand has drawn a rough sketch-map of St. Aillant, now tightly creased, which Liz opens across her lap. "There's a disused priory or something ahead. Turn right there and follow the road around. Past the petrol station."

"Fine. Yes. It's actually near where he used to live last time I was here. Shouldn't be too difficult to find. Should recognize it from the photograph anyway."

*

I have been out of bed for an hour or so. I fold back the wooden shutters, look out on a lawn scarcely deserving of the name - parched, patchily brown, vainly striving for the greenery of wetter climates - and set about preparing myself breakfast. Ferrand and Annette have left us food enough for our short three day stay, with advice on perishables, and where to buy milk close by should we need it. A suitably instructed neighbour calls around with bread, a large crusty loaf, almost perfectly round, with white interior, spongy yet featherlike. Difficult upon which to spread anything even remotely viscous. I cover three slices with an unidentifiable fruit preserve, taking bites alternately with a soft, crumbly, and sharp-tasting cheese. I drink two bowls of filtered coffee, leaving the same amount on the stove for Liz; and read once again, the welcoming message.

"Dear Bernard.

Hope you had a good journey and that everything goes smoothly. Sorry not to be there to greet you but see you sometime, no doubt. Stay again on your return journey, if you wish. Leave key with M. Frobert as arranged,

Best wishes,

F., A., and children."

An odd postcard, a sun-kissed beach on the front, a bell- towered Yugoslav stamp on the rear. But no confession to 'having a good time'. Perhaps because Ferrand always appears to be having a serious time. He is the only conscientious foreign language assistant that Steynmouth High School has ever had, at least during my short time there and from what I've heard of previous postholders. He put in more diligent effort than all those who either preceded or followed him, and he worried about his classroom performance to a level beyond that warranted by his measly recompense. He conveys the impression of being consumed by meticulous perfectionism. Some of his predecessors and successors by contrast, had been blatantly imperfect. Marguerite, who absconded six weeks into her stay to share a sleeping bag and tent with the wayward son of a Dartmoor sheep farmer. Anne, whose vodka-fuelled lesbianism enraged parents and the wider community alike. Richard, whose indifference to his own body odour endeared him to no-one. Finally, Tazik, a lecherous Tunisian, whose obsession with sexual conquest left no place for subtlety in its retelling. "Tell me Bernard," he once arrogantly enquired, "have you ever, like me, made love in the Mediterranean with the waves gently lapping against your arse?" I always remember this enquiry, its confident beauty spoiled by the stupidity of its closing word.

In the final analysis, the only possible 'Euro-friendship' that I could have struck was that with Ferrand, brought about by and cemented through, our joint passion for football, a weakness which in Ferrand's case, had its origins in a past year's attachment to Liverpool University, and his being swallowed up in the football mayhem of that city. It was this enthusiasm that threw him my way. His sober concern for his teaching function might otherwise have consigned him to the shelter of Warren's wing, but the luminary of Steynmouth had no patience with anyone who showed even a minor interest in ball games, or, of course, in games of any sort. For Warren. life is never for living, but always for doing. He steers well clear of fun. Backslide and he ends up with fiascos of the barbecue type.

*

St Aillant has, what in cliché ridden terms, the tourist brochure might describe as an 'attractive, timeless air'. Warm, stone-built houses with broken-slatted and rusty-hinged wooden shutters; small window-balconies fronted with unambitious wrought iron railings, a modest central fountain decorated each day with fresh flowers; and a rustic silence contributed to by the diversion of through traffic via an almost coincidental by-pass, a girdling circle of lanes recently widened. Its long main street, winding vaguely North-South, lies snugly between the tended vineyards of the hillslopes to the west and the more spacious prospects towards the Saône to the east. Ferrand's new house, white with red-tiled roof, is one of the few modern ones to be seen in the village. It occupies the former orchard of a large dairy farm in a slightly elevated position overlooking the post office square, where also, is the incongruously titled 'Cafe Americain', a rendezvous entirely French and sometimes, as in its stocks of wine, solely Burgundian. M. Thibault, the proprietor, has a memory of at least moderate note, warmly recognizing me when at around two o'clock in the afternoon, I call in to say hello.

"It must be six years, Bernard?"

"No, no. It's only two."

We settle for three.

"And this is your wife, huh?"

M. Thibault smiles at Liz. He is not alone in his admiration. Her entry has turned other male heads, notably those gathered around a corner table whose safety seems threatened by a Heath Robinson styled coffee apparatus, precariously balanced on the edge of the neighbouring bar, but the possibility of whose collapse, the middle-aged regulars obviously regard as remote. She looks confidently ahead, unembarrassed by the essential familiarity of the experience. Tall, almost Nordic, aloof, challenging. She has got out of bed just before lunch, her first meal of the day, my second; saucisson, andouille, cheeses, and green salad; bread, fruit; and coffee left over from breakfast.

"No monsieur. I'm an old friend of Bernard's."

"Ah ... you make vacation together!"

"Precisely."

"Yes. Precisely, Mademoiselle."

Somehow, she feels that the word precisely is being used to varying effect, for her, the setting of a barricade between herself and me, his, a version based on male innuendo. This conflict of understanding accurately pinpoints the difficulties inherent in the whole adventure, She and I have for long operated magnificently as friends, conversationalists and drinking companions, but translate this to foreign soil and it presupposes certain consequences. M. Thibault had made his assumptions, and no doubt, they accord with my ambitions, which I still have, despite the pre-holiday pact. Here's how I see it: she feels that even if she decides at some stage to make love to me, which is how I guess she looks at it, then the holiday will have taken away her independence of choice. The occasion will have dictated the event. It doesn't matter at all that she knows me to have no rival, real or imagined, for her attention, but rather that her decision as to when and where might be pre-empted by nothing other than the inhalation of French air. Not to mention the possible impact upon the tourist component of the holiday, disappointment or anti-climax souring subsequent sightseeing, or alternately delight and obsession (which for that matter, could be just as well experienced in Steynmouth) relegating a once only foreign visit to nothing other than a backdrop to a physical interlude. The 'treaty' - daytime friendship, night-time nothing - she sees to be poorly constructed, perhaps untenable, but very necessary. With one night behind us, its basis remains unchallenged.

And so, it remains throughout the three days at St. Aillant, throughout the hillside walks, the picnics washed down with bottles of Aligoté, the evenings sat talking on the terrace off the lounge.

*

The misfortune of Lyon is that it lacks glamour, the charisma of Paris, the Mediterranean frontage of Nice. City number two tends to get avoided. Tourists take in the Capital, then move on to smaller provincial centres or to the beauty of the countryside. London, Oxford, the Cotswolds but not, definitely not, Birmingham. Lyon might thus feel unjustly maligned. For whereas the second city of England is built amid the anonymity of a plain, in small part, despoiled by a history of mining and metalworking, its French 'equivalent' has a physical setting which lends something of value to its occupation by man. Perched high to the West is the Basilica, whose hilltop site is most interestedly reached by funicular railway and from where we are afforded a panorama of the city, stretching to the horizon over one-hundred degrees or more of exposed view. Immediately beneath, is the Old City, a labyrinth of narrow streets set back from the riverside promenade along the Saône, an enclave of cobbled alleys, small eating houses, peeling paint, smelling drains and renovated craft shops. Between this first river and the Rhone beyond is the city core, of wider, straighter streets, large retail premises, fountained and statued squares. Looked at from above, the two rivers run like green threads, the foliage of their waterside avenues cutting two sharp lines through the beige and yellowy stone of the mass of building. At even greater distance, receding into the indistinct - and therefore, rarely ventured into by the visitor appraising the city from the Basilica - the eastern fringe sprawls outwards in a grand manner whose very size denies it the intimacy and appeal of the two more adjacent zones.

"Mmm … it's big." Elizabeth gives no hint as to whether this is a statement of observed fact, a murmur of appreciation, or a grunt of disapproval. It quickly shows itself to be an expression of bewilderment - 'where do we go from here?' It's unusual for her to present me with the responsibility of decision making. Even at St. Aillant, she stood firm on our agreed wants rather than yield to my recommendations. But here, she bows without struggle to what she supposes my talent might be, the trained eye of a professional geographer. To Liz, the confident certainty of the city map, with its recognition of distinct points of interest, seems foolhardy up at this height, as if it were impossible to reduce a settlement of such size to a piece of stiffened paper, and then to arrogantly differentiate its various parts. Me though, I should have the expertise to reconcile ground and map. Let him get on with it!

" … though we must make sure we get to the Museum. Apparently, it closes at three 'o'clock on Saturdays."

"Okay. Well look, while we're here, we'll take a glimpse inside this thing." I nod my head towards the

Basilica behind us. "And then, what I suggest, is that we take an early lunch in the Old City. If we forgo the railway and walk down, we apparently pass a Roman amphitheatre."

"Do you want to see it?"

"I presumed you might."

"Well how well preserved is it?"

"Blowed if I know. Does it matter?"

"Yes. In a way. I don't seem to have the powers of imagination necessary to reconstruct original forms, you know, from lifeless ruins. It's almost a waste of time gazing on. Now a fully-fledged working amphitheatre or coliseum, that would be different."

"Working?"

"Yes."

"You'd like to see men being eaten by lions?"

"Grr … " She smiles a wide smile, tossing back her golden framed head, a lioness with the mistake of a mane. She leans forward and steers me towards the Basilica. Afterwards, we take the train down!

It becomes rapidly obvious to both of us that were it not for its high vantage point, the Basilica would attract few visitors. A nineteenth century afterthought, not held in local affection, its heavily marbled interior dismays the onlooker. If religion were about light, then here is its reminder of the alternative facing the sinner. A sombre, chilling darkness with no human warmth.

"Look, Bernard, I just don't follow that. Chilling? I always thought Hell had exceptional warmth. Too much of it for comfort, let's say!"

"Oh, who could believe that? How could it possibly be hellish to be instantly consumed by flames? Now being locked away for good in somewhere like this, that would be different."

"I have a feeling our conversation is inappropriate."

"Irreverent?"

"Maybe."

"You worried?"

"Ought I to be?"

"Well ... doubt it." I pause and look around reproachfully. "It's funny isn't it how one religion can inspire such different architecture."

"This and Reims?"

"I was thinking more of this and Byschurch Presbyterian Chapel!"

"Byschurch?"

"Yes. Don't look so surprised. I've a chapel-going background! And I compare everything with my former spiritual nest."

"I bet!"

We do the decent thing, shift the frivolity of our conversation outdoors and move down to the Old City.

*

"Bernard, will you lead prayers before next week's meeting?" The Reverend Gwilym Evans-Hughes, Minister at Byschurch for some ten years, enthusiastic, boyishly middle-aged, craggily handsome, energetically Christian, and unfortunately, likeable. Difficult to say 'no' to.

"I'm not sure I'll be able to be here next week, Mr Hughes."

"What? You Bernard! You've not missed a Wednesday night session for a long time."

"It's just that… "

"It's just that you'd prefer not to lead prayers. Of course! Look, I don't mind what you pray about. Just get in some fleeting reference to this session's theme."

"Theme?"

"We do have one, somewhere among the music and table-tennis."

"Yes. We're bound to, I suppose."

"Bound to? Only by the proper dictate of our conscience, Bernard. The Somali Irrigation Project. S.I.P.! I'll charitably assume your forgetfulness to be a leg-pull. Fit in a mention somewhere between 'Dear God' and 'Amen'."

"I'll see what I can manage."

"You'll have to, if you want to carry on using the Youth Club as a hunting ground!"

Blackmail from a man against whom it's impossible to take real offence. Realism from a man who admits the futility of placing Christ in direct competition with the more fundamental yearnings of adolescence. It is, after all, a question of getting bodies onto pews. One carrot for sixteen-year-olds, others for the young marrieds, the old marrieds, the aged bachelors and spinsters, widows, and widowers. The Reverend Evans-Hughes has a week-night gathering to suit all in turn, five separate opportunities to say 'Goodnight. See you Sunday.' Some members of the Community, however, appreciating the short step from involvement to entrapment, decline the invitation. Not every Byschurch teenager is willing to seek secular enjoyment via a church-going obligation, unlike me, whose *upbringing has been so fully 'in the Faith' that mere venue has ceased to have much significance. A worshipful life is so much part of the image that Elspeth Davies presents to her husband and son that it has become thoroughly unremarkable. Every day to me, is no more mystical than the soggy cornflakes which confront me each morning, milk helpfully added long before my arrival at table. Mealtime grace, cake making for the women's meeting, flowers for this, fund raising for that. Nothing in religion to fire a boy's imagination. No revelation beyond common duty. Creche to Sunday School to Youth Club, a growing up, not to be questioned in mother's presence.*

"To Bernard. On his departure to university. From the Minister and Congregation of Byschurch Presbyterian Church of Wales."

"I ... umm ... thank you, Mr Hughes." I fumble at the New English Bible, its green, red and white dust jacket hanging loosely off the binding, a victim of my embarrassed acceptance of a genuine gift. These people see me as a loss to themselves but are confident of my ambassadorship outside. I will never deliberately encounter them again, nor their like in London or Steynmouth.

"Dear God ..."

I peer straight ahead, glancing down only intermittently at the sketchy prayer outline. Ten rows of bowed heads, the Reverend Evans-Hughes in the centre. Here and there, renegade opening of eyes. Deborah looks cheekily at me, then mockingly pious.

" ... we are here, as every Wednesday, to honour you and to acknowledge your sometimes-bountiful generosity in our lives... "

'Sometimes?' Deborah clasps her hands to her mouth, suppressing a chuckle. She's fearful that I might stray hugely off message or say something even more

clumsily irreligious in its phrasing. She shakes her head violently from side to side, mild amusement giving way to alarm as to where I might be going next. Signalling that enough is enough for now.

I sense her disquiet. I look down at my paper and the key words that I had hastily scribbled beforehand. I'm conscious that my flippancy will earn me a reprimand from someone I am anxious not to offend. But the skeletal nature of my prepared notes donates them an instant flexibility, and I immediately adopt a more courteous and exaggeratedly respectful delivery, banishing Deborah's blushing which has not been on her own behalf, but needlessly for Mr Evans-Hughes, who's heard even poorer invocations from other youth club members in the past.

" ... a generosity that reached a climax in the gift of your Son, for whose death, we are eternally grateful, and without whose sacrifice, our own lives would be immeasurably poorer and without hope of fulfilment ... we thus take delight in meeting here together, hoping that any message you have for us, will strike a responsive chord ... Let us react to your promptings with proper responsibility, compromising our less-worthy instincts, wary of our inexperience, bowing to your guidance and greater wisdom. Amen."

It's then that I see Mr Evans-Hughes's raised eyebrows. I've been so preoccupied with appeasing Deborah that I've neglected to mention something so important that it hasn't warranted the precaution of a written jog to memory. Quickly, before people get to their feet, I blurt it out.

"P.S. We're doing our bit for the Somali Irrigation Project. Keep doing your bit too ... Amen."

*

"So, are you going to send him a postcard?"

"Who?"

"The Reverend Hughes-Jones, Evans-Davies, Parry-Thomas or whatever his name is. You could tell him you've been in the Basilica."

"Ooo … ooh. He's a chapel man. Wouldn't like that!"

"Okay then, but what about postcards back to Steynmouth? We could be joint signatories and cut the cost." Liz asks the question without looking up from the plate, paying full visual attention to the difficulty of cutting neatly across the crumbly goat's cheese that she's strangely ordered as a starter.

"Well, even better, why not just send one to *The Green Man?* It can be passed over the bar when Bill and the others drop in. Problem with your cheese by the way?

"Slightly strange taste-wise. Difficult texture-wise."

"Want to send it back?"

"No! Don't want the hassle, especially when your French is as limited as mine."

"Really. I'd have thought a facial grimace would have said it all, a wave of the hand."

"Maybe, but never mind. I think I'll just give up on it, and hope that what follows will be better."

"It's agreed then. Just the one postcard."

"Yes, I suppose so. Though perhaps Clive ought to have his own."

"Clive!"

"Yes. To stop him feeling persecuted. Give him some personal recognition. It's selfish really, but I don't want to give him any grounds for having a go at me afterwards. Remember, I have to work with him. And I'm still in his bad books for what I said to him at Warren and Sarah's party."

"I thought it was him who drove you out?"

"Well yes. With Amy monopolising you, I couldn't face him latching on to a free me."

"You could have looked us out. Not like you to be shy."

"Oh, sod it. I just wasn't in the mood."

"Okay! But what was it you said to him that makes an olive branch so necessary now?"

"Oh, you're right. I'm probably overstating the case. I don't suppose he paid much regard. You know he'd been looking at some well-paid civil service job in Singapore. Reckoned he stood a good chance of getting it."

"How come?"

"Search me, but he seemed offended when I reminded him that whereas he was sent to Steynmouth, he would have to compete for top money in the Far East."

"Aw hell, I don't suppose he heard you above the square-dancing."

But it seems he had heard. Liz's words had invaded his beer and scratched their way down to his stomach. It had heaved in discomfort, and then subsided back as he sought to reply. But there'd been only a hiccup of air. No words.

"Well, whether I annoyed him or not, I'm still inclined to send him a card. I can do without being on the receiving end of his petulance when I get back. I tell you: he seems to have been even more odd than usual lately. Pretty well ignores the tasks he once enthused over. How he hasn't been reprimanded, I don't know. God knows what sort of testimonial he'd be able to hand over to the Singapore selection board."

"More odd? Oh, I don't know. I think much of it is cultivated. He delights in his strangeness, don't you think? Though I suppose that's pretty strange in itself! In which case, perhaps you won't be forewarned of any moment of crisis. If it ever happens. Nothing he might do could ever stand out as a signal amid the whole barrage of idiosyncrasies. I shouldn't count on your postcard as an insurance against anything."

"You're right. I think! It's just that he's been making me feel increasingly uncomfortable. I can't decide whether I despise him, feel sorry for him, or what."

"Well, let's not give him too much of our holiday attention. We'll decide on the postcard business later. What do you want to eat next?"

The rest of the lunch was acceptable, but forgettable, in perfect keeping with the moderate price paid. A thin, tender slice of veal, in juices suspiciously derived from some other animal, with overcooked ratatouille, green salad and slices of baguette. Strawberry tart, open topped and heavily glazed and some red wine or other. Away from St. Aillant, where I acquired soundly based preferences, price determines choice of bottle. Neither me nor Liz have the social poise or expertise to specify a label, nor are we sufficiently charlatan to enter any such pretence.

Once outdoors, we walk slowly towards the Saône, stay for a while on a bridge across, leaning over the balustrade, delighting in the freshness of space after the tight and high-sided streets behind us. Then, on to the city centre proper, eventually leaving ourselves an hour to comply with Liz's desire to visit the Musée de Beaux Arts, where we rush from floor to floor, and leave with a lasting memory not of its Impressionist masterpieces, but of its entrance arch, a dark framework to a sun-baked interior courtyard with a glowing sambucus. Then, more pavement bashing, hotter feet, increasing tiredness and the search for overnight accommodation. We find ourselves walking behind a young woman, dark-haired, coffee-skinned, slim, in white top and shorts, both widely slit and laced at the side. We book into a small lodging house in the 'Red Light' district. But nothing in the ambience of that Quarter tears down our holiday pact. The next morning, we each push back our separate duvets.

*

Travel with Liz and you travel with someone with no self-declared history. A creature of the moment, she yields little of herself to enquiry. During my acquaintance with her, I've pieced together her past from a collection of silent responses, cautious evasiveness, confessions, suspicious in their deliberate construction, and transparent untruths. A partly assembled jigsaw puzzle of a now accent-less North Country girl whose parents are either dead or alienated, certainly not the object of any current affection. Intelligent, but not of admitted education, assured, but through genetic disposition or confidence-inducing upbringing? Not that it matters. Her mystery has its attractions. The thought that she's been created as a twenty-five-year-old woman appeals to me. This way she has no romantic past whose memory might dilute the romantic present which I hope to engineer. The obvious counter argument is that a 'life-before-me', providing it's been less than completely happy, might serve to cast me in an exceptionally favourable light. But this rarely crosses my mind. Generally, I try to juggle her obscurity into something which adds strength to my own position. But it's not easy. By contrast, she has the strategic advantage of having learned everything about me from foetus through to the man now driving up the narrow mountain road above Chambery.

Her prevarications are born partly of her conviction that her past is irrelevant to how she ought to be thought of today. Appraisal should be entirely contemporary, without the dubious benefit of scrutinising the mould. Too many people, in her experience, are obsessed with the inconsequential morsels of her life history and she has never supplied her inquisitors with any information which she regards as of no current consequence. Never, that is, until the conversation which, ten minutes later, I rightly recognize as the first signs of thaw.

"You know, we've still done nothing yet about the postcards."

"Liz, I didn't think you'd be so preoccupied with token messages home."

"I'm not preoccupied! But if you want them to arrive back before we do."

"Yes, you're right. Perhaps today, if we can find the time."

"Fine … Listen … You know when you send a postcard to Byschurch, do you do so out of a sense of duty or because you really want to?"

"Why? Anyway, I'm not sure they're easily separated. Probably a bit of both."

"Umm. Would you say that you genuinely love your parents?"

"This is getting a bit heavy, isn't it?"

"Aw, c'mon Bernard. Answer the question."

"Yes, I suppose so. It's just that it's difficult to articulate it. I mean, when you are a young kid, they train you to tell them how much they mean to you. Then you retreat into your adolescent shell, too embarrassed to display your feelings for them."

"But they're there all the same?"

"Yes. You just don't admit it. How can you? It would somehow demean your peer associations."

"And what about now, in your late twenties?"

"Well, I enjoy their company. I don't know if that says anything significant or not."

"Oh, what the hell. With them both alive, you don't have to think on them too seriously."

"Sorry?"

"Well, you can embrace them or ignore them as you wish, knowing that tomorrow, you can change your mind and rectify yesterday's mistakes. They're just there, like Nelson's Column."

"And you're in a different position?"

"I think I was a sod of a kid."

"All kids are, at times."

"Yes, but most have the opportunity to follow it up with a properly adult relationship with their parents. A sort of unstated apology for all the tantrums and tears."

"But not you?"

"Not with my mother, no."

"She's dead then?"

"Yes, since I was fourteen. A road accident. I now think of her going as cutting off my words to her in mid-sentence. She only ever received the parasitic love of a child, never the respectful love of an adult daughter."

"Would you have made the transition?"

"Who knows? I'd like to think so."

"So, as you see it, her premature death left you both unfulfilled."

"And me threatened."

"By what?"

"Mortality. More so than if it had been dad who'd gone."

"I don't see that."

"What I mean is, people usually profess to love each parent equally. They might admit to liking one more than the other perhaps, but beyond this, they claim the same fundamental bond with each. Well, I think that's nonsense. The death of a mother is always more devastating to a daughter than to a son and vice-versa for father of course."

"Why, for heaven's sake?"

"Well, because it places you right in line as the next female or male to go. You're the branch that's hanging off the family tree, waiting to fall to the ground. There's nobody between you and oblivion."

"And gender matters in all this?"

"I think so. There's an element of selfish fear. Greater grief at losing the parent of the same sex as yourself."

"Then you'd not be so sorry to see your father go? He's still with us?"

"Oh, I'd be sorry yes. I like him. But I'd not be upset for my sake."

"Look, if you don't mind me asking, where is he Liz? You never seem to troop off on some dutiful visit or other."

"Oh, he's still up there in Bolton. Grocering away. Stepmother too, goddam her. He despairs of me, a bit. Thinks I'm irresponsibly impulsive. He expected a lot of his only child. Has never really forgiven me for leaving Exeter so soon."

"Exeter?"

"University."

"How soon? Did you last the week?"

"Fifty-two of them. Or rather thirty, to take the mockery of the academic year."

"Why?"

"Aw hell, students mainly. The boring sameness of it all."

"Yeh, but more boring than the Steynmouth tax office?"

"Well, as boring but without the financial rewards."

"And Steynmouth itself?"

"Ah … well, I threw in the Exeter towel in June, so not wanting to return north to the company of dad's new woman, I just moved down the coast to work as a holiday season waitress. When that was through, late September, I moved on to the more permanent pastures of the tax office. In the meantime, I'd met Amy. Get a close friend and you're disinclined to move away and start all over again."

"What? Amy winning out against your much-vaunted independence?"

"I don't see the contradiction. It was my choice, and anyway, she wasn't the crucial input, just part of the whole parcel. I'm a convert to the West Country. You can set yourself aside from London-inspired idiocy. I don't feel banished in any way, not a frustrated sufferer from some Dick Whittington syndrome."

"So contented then, as to have no need of future plans?"

"I have some plans, though it's perhaps an overstatement to call them that."

"Let me in on some of them."

"Well, they're not plans in the sense of conscious strategies for the future, just personal hopes."

"Involving other people?"

"I suppose so, in so far as gregariousness is forced upon us."

"Yes, but people with names? Known to you now, as opposed to persons yet to be met."

"Are you enquiring after yourself, Bernard?"

I concentrate hard on the road ahead, recognizing for the first time its sharp Z-bends and poorly cambered corners, hazards which were incidental when conversation threatened no demolition of my dreams. A sudden learner-driver, I mutter a reply. "Well, perhaps I am, but prematurely maybe. Don't answer."

"As you wish, but …"

"But nothing. Just let me say thanks for what you've said so far."

"But it made no direct reference to you."

"No. But it's the first time I've heard it. And I doubt many others have."

*

I chose La Clesaz on the casual recommendation of a colleague at work who'd had the misfortune to accompany a school holiday party there, but who's claimed it to have great merit, provided you weren't encumbered with the responsibility of child-minding. "Yeh, great centre for Chambery, Annecy, Aix-les-Bains, all close at hand. Plus, good walking etc. when you don't feel like gobbling up petrol. Small place, but with three or four friendly hotels. Try the Mont Brunard."

But I'm always sceptical of holiday recommendations. Afterwards, disasters are relegated to the status of minor mishaps. Day-to-day pleasantness is promoted to the rank of major excitement. "Yes, we had a wonderful time. Yes, we'd certainly go there again," and so, it must have been with the person who's suggested La Clesaz, much retrospective embellishment. When I think about it, I ought not to have been fooled. I've only to recall the clinically selective retelling of my own past holidays like the Chapel Youth Club fortnight in Weston-

Super-Mare, whose memory now emphasizes the unsupervised cavortings of afternoons rather than the adult-guided prayers and deliberations of earlier in the day. The late teenage descent upon Butlins with Philip and others, now recollected for its corporate but celibate merrymaking, rather than for its individual sexual frustration. And the more recent school party to the Middle Rhine, whose rare humorous moments are now sufficient to eradicate the memory of the time-filling chore of being teacher-in-charge. Since I am, therefore, no stranger to this latter role it's less than sensible of me to embrace the recommendation of someone whose only experience of a place was doubtlessly tainted by having kids in train, but who subsequently, would try to save his personal reputation by pretending that his choice of location was a stroke of genius. So, La Clesaz could be better!

The convenience of its situation is illusory and could be suggested only by an atlas lacking any representation of relief. Its tortuous and steep approach roads render it forty minutes tiring drive from Chambery in the valley below. This would be of little concern in winter when the village attracts a clientele of willingly imprisoned skiers but its operation as a summer resort is very much of an afterthought, a means of avoiding complete seasonal close-down. However, with no snow on the ground the immediate attractions of the neighbourhood are quickly exhausted, leaving the visitor no option but to take to a car and begin each day winding down the mountainside. But before this necessity comes to prevail, Liz and I spend two days walking away from the hotel. On day one, along a flat path alternately passing through pine forest and open meadow, the former remarkable for its large and seething ant hills, the latter for its large and seething dung-heaps, the offerings of well-tended, soft-eyed brown cows, large bells hanging noisily from their sagging necks. Day two is a more exerting climb to a prominent stone cross which stands perilously above the main valley below and casts an inquisitive eye over the urban behaviour of Chambery.

"I didn't know you were an expert on flora!"

I'm not, but I've recognized the large purple flower as the most popular herbaceous item back at the Davies garden in Byschurch. "Bernard! Don't kick the ball into the Centaurea!" Here, it's a prolific roadside weed.

Leaving the road, we reach our destination via rocky limestone outcropping irregularly between short, springy turf.

We sit down alongside the Cross, tired after an hour and a half's effort. Liz shakes her head, attempting to give some free flow to hair now sticking together in the heat. Her jeans, tight at the top but flaring downwards from mid-thigh, are rolled up to knee height, revealing shining, graceful shins which descend incongruously into large socks and boots. She pushes her right hand inside her white cotton blouse, just below the neck, easing the fabric off the skin and fluttering her fingers to introduce air whose stagnant thundery nature offers little hope of relief. More adventurously, I unbutton my shirt along the greater part of its length, leaving its red, black and white check hanging limply to each side. I lean back on my elbows, suddenly desperate for Liz to follow suit, to expose her breasts, to turn towards me, to signal the start. I've felt more confident these last two days but still not so as to show my hand at any time, other than what I judge to be the optimum. Which proves not to be now, for she suddenly sits bolt upright, asking touristy questions about the view displayed before us. Our being at this precise place is the result of an orgy of written praise in the information pamphlet picked up at the office of the Syndicat d'Initiative. The Cross is a 'most magnificent Belvedere', according to the person who'd penned the English language edition. The document shows all the enthusiasm of a translator whose linguistic talents, though not good, were probably the only ones available to satisfy the Syndicat's demand for cosmopolitanism but within its modest budget.

" ... and in summer, a climate dry, an air very pure, permitting to holidaymakers rest and repose, profitable to health. The forest of pines, crossed by routes and shady ways, offers easy walks and without danger. You can pick up flowers of the woodland and accumulate numerous varieties of fungus. The plant life will astonish you by its abundance ... You will find sympathy in the hotels, a plentiful kitchen, and always some prices which are reasonable ... "

Well, true enough in its way. Back from our walk, we are met at the door of the hotel Mont Brunard by the proprietress, Madame Varzier.

"Oh ... 'ow are your poor legs and feet? You 'ave an appetite, yes? Good. This evening, there something special on the table. You go and wash now. Relax for a while." Her welcome supports the Syndicat's claim of sympathetic hoteliers, and its promise of good and affordable eating. Not so genuine, however, is the invitation to wash, for it has already become apparent to us that turning a tap is no guarantee of water.

"Yes, Monsieur. It sometimes 'appens during a dry summer. We are so 'igh up that the pump cannot manage to bring the water. The 'ole village suffers Monsieur. We 'ave to accept it. It will be back by the morning you see. They will send someone from Chambery to make the repair."

It's four days into our stay before I discover that the Hotel Mont Brunard is unique in the stemming of its water flow; that the neighbouring hotels are not similarly affected; and that the low level of summer income sees Madame Varzier turn off the supply at intervals, so as to save on heating expenses. No water means no hot water.

"No, no, Monsieur. You must be imagining that. Everywhere is the same … What? Not at the Hotel du Neve? I can't believe that. There must be some mistake."

But mistake or not, there are fewer failures of supply for the rest of our short stay. Less a sympathetic hotelier, more one reduced to honesty.

The drought at the Hotel Mont Brunard might, in fact, have aroused even greater resentment were it not for the incident of the 'Scots Lady in the Shower'; an event which I'm sure we will later look back on with considerable amusement. For three days, we've suffered from the uninvited presence of this woman at our dinner table. One Mavis Gallagher, fat, noisy, intolerant of being abroad. She'd been midway through a shower when Madame Varzier closed the main valve. We'd met her on the stairs, soap-covered body swathed in a bright pink towel whose colour was matched by the angered burning of her face.

"My God! How am I going to get this soap off? If it's like yesterday, it'll be hours before we've water again."

She'd stumbled past us in a desperate attempt to get from ground floor shower room to bedroom as quickly as possible. There, she might avail herself of some last trickle from the wash basin, for in defiance of every law of plumbing, the water seemed to disappear from lower to higher levels in that order. In the event, she'd been too late even for this minor degree of salvation and had growled incessantly all through dinner, a meal which we ate with some difficulty. Our mouths hadn't known which shape to assume, whether for laughing or for chewing.

In a very real sense, it's the absurdity of our being here that's makes us stay at the Mont Brunard for seven days with activities on the last four thus sandwiched between the tiresome drive to and from the valley, trips to Aix-les-Bains, Annecy, and further afield to Chamonix. But it's worth the evening's return to the world of Madame Varzier not least of all perhaps to witness the latest turn of events between her and the Moroccan.

In the absence of the elderly Monsieur Varzier, away on business since the day we arrived, his young wife has sought to take full advantage of still being in her early thirties. With only a few summer customers for whom to cater, she needs little in the way of hired staff, typically just one boy in his late teens, acting as kitchen help, barman and fulfiller of fantasies. This year, his name is Mounir, tall, slightly stooping, fuzzy haired and with two gold-capped teeth placed centrally in a less than friendly looking mouth. Liz is the first to spot the relationship, to suggest that daytime chores give way to night-time frolicking.

"Impossible." I disagree.

"Why not? You can sense it."

"Practicalities render it impossible."

"Practicalities? With hubby away?"

"Her trousers. Removing them would be about as difficult as stripping stove enamel off a household saucepan. They're old man Varzier's guarantee of faithfulness."

The garment in question is in fine white corduroy, gleaming fresh each morning but presumably having been cleaned in situ. This is sprayed-on textile whose obvious permanence of fit would surely frustrate the young Arab.

"Rubbish Bernard! I tell you the old man's long foregone any exclusive call on his wife's favours. She's just a welcome status symbol to him and he knows she's likely to succumb to some fledging male or other. He's getting what he values most out of her. A good day's work!"

Liz's suspicions are soon confirmed in a most unexpected way. It's about one o'clock in the morning. She's been asleep for maybe an hour, and it has taken no little time for her to adjust to premature wakening, to focus hazily on the silhouetted figure moving towards her from the light of the open bedroom doorway.

"Bernard? Is that you?" The enquiry is rough in tone, slightly disapproving of my supposed entry. Some weeks later, she will tell Amy that her question also had an air of excited anticipation. Of desire, surfacing without inhibition or caution from the realms of drowsiness. For me, it was a missed opportunity, one never made apparent in the rationality of daylight.

"Eh … Pardon? … Louise? … C'est moi, Mounir!" Then he crashes heavily to the floor, confused by the unfamiliar distribution of furniture in a room entered into in drunken mistake. He lies there groaning, watched over curiously by an immobile Liz, who, once she's appreciated what's happening, purses her lips into an amused smile. His error of destination has been only a minor one, geographically. Within seconds, an alarmed Madame Varzier arrives from the unoccupied room next door, an agreed rendezvous which offers no formal insult to the bed of the married couple. Glancing at Liz, she gathers her towelling bathrobe more closely around her otherwise bare and beautifully contoured body. The white trousers are nowhere in evidence. She'd prods her lover to his feet, and ushers him somewhere or other, presumably not to his original goal. Mounir that night, is too insensible to perform properly.

"Thank God she came to remove him," Liz says laughingly over breakfast. "I'd have had to fetch you otherwise."

I look up from my coffee. "Really? I've almost given up on you paying me a night call this holiday." Talk of tripping the corridors in stealthy anticipation had highlighted the absence of such thrills from my own experience. I guess I look, and sound peeved, probably unwisely.

But her reaction isn't entirely what I might expect. "You knew that before we started. Not this holiday, you're right. But soon, someday soon."

*

We leave La Clesaz on day eight, and motor slowly back towards the Channel coast. Two days among the lakes of Morvan, two days in Paris. We disembark at Folkestone and drive immediately for Steynmouth, wondering why we haven't opted for a more westerly crossing. My hair, lightened by the Sun, has grown beyond its usual length. Liz has tied hers back for the completion of the journey. Viewed quickly through front windscreen, we might easily be taken for brother and sister, faces suggesting derivation from the same gene pack. Indeed, the only way in which our holiday relationship has gone beyond that of close blood relatives has been in its eventual promise for the future. On balance, I console myself, we have lived in each other's daily company for three weeks and have finally replaced the initial platonic understanding with a suggestion of better things to come. "Vive la France!"

Chapter 5

Back to School

The September staff meeting, held the day before the start of term proper, draws the curtain on the temporary escape of the summer break. The Steynmouth High School show is on stage again, and I've grudgingly to return to the professional role expected of me by my youthful charges, their parents, and my non-too-bountiful paymasters. The platform for my presumed talents is a complex of buildings whose variety of style reflects the uncertainty of contemporary educational thinking. Old red-brick Grammar school buildings, with tall Georgian-paned windows, stand alongside equally solid but more glass-dominated extensions built to accommodate the products of the post-war baby boom. But both are now engulfed by the fragile, prefabricated additions consequent upon comprehensive reorganisation: a maze of hastily erected units in fading red cedar.

It's within this physical hotch-potch that some teachers, whose working lives were previously eased by the beneficence of the selective system, now struggle to come to terms with the new challenge posed by the non-academic child. This client's interests are vociferously defended by the younger members of staff, persons selected in accordance with their 'commitment to the ideals of comprehensive education'. This was something to which I had to notionally subscribe during my regrettably successful interview of some four years back. My problem, in life in general I suppose, is that I basically don't know how to react most effectively to stupid behaviour, which if truth be told, can manifest itself across a wide range of intellectual abilities, not least of all, within the context of this staff meeting. The pupils where this trait is most frequently encountered fill up about sixty per cent of my working day. I relate to them by often digressing to talk about something other than the subject material that it's my paid duty to put across. It is to justify my receipt of this remuneration that my misguided conscience insists I attempt to *teach* at intervals far too frequent for my own good. Much better to respond to queries about whether Mandy should agree to see Richard from 5E this evening or talk about football, or absolutely anything, in fact. I'm quite good at going off track. It is against this reality that I am bemused by the unrealistic ambition and the deluded self-importance of many of my colleagues.

I look down at the discussion paper placed before me …

"STRATEGIES FOR OVERCOMING RESISTANCE
TO PASTORAL CARE.
As long as the functional relationship between guidance /
counselling and academic achievement and vocational
preparation is clearly perceived, both staff and students
will participate willingly with common goals in sight…
Inter-personal development within the 16-19-year-old
cohort is intrinsic to the Counselling, Complementary
Studies and Social Education parts of the curriculum…
Any change from the 'Hidden Curriculum' to the 'Overt
Guidance Curriculum' will need serious consideration and
willing acceptance on the part of students and staff… It is
clear that the development of Guidance and Counselling

must depend on consensus agreement regarding clear functional relationships between Pastoral Care and Academic and Personal performance ..."

All of that is embedded within the preamble. There's more following on behind. What the hell does all this mean? My brain is in complete meltdown. It looks to be the potentially most time-consuming item on the agenda, 'The Sixth Form Guidance Programme'. As I read part of it, the business of the meeting continues around me: the welcoming of new members of staff; the changes in timetable structure; altered procedures for pupil registration. I make neither written nor mental note of any of them, turning instead, to doodling in the margin of the discussion document. First to appear from my pen is a highly decorated 'G', like some substandard initial letter from a Medieval religious tract. Beneath this, I write down words to which it offers entry; 'g' for guidance, Guinness, grimace - I make an appropriate facial contortion, confident that I'm the centre of nobody's attention – gravity, gorilla, guerrilla, Gallipoli, gonorrhoea. This takes me towards the bottom of the page where an expectant three-inch expanse of blank paper beckons a more adventurous hand. I draw a face, round, with narrow eyes, round nose, round mouth, like an astonished elderly Polynesian. I still have some space left and fill it with an unflattering and exaggerated profile of Warren, who is sitting sideways-on some small distance to my right, forehead too high, nose too long, hair too thinly curled, spectacles too dominating, chin too absent. Yet not untrue.

"You'll do that then, Mr Davies?"

"Sorry?"

"You'll look after Mr Raybould for the first few weeks, as is our practice with new colleagues."

"Oh … Yes … of course."

The penalty for not listening to the tedious outpourings of George Pointer, Headmaster, is to find yourself allocated responsibilities whose exact nature remains a mystery. In this case, it's the identity of Raybould which is the mystery. No doubt, he's been introduced as part of the preliminaries. Somebody will know who he is. Even so, I'm hugely uncertain as to my own role as guardian and wet nurse. I'm not aware of any usual practice in this field. The only familiar practice I could admit to, is that of Pointer's introducing some new burden, as if it's been part of one's job description since the Big Bang. Probably, it will entail simply demonstrating to Raybould, the mechanics of form-filling, fortnightly pupil assessments, the paraphernalia of being seen to be doing what's expected, or maybe not. Maybe, some major new initiative, some sort of shared responsibility between experienced and inexperienced, on this occasion, with the doubtlessly alert novice knowing more about it than his approved mentor.

"Fine! You'll start tomorrow then."

"Yes … umm … if that's thought necessary."

"Thought necessary Mr Davies? Let me see if I've got this straight. In your opinion, we could reasonably postpone your chaperoning of Mr Raybould?"

"Well … no … not if would cause difficulties."

"Which it most surely would. So why question the necessity of an immediate start?"

"I ... uh ... didn't mean to really. Just a turn of phrase."

"I believe the word 'just' cropped up in the excuses offered by the Light Brigade, Mr Davies."

"Is that so?" By now, I'm resentful. I feel that Pointer's plodding sarcasm has now scolded me sufficiently for my daydreaming.

"Well, let's just say I suspect it was. My point is that turns of phrase, as you put them, should not be lightly tossed into the air like some carelessly aimed confetti, lest as here, they miss their target. An educated mind should instead, aspire to consistently relevant thought, impossible when people don't attend to proceedings!"

George Pointer is almost unbelievable. It's impossible, as I've found, to accurately portray him to others without being accused of painting a grossly exaggerated caricature. But I've no doubts at all. Here is unrivalled pedantry and pomposity. It is real alright.

"You're right Mr Pointer. My thoughts were elsewhere."

"Is this an apology?"

"It's more a recognition of your powers of perception."

"Well, thankful as I am for the accolade, they don't stretch to full mind reading, so perhaps I might enquire whether these thoughts of yours were constructively elsewhere, Mr Davies, dwelling on some grand design for the school year ahead?"

"On some design, yes."

"Perhaps you'd like to let us in on it then, Mr Davies?"

"Umm ... well it's just in outline form at the moment, in sketch form you might say." I resist the temptation to look down at Warren's pencilled head.

"In which case, how long before it reaches fruition, before we can all benefit from your obviously peripheral deliberations?"

"Well actually, I think I've reached a state of impasse." Warren offers no scope for further cartoon treatment by my inartistic hand.

"Perhaps then, you might put your problems aside for the duration of this meeting and return to them at some more private moment?"

"Of course, headmaster."

This insincere proffering of full title is the signal for the end of the skirmish. It recognises reluctantly the undeniable authority of the man-in-charge. A man so in charge that my self-inflicted predicament has caused no muted giggles of amusement among the other assembled subordinates. There is never a meeting in which some member of staff isn't treated with less adult politeness than would be accorded by the same man to the most loathsome of pupil miscreants. Even the unsuspecting Raybould's turn will come.

Yet, this very boorishness and bullying arouses little or no open revolution. My own frequent acquiescence in the general servility makes me despise myself on occasion, though only momentarily, until I recall the folly of taking it all too seriously. By which I mean, seriously at all.

*

One of George Pointer's most interesting habits is his 'flickering of the lights', a regular Monday to Friday occurrence whose title I coined from some past amusement at an entry in a Seventeenth Century coroner's report recounting nine deaths from 'rising of the lights'. Admittedly, George's actions never contribute to anyone's deaths, physical death, that is. But sometimes, to death of principle.

It's all to do with staff attendance at morning service. The headmaster of Steynmouth High School doesn't see this as a matter of personal conscience.

"You don't wish to attend, you say, Mr Davies?"

"No. That's right."

"May I remind you that daily worship is compulsory under the terms of the 1944 Education Act?"

"For pupils!"

"So, you prefer to put up your feet for ten minutes each morning, to fill the ashtray?"

"I don't smoke, Mr Pointer."

"But you clearly give priority to relaxation over obligation."

"Perhaps. Except that I can't be obliged to say prayers and sing hymns."

"Ah! You're standing on principle then, Mr Davies."

"Well, some mornings I might want to relax, as you put it. On others, I'm energetic enough to think that principle is important, though far be it from me to glorify my stand with so grandiose a label."

"Principles, Mr Davies, cannot be overvalued and in this case, the only principle that matters is that of responsibility, of being in loco parentis, even if this entails a token mental kneeling at the altar."

"I beg your pardon, Mr Pointer but let me point out that if it is our task to mirror parental activity, then you'll have next to no staff at morning service. As I recall, most mums and dads, or just dad it was, in my case, dispatch their offspring to Sunday School just to get them out of their own hair."

"Might I suggest Mr Davies ..." - the exaggerated politeness of title and surname is a characteristic feature of conversations between George and his members of staff - "that the humility that comes from recognizing the majesty of your Maker, might help efface the impertinence sometimes displayed in your dealings with authority!"

"I'll certainly bear that in mind, headmaster!"

But I remain one of seven recalcitrants who at ten minutes past nine each morning, witness the groping hand of George Pointer appear around the staffroom door to rock the light switch back and to. The alternate dimming and brightening, is a reminder to us all, of our duty to toe-the-line of religious observance, a sort of Damascan prompt, but one never heeded, since experience has taught that to stand up to George's initial bluster is often to take the wind out of his sails. The pity is, that on this and other matters, most combatants spinelessly cave in during the opening skirmishes.

One morning, six months back, there was no 'flickering of the lights'. Instead, George's deputy, an unwilling agent, adopted a more direct line.

"Why don't you lot get up off your arses and give old George one less problem to worry about? Make all our lives more tolerable."

"Please Cyril! Such language in the presence of ladies." I winked across at Marion, an evangelizing atheist, and an un-shockable woman whose own vocabulary is so florid as to make Cyril's exhortation seem the most delicate of requests.

*

"Perhaps then, the meeting could now move on to look at the working paper you hopefully, have before you."

George raises his eyebrows and looks around, as if in expectation that at least some copies might, by now, have been converted into paper darts. This is the suspicious reaction of a man who attributes to his staff the sort of impulsive immaturity that thirty years being in charge of children has led him to assume is normal human behaviour, and which demands rectification from above. His mission in life is to elevate the conduct of others to a level above the destructive and the reflex, though his tactics are usually those of the intuitive demolitionist.

Satisfied that all is in order, he lowers his eyebrows back to his memo pad. Large, black, bushy brows that cast a speckled shadow over his eyes and make their precise movement and stare difficult to follow. He scratches at his head, his finger disappearing into luxuriant and wiry hair whose colour and density belie his approaching retirement. Before returning his hand to the desktop, he taps at his skull, three times, as if punching in some sort of thought code for the debate ahead. Like all such staff conferences, its outcome is certain: decisions are made in advance of open deliberation. This means that George's anxieties are occasioned not by worry as to his own ability to convince, but rather by concern over the smooth conduct of the token proceedings ahead.

"As it stands, ladies and gentlemen, the document represents the end product of last year's staff working party. But it's in no way a programme or strategy that's ready for implementation. I hope today's discussions might go some way towards translating our objectives into practical reality. If the members of the working party can gain some insight into the staff viewpoint overall, then they can come back later with some definite proposals for action. Any immediate thoughts on this?"

George looks around, his general enquiry being in fact very specific. His inquisitive gaze focuses expectantly on those whose views he actually wants to hear. He is in the position of a man whose twilight professional years are having their tranquillity compromised and squeezed by the insistent clamourings of the Inspectorate. To smoothly implement change at Steynmouth, demands that he listens not to my scepticism nor to Warren's bandwaggoning, but instead, only to the tolerant middle ground, where mild suspicion is enfeebled by resignation as to the inevitable.

My minor contempt is well known, but seldom voiced in a formal arena. But Warren is a great man for the public eye, a mouth difficult to muzzle. He pushes his glasses firmly to the bridge of his nose and begins a lengthy observation, unstructured and delivered at such speed that even the most diligent listener can catch only the occasional frenetic snatch of heated viewpoint.

"Mr Pointer, I wonder if ... we are talking here of pupil acceptance of Guidance and Counselling; the need for them to recognize its existence, to see the teacher as something above and beyond a purveyor of knowledge ... Surely, in seeking the co-operation of the pupils, in wanting them as partners in this venture, we ought to admit them into the planning stage, to reconstitute the working party with proper pupil representation. Only then, can we achieve anything even remotely approaching consensus ... Everything possible must be done to remove the barriers between teacher and pupil, to forge a new and open alliance to the mutual benefit of both parties ... And finally, ..."

This is all too much for Major Warlby. It's a far cry from the parade ground strictness of his former military career or indeed, from the respect for age and authority which he still attempts to engender among the uniformed members of the school's shrinking cadet corps. This mini army, now only six recruits strong, is a relict institution, inherited along with its leader from grammar school days gone by. When the Major goes, so will it.

"Poppycock, Mister Metcalf. Absolute poppycock!"

Warren is addressed in formal terms not out of distaste for his progressive ideas, but as part of the normal order of things. In the absence of Sergeants or Generals, then plain 'Misters' will have to do.

"Let's talk some sense. The sort that comes from generations of experience. That kids are kids and adults know best. You'll never get the kids to acquiesce in that. I'm all for overt, as opposed to, hidden guidance, but let its authoritarian bias be firmly declared for heaven's sake, not some wishy-washy peace so as not to rock the boat. If they don't obey orders, they fall out. Damn good training for the outside world."

This strikes me as being generally sound. It might seem the sort of reasoning you'd expect from one accustomed to receiving and giving orders, but the truth is, that the kids prefer the Major to Warren. He's actually able to convey to his pupils an enthusiasm for life outside of the command structure and marching. Also, he's a poet, sensitive in his quiet moments, and a man whose views are not to be instantly dismissed on sole account of their hierarchical context.

Warren makes to reply … but the alert George Pointer, seeking again to restore advantage to the emasculated centre-ground, bumbles some sort of conciliatory nothingness.

"I think that at this stage, we see something of the opposing stances that via conscientious effort, we can fuse into some sort of sensible and agreed approach. Now if …"

"Mr Pointer! Do you envisage consulting the troops or not? We need an answer. I, for one, cannot acquiesce in anything decided for me by those for whom I am responsible."

"Umm ... quite, quite, Major Warlby. The whole idea of debate is surely that no-one decides anything on behalf of anyone else. We are looking for a workable compromise. My ideas... "

"Are unworkable, Mister Pointer." Warren is red-faced in his adventurism. "Assuming that is, that you intend to impose a pastoral system upon pupils without actively seeking their ideas."

"If I may be spared the role of the boxing glove - I feel as if I'm being passed between your fist, Mister Metcalf, and that of Major Warlby - it seems to me important that the pupil body be seen to be consulted, towards perhaps the end of our discussions, basically to placate the precocious. I propose then that we accord the boy and girl presidents some sort of minor formative role, perhaps by having them in on our final session, and convincing them of the selfless nature of our intentions."

"Formative!" Warren snaps his pencil.

The major gives a half-satisfied smile. The face of a man content with a half victory. His battleground experiences have instilled in him an appreciation that conqueror and conquered are often equally scarred. Thus, he has the advantage over Warren of almost always stopping short of overheating. The redness of his complexion is the result not of hypertension induced by conflict, it is rather a sweaty glow which has remained with him since the sun-baked days of campaigns in the North African desert, after which the irksome George Pointer poses no threat to his personal equilibrium.

*

The only time that I have ever seen the Major in genuine temper was one lunch hour, when his moustache twitched in high annoyance at the insistent and taunting Republican mouthings of a junior colleague.

"Sir! In days gone by, your flow of disrespect to the monarch would have been stemmed by the royal axe smoothly parting your spinal cord. My fist might be a far blunter instrument, but at least the discomfort it conveys will last a damn site longer. Be warned."

"Hey, no need to get uptight, old chap!"

As the Major rose to his feet, he caught the leg of a coffee table, dislodging books, lunchtime sandwiches and two vacuum flasks, an incident so spectacularly unusual that the sheer volume of excited buzz around the staffroom served to remind him of who he was. Not a two-bit bar-room brawler, but someone whose values were so obviously the right ones that they needed no defending against the passing political enthusiasms of the young.

"I say! Quite some chaos I've caused here. Not to worry chaps. I'll fetch in a couple of boys to clean it up. Unless that is, that something so feudal, arouses the wrath of our egalitarian friend. In which case, having instigated the whole bothersome business, he might care to wield the mop himself. What do you say, brother?"

"You silly old fool!" came the reply.

But this time, the Major was so self-assured as not to answer at all: no words, no blows.

*

Discussion on and around the Guidance Programme continues for a further three quarters of an hour, during which time, I sink further into my chair. Major Warlby moves increasingly towards sleep and Warren persists vainly in his one-man crusade. It isn't that there are no others of similarly radical disposition. They, however, hold the contrary view that progress is best achieved not by heated confrontation with authority, but by relentless background manoeuvring, the achieving of small changes, whose combination makes greater change inevitable, boxing Pointer into a corner not of his own making. In this way, the dispensation with school uniform had come about, not as a result of parental impecunity or liberal concession, but as the imperceptibly achieved outcome of a deliberate slackening in the will of some to uphold the rules. This meant that eventually, the absence of caps, ties and blazers had to be sanctioned from above, an unknowing tribute to the efficiency of the quiet plotters. "It seems to me," said the great George Pointer, "that our efforts to encourage decency of dress, although not necessarily doomed to failure, should our wishes be resolutely to the contrary, are likely to demand an intensity of effort that would detract from the more important functions of an educator. I think, therefore, we will have to move with the times on this one, though please, ladies and gentlemen, let us keep a watchful eye on cleanliness. And by the way, no denims!" But the wall had been breached.

Warren then, is not so much a lone voice, but a lone tactician. He enjoys with others, the dream of a pupil-teacher body harmoniously motivated towards the same end, the production of an army of socially skilled, optimum achievers. A joyously modern and relentless charge against the sterility of all that's gone before. He is in a noisy hurry. His co-aspirants are content to manipulate over the longer term. Thus, I think, both are doomed to failure, Warren because his clumsy vociferousness embarrasses his cause and forewarns his adversaries, the others because their quiet gradualism is conceptually weak. In the context of any one peer group, it takes such slow effect that the prodigies are only half-moulded at school leaving age and are then quickly shaped back into the ways of the real world. So, the school uniform issue was not an issue at all. At the end of the day, Pointer is still there to bore the pants off everybody, and his naive opponents are equally boring in their victorious elation. Strangely, although belonging to neither of the two reformist camps, revolutionary nor gradualist, I find it is me who is accused by George of seeking to demean him through what he judges to be repeatedly truculent behaviour, even though generally, my instinct is to let everything simply drift by.

"You're quite wrong, Mister Pointer. You ought to save your persecution for those who would cut your throat tomorrow, given the chance."

"Oh no, no. Warren Metcalf and his cronies are just noises, whereas you are genuinely awkward."

But it's a very passive awkwardness. To seek to damage George, is a task that I could never warm to. The man's safety owes everything to the inadequacy of the tactics employed against him by those committed to his downfall. As for me, most of my energies are reserved for time other than that spent at work.

*

Some hour and a half or more into the staff meeting Warren's voice is still the most obtrusive, and the most unheeded. I've used the last ten minutes to embellish my earlier portrait of him, adding a large balloon issuing from his mouth and containing one of his typical zealous mouthings. In a duplicate profile, alongside the first, a blast of fire passes through Warren's lips, popping the balloon. The word 'BANG' is inscribed above the furious flames. Where temple meets forehead, a huge angered vein stands out, its outline fringed by a series of short parallel strokes of the pen, effective I think, in their suggestion of impassioned throbbing. Leading down to Warren's ear, is a large trumpet, not dissimilar in its lack of proportion to one perched above an old gramophone, and into which, an unidentified puppet-master's voice is exhorting him to yet further efforts to achieve his various goals.

It's at this stage of proceedings that I make the decision, not hastily arrived at, to reorganise my social life. I can stomach no more of Warren, in or out of work. From now on, my Wednesday evening seat at *The Green Man* will remain gloriously empty.

Sarah, I won't miss and she, not me, especially after my recent mirth at her liking for seven-hundred-page historical novels. As a librarian, she feels her literary tastes to be beyond even jocular question. Liz,

I prefer to meet in less crowded company, and never in Clive's. Bill will look me up whenever he needs someone to buy him a pint. Only Amy causes me some hesitation. I'm afraid that to see her independently of the group will suggest more than is intended. Yet I don't want to shut her out. She's a friend but one rarely met in circumstances other than those which play equal host to Warren and Sarah. It occurs to me that my being in this latter company so regularly, elevates my relationship with them to a level above that of mere acquaintances. If so, then it's a strange appraisal that recognizes friendship as something determined by weekly occasion rather than by inner fondness. Yet, perhaps it's the only really workable rule of thumb: affection often proving more ephemeral than the tolerant acceptance of those met on a less intimate basis. I find myself thinking about Philip and the frightening uncertainty of much of our conversation on my last visit to Byschurch. Then, Deborah, whose marriage must surely have wiped out any residual depth to my relationship with her. I suddenly feel lonely, but not so desperately as to ditch my new resolve. On balance, Wednesdays have offered a lot that's been positive, the introduction to Liz, Amy and even to Bill, but against this, there now has to be set the need to enjoy life. The only pleasure offered by Warren, Sarah and Clive is the perverse one of leaving or avoiding their company. Now, I need to make their absence the normal run of things.

When I come to think about it - and the distant deliberations going on around me offer no intrusion - my voluntary association with Clive is especially despicable, a horrible self-betrayal that I must now put right. It's remarkable that Steynmouth or anywhere else, could ever have served as the arena for the resurrection of our formerly unhappy partnership of student days. I now have to do what I should have done one December day on the platform of the underground station.

*

I'd spent the afternoon at the Geological Museum, taking in an exhibition on crustal movement, a topic I'd always found interesting in spite of its compulsory presence amid the material which the university expected me to master. At four o'clock, I picked up my coat, short blue gabardine with a simulated fur collar, and walked out into the chilly air of Exhibition Road. I bought a 'hot dog' from a roadside vendor and ate it with my leather notecase squeezed firmly between my legs. The numbing cold caused my cheeks to redden and the effect was heightened by ketchup oozing from a bread roll whose width was not easily reconciled with that of my mouth. I found myself short of a handkerchief and returned to the museum to make use of the paper towels in the Gents' washroom. This irksome retracing of my steps was made further necessary by the protests of my bladder, unsuspectedly full on my departure and responding quickly to the cold outside. The same doorman insisted that I yet again display the contents of my case. I couldn't for the life of me imagine what possible motive the I.R.A. might have in causing an explosion in a building full of rocks, many of which were quite used to fiery extravagance at the time of their birth.

My second departure, made in more hurried fashion, saw me quickly in the long pedestrian subway leading to

South Kensington station, but still no more sheltered from the unfriendly weather than I'd been up at street level. The heavy cold air drained down into this brick-lined burrow and forced its unwelcome way into the lungs of the human passers-through. Here and there blue-fingered buskers picked painfully at ice-cold guitar strings and burbled vague folky dirges. I hunched forward, partly to avoid their begging stares, but mainly to assume a warmer posture and in doing so, became conscious of shedding height. This obviously was one reason for the majestic tallness of the lithe and muscular East African nomad, herding his cattle with shoulders well pushed back against the powerful tropical sun. Thus too, the squat Eskimo, too fearful to stand straight against the nastiness of Arctic blizzards. I quickly judged myself to be a more seasonal being, altering my stance in response to the vagaries of the British climate.

I scurried through on to the platform, now quite busy in anticipation of the imminent rush-hour. I ignored the unintended brushings against me, so much so that I responded only very slowly to a more deliberate tap on his left shoulder.

"Are you going back to the hostel?"

"What? ... Sorry ... Oh, hello Clive. What are you doing here?"

"Are you, or aren't you?"

"Yes, why?"

"Well, you could perhaps save me a journey. Take my stuff back." He lifted a giant and obviously heavy briefcase into the air, immediately dropping it back with a solid thump on to the concrete floor. "Then, I'll be able to make a direct journey into town and on to the theatre."

"What are you going to see?"

"Conduct Unbecoming."

"As is this!"

"I beg your pardon."

"Well, lumbering me with your rubbish."

"The product of a hard day's work old boy!"

"Day's? Could be a decade of diligence inside that sack of yours. In any case, what's a classicist like you doing here, amid science and technology?" I somehow neglected the V and A.

"The Classical World, Bernard, is unconfined by subject or chronology. Its influence is everywhere. Come on now. To carry one's bag is to ask very little of a friend."

"Not when he already has his own and might for all you know have plans to do other than return home himself."

"Do you?"

"No."

"Well, come on then, don't be churlish and anyway, I've something more important to ask of you. So, don't let's make an issue of the minor item."

"Something else? What? As an afterthought to my being your porter?"

"No, not an afterthought. Actually, it's something I've been wanting to mention for some time."

"Oh, what the hell? Fire away then."

"Well … not here exactly."

"What then? You now want to postpone this mysterious request."

"No, no. It's just … well … perhaps if we could retire to the far end of the platform. Somewhere less conspicuous. More private."

"Clive! I've a train to catch."

"It won't take a minute, honestly."

"Okay, okay, I'll give you until the train arrives. Which is probably less time than you claim to need."

Clive stepped quickly sideways, anxious to say what had to be said. Surprisingly lacking in curiosity, I followed, less deliberately.

"Come on, Bernard! You're the one who says he's in a hurry."

"Yes, but not necessarily to hear your request for a favour. It is another favour, I presume, on top of carrying your bag?"

"A favour? Yes, it is but not such an everyday one that I'd want others to learn of it."

"Oh, get on with it."

Clive shuffled his feet, looked carefully around to assure himself of confidentiality, and began his half-whispered request. The manner of his delivery was such that only a small portion of the air expelled from his lungs was utilised in the speech process, the rest of it showing up as spurts of mist in the cold late-afternoon air.

"Let me put it this way. Would you subscribe to the view that, as individuals, we men are the frustrated victims of supressed aggression, deprived by the niceties of society of the outlet of a good therapeutic bash at someone else."

"What? I don't know! But what I do know is that this investigation of our primitive urges is out of place in the context of South Kensington station in December."

"No. no. Look ... not so loud. Just give me a minute Bernard. I feel, sorry, have felt for quite some time now, that I need to hit somebody, not to put too fine a point on it."

"Really! Well how about getting off your arse and looking for a more acceptable outlet for your aggression, say the sports field?"

"Look Bernard, you know my opinion of sport, the pastime of egotistic bullies."

"Apart from which, you're no good at it."

"True, but not relevant to my basic opinion. In any event, to get back to what I was saying, the trouble is I want to hit out but not get hit back."

"No kidding!"

"And that's just where I was wondering whether you might be of help."

"Sorry Clive, but you've lost me. If you want instruction on how to hit and run, then I'm not the person to offer it. No experience."

"No, no. See, I can't just thump the man in the street; any man … if you see what I mean. I need a willing victim, someone to agree in advance that he won't retaliate. I really need this Bernard and it's a question of who to ask."

I stared disbelievingly at him. "Now wait a minute Clive. You're bloody crazy if you think I'm your man. No volunteer chin here mate! Drop it. Let me just say that I've a bad memory. I'd probably, through no fault of my own you understand, forget all about the deal and sock you one back."

"Please Bernard, quieter please, just hear me out. Half of your objection to the idea stems from nervous anticipation of the event. Whereas, if we put the whole thing on ice, and then I just whack you at some unexpected moment, it won't be so bad. No time for preliminary worries."

"Clive. You really are crazy, you know that. Where do you suggest this little one-sided confrontation takes place?"

"That's just it; what I was saying a second or so ago. It's best left on the table until I feel the need. Just so long as you don't get upset when it happens."

"I surely would do, Clive. Let me warn you of that in no uncertain terms. Look, here's the train and by the way, your bag can accompany you to the theatre."

I moved forward quickly, pushing my way through a group of staring travellers whose curiosity had been aroused by my loud dismissal of Clive's proposal. I stepped ahead of them onto the train, turning as I entered the door to look back over their shoulders to where Clive, now given up on secrecy, was shouting defiantly that his idea could not so easily be put to rest.

"I'll do it Bernard, you see! You'll understand at the time. I'll do it!"

*

The staff meeting has ended after two and a half hours, a crazily enervating experience, given the rigours of the new term ahead.

"Hello! I'm Barry."

"Barry?"

"Yes, Barry Raybould. Mr Pointer mentioned me to you during the meeting."

"Oh yes. Pardon me, but he didn't mention your Christian name, or did he?"

"No, no; he didn't. But I thought that …"

"Yes, of course. I'm Bernard. From my hazy recollection of what went on in there, I'm supposed to introduce you to the ways of this place."

"Yes. I believe so" Raybould laughs nervously. His manner is hesitant, not the passing hesitancy of a newcomer, but that of the perpetually self-doubting. He looks ill-fitted for the job, in my opinion. Physically unimposing, quiet of voice, a probable object of future pupil misbehaviour.

"You're sure teaching's what you want?" My question is smilingly put, but indelicate in its reverse implication.

"I believe I'll adapt. At least, I hope so."

"Oh, you'll be okay." My reassurance, despite its casual utterance, is likely to be an accurate forecast. The taunts of an unappreciative audience will probably never heighten Raybould's uncertainty to a point where it will overtake the soldiering on, dictated by his conscience. Such doggedness, by contrast, can never be mine. At some stage or other, I might well decide that enough is enough.

Raybould walks alongside me, obviously intent on pursuing our courtship, expecting me to say something further.

"Look, Barry, I'm actually off to the car now. I'm sure we can find some time tomorrow for a chat. Can I offer you a lift somewhere?"

"No thanks. I've found accommodation just around the corner, within convenient walking distance."

"Fine. See you again then."

"Yes. Nice to have met you."

We leave the main door together, Raybould turning right towards his bed-sit, and me to the left. The staff car park is up against the gymnasium wall where an anonymous aerosol artist last year inscribed the now fading slogan, "Increase the Nation's I.Q. Kill a P.E. teacher." A small group of six of my colleagues is buzzing searchingly around the various cars. One of its members turns back towards the building, his eyes scouring the path before him.

"What's up?" I'm hoping no help is needed.

"I've lost my bloody car key," snaps Warren.

"Oh dear!"

I hope you're not being facetious Bernard, because I'm strictly not in the mood."

"No no. Hang on now. Before you bite my head off. I think I can be of help. Your car key you say?"

"Yes, yes. My car key! You've seen it?"

"No … but …"

"Bernard! If you're …"

"Let me finish. I've just seen Major Warlby in the corridor. He's your man."

"You mean he's found it?"

"Well, not exactly."

"For Christ's sake Bernard, what do you mean then?"

"Just look him out, Warren and your problems are over."

"Okay, okay … but this had better be genuine Bernard."

Warren runs towards where the Major has reportedly just been sighted.

I shout after him. He's your man for khaki, Warren!"

Chapter 6

Something to Report

Wednesday nights at *The Green Man* now comprise Warren and Sarah, often alone; sometimes Clive, inexplicably; once Bill, accidentally, forgetful of the new non-arrangement; occasionally Liz, out of concern for Sarah. But never me. By late October, I've absented myself from seven possible sessions. My unilateral decision has served as a catalyst for further disintegration. The more muted but basically similar response from other quarters has flattered me.

Opting out, has proved, however, to be a decision whose soundness is not easily admitted, even as a wise desertion of what's gone before. Its implications are not clear-cut. Reorienting my social life, both solves and creates problems. Whatever its failings, the group was a vehicle for social exchange outside of its own claustrophobic existence. After all, even Warren has thrown a party to which smiling faces were invited and such events, however infrequently held, have more to commend them than the sporting seriousness and sterile bar side conversation I've since encountered at the Steynmouth Squash Club.

I now play squash on Wednesday evenings, regularly, replacing my more fitful enthusiasm of yesteryear. The club itself, occupies a revamped riverside warehouse, the ventilation fans at the front of each court sucking in unwelcome quantities of fishy air to the discomfort of gasping combatants. The basic seediness of the premises goes unrecognised among its image-seeking patrons with whom I feel my flirtation will be short-lived. The fun component is barely present. My opponents regularly enter the fray with a gladiatorial scowl. They become offended when I laugh at the less-than-expert shot, the unexpected bounce, when I win without delight or lose with no semblance of dismay, when I show little inclination to indulge in lengthy post-match analysis over the drink which my physical state demands.

"I noticed you changed your tactics mid-way through the second game."

"Really?"

"Yes. Meeting my serve earlier, playing fewer angled shots, aiming for more pace."

"You noticed all that?"

"I'll say. You're difficult to play against. Very unpredictable."

"Oh, I just get tired of concentrating. More bash and less brain as the game wears on. Like another drink?" There are few people more tiresome, I think, than members of the sporting community. The blazered and pompous athletics official; the big-bellied and boastful rugby player; the pampered prima-donna of the tennis court. Even my own spectator addiction to professional football is despite my dislike for the lifestyles of many of its practitioners and their afternoons at the betting shop.

*

Not that there's ever any chance of facing Bill in sporting conflict. So, there's developed instead a regular Thursday lunchtime chat aside the bar of the *Lamb and Flag*. This dingy, establishment situated almost next-door to the abandoned, but more attractive, *Green Man*, has little to commend it other than it meets my determination not to return to old pastures. A soft, flour-dusted bread roll filled with limp lettuce and overripe tomato, washed down with a glass or two of tepid shandy, gives the whole thing an air of disgusting ordinariness. The need to maintain sobriety for an afternoon's teaching makes Bill's company marginally more tiresome. He's admittedly a decent sort, and I've felt compelled to offer my fat friend some social compensation for the demise of the Wednesday drinking circle, but this gesture does little for the well-being of either of us. Without an audience for his personal cocktail of jollity and concern, Bill is essentially uncomfortable.

"How are things, Bernard?"

"Fine."

"You mean that you don't miss the get-togethers at all? Even allowing for Warren and Clive?"

"Right."

"Well, I'll tell you. I miss them. Without Wednesday nights, it's like being locked out of a benevolent prison. In its way, the group helped me evaluate myself and my stance on things."

"Not with me it didn't."

Bill places his glass down on the table and lets the subject rest. He recognizes that Warren might well have been an eager and serious conversationalist, but I'm a more trustful companion.

"Your round. Oh, and order the salad rolls while you're at the bar."

Which means pay for them. Bill is still unemployed, and the summer bounty from his sale of coastal paintings has long since been spent. Some of it on two blue suede patches now stitched boldly on to the elbows of the red sweater.

*

The Reverend Keith's telephone, temporarily mine, has a shattering ring, amplified out of all proportion to the needs of a normal ear, but installed with meticulous foresight at the possibility of impaired hearing come the time of eventual ministerial retirement. In the meantime, it causes me to run in answer, desperate to halt its raucous summons.

"Hello Bernard. Glad to have caught you in."

"Amy! Nice to hear from you."

"Yes, well, I haven't seen you for some three weeks or so now. Look, I know it's very Charlotte Bronte and all that, but would you like to come around to tea on Sunday afternoon?"

"Delighted."

"Fine. I'll ask Liz too."

"Any special occasion? We'll not be blowing out birthday candles or anything?"

"No, no. Nothing celebratory. Just I'd like to see you, see you both for that matter. Liz has been away you know this last fortnight. Some training course or other up at Bristol. Gets back this Friday evening."

"Yes, I know."

"Of course. I suppose you would." Her voice is suddenly less than cheerful.

"Any special time?"

"No, no. Come over when you like. Say after the football on T.V.!"

"I might forgo that for once and come straight over after lunch. Give you a hand with the scones. Help whip the cream."

"Bernard, it won't be that twee!"

"No, sorry. Look, anything you'd like me to bring?"

"Well, a bottle of wine maybe."

"Wine? I thought we were talking about tea."

"Yes, but you'll not be in any rush to get away. We can sort of work our way through into the evening. I'll ask Liz to bring a contribution too."

"Fine. Sounds better all the time. I'll look forward to it. How are you by the way? Honestly, I've been meaning to call."

"Hold it, Bernard. I'm always sceptical about intentions not acted upon. See you Sunday, okay?"

"Okay."

We both wait for the sound of disconnection. It seems there's more to say. But it goes unsaid and the line is waveringly closed, equally timed at each end.

*

It's marginally easier parking outside Steynmouth railway station in October than during the hectic days of summer arrivals and departures. Unashamedly, I draw my car in close alongside a shining black Mercedes, whose gleaming radiator grill is topped by a gently waving civic ensign. For one ridiculous, but horrible moment, I imagine the mayor having spent a night or two with Liz in Bristol. Debauchery at the ratepayer's expense and now, to be chauffeured back home to the unsuspecting mayoress. This fear is expelled by the appearance of the municipal leader, a large Pickwickian figure who, even if of the mind to entice, would hardly be likely to allure. And so, he would have remained but a fleeting occupant of my thoughts, were it not for the fact that the Mercedes' passenger door is too wide to open adequately within the narrow gap between the two cars.

The chauffeur, a slight, almost emaciated man, stares accusingly at me. "Excuse me, sir, but perhaps if you reversed out, then I could allow the mayor to take his seat in the car. It's all a question of room you see."

"Well, I can see he needs a lot of it." I'm deliberately ignorant of the inconvenience I've caused and look around curiously. "Listen, if you were to reverse out, then there'd be more space for His Worship to get in and what's more, you could drive straight off. Whereas, I'd have to vacate this parking space, and then move back into it to await my passenger. Now, which is the least bother, eh?"

"Hello!" Liz's arrival, with small blue suitcase in hand, has gone unnoticed. She breezes in, unruffled by the experience of West Country rail travel, and unconscious of the debate into which she now intrudes.

"Hi!" ... "Hello." A double fanfare, the mayor echoes me with an independent greeting of his own and then beats me to the punch with a conversation opener.

"It would seem, Elizabeth, that the manners of our respective chauffeurs hardly bear comparison. A civilised request from my side that your man move his car but intransigence and rudeness in return."

Liz maintains a glorious equilibrium. She has the sort of fine-tuned alertness that guarantees quick adjustment to the unforeseen. Added to which, she's already encountered mayoral brashness - over her spilling of coffee in the buffet car - and has conquered it via delicately flirtatious behaviour, which she now sees needs further deployment.

"I'm sure, Councillor Le Bryce, that my friend meant no offence. I mean, he probably took the view many might take, that you are, after all, a servant of the people, and not in a position to command their obedience. Oh, and by the way, your mention of a ticket to your Christmas Ball. Perhaps, since the lady mayoress is, as you say, likely to be too ill to attend, then I might take you up on your offer. I could give your secretary a call nearer the time."

"Yes, yes. Of course, Elizabeth. It's all been a misunderstanding. Look, by the time you've loaded your luggage, we can most surely be out of your way. Reverse the car, Stanley old chap. I'll hop in out here. Jolly nice to have met you, my dear. Best journey back from Bristol I've had in a long while."

There follows mutual admonishment. Liz to me, for having been needlessly obstructive to someone merely being the product of his class. Me to her, for the tasteless employment of her face and body. To which she replies … "Bullshit! And if I kiss you, will you lift my case?"

We laugh. She moves instantly sideways into the fold of my arm and presses her cheek against my shoulder. Then frees herself to walk briskly to the car door.

I lift the case without being kissed.

*

Liz's second floor flat, rented from a Londoner who has long since lost interest in Steynmouth, has that hybrid feel of an intruder's stamp upon someone else's property, although in this case, the essential insecurity of tenancy serves to dilute her impact. It isn't that the place fails to announce her presence, but rather that it betrays the possibility of her leaving at short notice. Quick-assembly mail-order furniture that looks all set for instant pulling apart: lots of bright-coloured lightweight cushions, large but with no weight penalty come removal day; a small stack of six books on loan from the library, easily returned to Sarah's desk; no collection of solid hardbacks to pack into tea chests; light shades of white concertina paper, readily folded to nothing, or for that matter cheap enough to leave behind. At times, she envies Amy and her actual ownership of property. Her own walls are covered with paper posters and unmounted Athena prints, whereas Amy has indulged in solid-framed, glass-fronted originals which can't be rolled up. It's a matter of cut flowers as opposed to the established foliage of long-resident houseplants.

I follow her upstairs, pausing mid-way to switch the suitcase from right to left hand, this dictated not by weakness of arm nor heaviness of weight, but by the need to avoid a protruding gas convector heater whose modest output is optimistically meant to filter through strategically located, dusty aluminium grills, and thereby service the combined winter demand of bathroom, bedroom and kitchen. Only the spacious sitting room, whose elaborate cornice work and large sash-cord windows are conspicuous reminders of former Victorian elegance, has its own independent source of heat, a mock Regency gas fire with warm red ceramic radiants, essential in January, and welcome even now of a late October evening. Liz marches ahead and with six loud clicks of the control knob achieves an alarmingly explosive ignition.

"Leave the case in here, Bernard. I'll sort it out later."

We ought to be closer. Summer in France. Then Autumn car-rides, cinema outings, dinners for two. All enjoyable as occasions, but from my viewpoint, not yet a green light. At best, I've convinced myself of a flickering change from red to amber.

There follows some coffee, a chat about Bristol, jokes about the mayor, confirmation of Sunday tea at Amy's, background music, T.V. news, Carole King replaced by Kenneth Kendall and Kissinger, more coffee, Drambuie, but then goodnight. I'm disappointed but determined to persevere in a pursuit which is anyway now conducted in private, and thus, a vindication of my dismantling of the inquisitive assembly of Wednesdays past.

*

Though *The Green Man* had meant that Clive had usually been met in structured safeness.

The October staff meeting has just about made it. Originally scheduled for the fifteenth, it's been postponed three times as George Pointer falls repeated victim to the other demands on management. Working lunches with other headmasters, likely to drag on beyond four o'clock. Informal discussions at Shire Hall. Local P.R. missions. All preferable maybe to witnessing Steynmouth High School in daily operation. Therefore, his monthly address is finally rescheduled for the thirty-first. Opening words are delivered at four fifteen, closing homilies at six o'clock. In between which, Warren has waffled and Raybould has found his questioning feet. Time, I think, to ditch him, lest the novice's enthusiasm proves infectious.

It's a chilly evening when I walk out through the rusting wrought iron gates, held uncertainly on hinges set in partly crumbling brickwork. Exercise to-and-from work represents a recent steeling of resolve. The school is set in leafy suburbia. Substantial semi-detached houses of Thirties vintage, and well-established avenues of pollarded trees growing centrally within grass verges which separate road from pavement. It starts to rain. With my car once again out of action, I might march the six hundred yards to the bus stop or risk the two miles walk back home. The decision can be deferred for a minute or two.

In many a crime or suspense movie, the car or cab driver looks in his rear-view mirror and sees nothing other than the expected: concrete, tarmac, other traffic. But then suddenly, the usual becomes unusual. Not just cars behind, but one car, the same one that was there three or four blocks back. The tail is spotted. All within half a minute. A few feet of celluloid. It takes me a lot longer.

Once sown, the seed of suspicion has germinated hesitantly, and has struggled to grow in the absence of demonstrable nourishment. Any delay in flowering and it could all be relegated to the unsubstantiated. It started weeks back as a feeling of vague, unidentifiable discomfort. A sense of mild concern perhaps, but barely approaching the threshold of awareness. Fitfully, sometimes receding, sometimes escalating, it heightened to something that wouldn't go away, that drew the physical response of a sinking stomach and flushing cheeks. There was a war veteran back in Byschurch who would regularly spin around during his town centre walks, hopping exaggeratedly on his left leg, confronting his amazed 'shadow' with accusations of back-stabbing ill-intent. I've resisted the pressure to emulate such paranoia. Yet this evening, one minute into my journey, my resolve fails. I whirl around and stop abruptly, like some toy-room Dervish whose clockwork has suddenly snapped.

There, in the fading light, is Clive, shunting quickly sideways behind a strangely sculpted tree.

Jesus Christ! What the hell is he up to? A thought triggered by relief at the release of suspense, at the ability to identify the pursuer. Then anger, but against such an oft-directed target that I feel no need for instant confrontation. The whole thing is essentially silly and demands no more reaction than continued vigilance and curiosity.

But repeated occurrences over the next few days, at different times and in different places, with only token efforts at concealment, suggest a degree of planning and a strength of motive that cause my ease to abate.

"I tell you Liz, he's blown it. Now tell him, in some quiet corner at work, to lay off. Otherwise it'll be ... hell, I don't know. Just tell the fool to lay off. Okay."

But Clive continues to appear, staring at his quarry. Crazily confident of his own invisibility.

*

"And so, you see, we do have a problem here. One in which we need your help and alertness. Now, unless any of you have some final observation or other ..."

The fat policewoman is nearing the end of her address. She lies at one extreme of the range of sizes of uniform offered by the Steynmouth force. Her balloon-like white blouse is nevertheless stretched tightly across quite spectacular breasts. These are fortunately counterbalanced by an intimidating pair of legs, bulging calves inside laddered black stockings anchored down by heavily shod feet.

She speaks loudly, out of a face more finely cut than her body has a right to expect, pulling nervously at her hat which lies before her on the desktop, loosening its black and white gingham band.

What had been billed as a question and answer session has never been anything other than a quickly delivered monologue. Drugs, their use and misuse, and the role of the Steynmouth High School teacher in assisting the officers of the law. Now, she wants to finish. It has all been very much along the lines, 'This is a syringe'.

"I have an observation."

She looks disparagingly across at me, the man who is threatening to overturn her neatly loaded applecart. "Yes, Mr? ..."

"Davies. Bernard Davies. It's essentially that I think you've overstated the scale of the problem, locally that is."

"Really?"

"Yes. I accept that there's an influx of summer sun-seekers and surfers to the beach and that some of them roll their own, but as for the native teenagers, it's no more a widespread social phenomenon than is say wife-swapping among their parents."

Her eyebrows raise. "And you don't consider wife-swapping a social problem?"

"What I mean is, there's not much of it going on."

"In which case, Mr Davies, how do you explain the deployment of six members of the local police force, me included, to tackle the drugs problem?"

"I don't know. Fashion. Job creation. But not the essential scale of the problem."

"Mr Davies, drug abuse is now universal. We're no different down here."

"But we are, Sgt Livermore, we are. Steynmouth Quay is not Haight Ashbury in the late sixties."

"Hate Ashberry?"

"That's all right, Sergeant. I'll take your word for it." I see no point in further exposing someone who only minutes earlier, had vilified the primitive Amazonian Indian for his chewing of the coca leaf, equating his conduct with that of the urban heroin peddler.

*

"If you don't mind me saying so, I'm increasingly of the opinion that this is all down to our disagreement over the drugs issue." I seek some reason for what I see as deliberate non-cooperation on Sgt Livermore's behalf.

I've been referred to her by the desk officer who's suggested that, whatever the nature of my enquiry, it would initially be useful to speak to someone I already know. "It's the personal touch, sir. We feel it helps. Now, have you ever spoken to a member of the Steynmouth force before?"

Umm … no … Oh, wait a minute. Last year sometime. A Sgt Liver… something of the Drugs Squad. She came along to the High School to do a P.R. job."

"Fine, fine. I'll check if she's in. Your name? … Hello, Hilda? A Bernard Davies is here to see you. Asked for you personally… yes, straightaway? Okay, I'll send him up … Third floor, sir, far end of the corridor, door facing you."

"Okay, thanks."

The police station occupies a narrow triangle of land at the town end of the public park, an area which is, therefore, uncharacteristically free of vandal damage and litter. The end-of-building staircase which connects its four floors is housed in a rectangular column of smoked glass, which to one side, takes advantage of its elevated position above the town centre to afford darkened cross-rooftop views of the sea and harbour beyond. I take the cold steps of mock granite two at a time, quickly reaching the third floor. I push aside the well sprung fire doors and walk the length of a corridor empty of people but alive with voices, telephone ringing and radio blips from behind half-open doors either side. But not, it would seem, loud enough to drown my approach, for as I get close to Sgt Livermore's office, the door opens before me and my matronly confidante stands expectantly there, in curious welcome.

"So, you're being followed by a friend. I don't really see what you expect us to do, Mr Davies."

"I thought I'd explained. He's not a friend, well currently, not a friend. If he were, he wouldn't be stalking me like a refugee from a Hitchcock film set."

"Mr Davies. I wonder if - how shall I put it - I wonder if I might enquire as to the exact nature of your relationship with this man?"

"But I've already put you fully in the picture. As I said, he's an ex-university colleague and very peculiarly behaved."

"What I really mean Mr Davies is, well, is this all a lover's tiff?"

"No! It bloody well isn't! Look, he's unstable, screwed up. One of these days, he's going to translate some hang-up into action and the way things are, going I'm likely to be involved. See, if he were just a big but normal bully who wanted to work me over, fair enough. But you just can't forecast with him."

"Mmm. Well there's always a solicitor's letter Mr Davies. On balance, that's what we'd recommend. Objecting to the harassment. It's usually enough to bring most people to their senses."

"Oh my God! He's not most people, for Christ's sake. Surely, if one of your heavy mob were to knock on his door and put the real frighteners on him. That's all I'm asking."

"Sorry, Mr Davies. That's just not on at this stage. All we can do is to commit your complaint to paper, and suggest you refer to us again if the need arises."

"Hell's teeth. If it were the P.M. who was being shadowed by a developing looney, he'd be protected by Special Branch twenty-four hours a day. All I want is a humble bobby to tell this twit to leave off."

"Do try the solicitor's letter, Mr Davies. Our experience is that it's preferable to the sledgehammer approach."

"Oh please. I tell you what. I'll not bother you again, take up any more of your valuable time, until I've a bullet through my brains!"

*

Sgt Hilda Livermore is unperturbed. Liz and Amy are unperturbed, even amused. I'm very perturbed. Not amused.

Chapter 7

Marriage Counsellor Required

It's a remarkable reflection on man's desire to enjoy himself that the execution of his forebears becomes a cause for celebratory concern on each anniversary thereafter. Thus, it is not the memory of ridding herself of the tyranny of aristocratic control that leads France to rejoice every fourteenth of July, but rather the ghoulish recollection of the guillotine descending upon deserving necks. But at least, I say to Liz, the French do not seek to recreate the moment itself. They do not subject some stuffed effigy of a 'seigneur' to a mock severing of head from body. It is the British who, by contrast, regularly burn Guy Fawkes on the fifth of November each year and relish at witnessing human flesh set alight, not just thanks for the failure to destroy Parliament. It's all about fire, not about political and religious shenanigans.

I can feel my face reddening with the heat. Stretching forward, I poke the charred end of a stick into the edge of the blaze and work three baked potatoes on to the safety of the partly singed grass. Amy passes me three disposable plates of expanded polystyrene, each of which, in turn, I place in a position allowing me to scoop the potato sideways onto it, using the instep of my right foot. The centres of the plates partly melt in protest. "Liz has gone to fetch some forks. Should be back any second."

The bonfire is held in the town park, alongside the out-of-season paddling pool whose scum of sodden leaves floats miserably on its surface. Boarded up ice-cream huts, see-saws and swings with wet, mossy wooden seats, an annual convention for the members of the Steynmouth Chamber of Trade. Amy and her fellow shopkeepers are too busy of a Summer to bother with anything other than the ringing of cash registers and the banking of tourist money. Come Autumn, they can relax temporarily, before the locals dig into their Christmas pockets. She isn't really someone who likes to organise but has agreed to attend, even to promote, this particular exercise in merchants' self-help. Exorbitantly priced tickets, offering entrance to both the occasion and a modest lottery, yield profits which this year have been earmarked for the thematic redecoration of quayside shops. Plus, although she might not like the colour, the paint and its application would be free. "Both of you really ought to come along," she insists. So, Liz and I have made our respective donations to the brightening of our friend's home.

The unfortunate Guy Fawkes was consumed some half hour or so ago. The fire, initially rather unpleasant via its tinder of old furniture and car tyres, has now reduced to a large glow of hot embers, its imminent demise indicating the need for alternative entertainment. Mr Edmund Cecil Smith, a bulbous confectioner, known to friend and foe as 'Sweetie', makes the announcement …"

"And now, ladies and gentlemen, the fireworks display!"

He points to his left, where on a concrete square, expectant packages of gunpowder are festooned on hastily improvised scaffolding.

"I am pleased to announce that, this year, his Worship the mayor has kindly agreed to put match to fuse."

Councillor Le Bryce steps forward, his chain of office stretched to its gilded limit over a generous sheepskin coat. A few words of grateful thanks for the invitation, an apology for the absence of Mrs Le Bryce, and he pulls a box of Swan Vestas out of his side pocket. As he opens it, the upside-down inner tray spills out its contents onto the damp grass around his feet. Sweetie steps forward with the offer of a gas-filled cigarette lighter, and within seconds attention is diverted from the collapse of mayoral dignity to the whirring of Catherine wheels and the spouting of Roman candles. The short-lived display is modest in all but its finale, an illuminated invitation to 'SHOP IN STEYNMOUTH'. This is a tenuous connection with the fifth of November but then, as Amy remarks in defence, no more so than turkey and beer with the first Christmas Day.

I look out over Amy's left shoulder. "Liz is one hell of a time with the knives and forks!" Spending a generous percentage of my social time in the obvious company of two attractive women is not all that the jealous onlooker might assume. I am certainly not the object of any simmering rivalry for my physical attention, at least not in the lurid sense supposed by the suspicious outsider. Nor in the real sense of Liz's friendly resistance to my advances, and Amy's timidity to advance. All I am allowed at the moment, is an unrequited preference for one, without implying a shoddy dismissal of the other. There is no disparity in the level of social regard in which I hold them as friends.

But to others, I am just plain greedy, so that, when Liz returns, Councillor Le Bryce sees no reason for me to deny him the chance of reviving the acquaintance he had struck with her on the Bristol train.

"I'm sure you wouldn't mind, would you, if I introduced Elizabeth to some people I know. No, no, of course you wouldn't."

And so, she goes, inwardly scornful of the order to follow, intrigued at the offer of post-bonfire cocktails at the Le Bryce family seat and slightly scolding of me for having reprimanded her for being so long in fetching the cutlery.

*

"Thanks for the evening, Amy. A nice suggestion." I lean across her to push open the stiffly hinged door of the Imp, which has now agreed to work again, though probably only for a day or two.

"You're not coming up?"

"I hadn't thought to."

"Out of disappointment?"

"At what?"

"At ... you know ... oh, c'mon, forget the chivalry. The important thing is that I'll never regard myself as a consolation prize. So, let's have a drink! I've some brandy to warm you up. It's a while now since the fire went out."

"Okay."

"Good."

"Amy."

"Yes?"

"Cheers."

*

Four 'o'clock Fridays are somehow glorious. Each week, it is tempting to imagine that the two days ahead will last forever, that Monday morning is destined not to come around. But reality won't be denied.

"Okay, then. I'd like you all to finish that exercise for Tuesday next."

"But sir, I've finished it already."

"Well, lucky you, David."

"Yes, but sir. My dad will want to know why I've no homework."

"Tell him it's because you're efficient."

"But sir, he'll not believe me. There'll be trouble to play. Last time this happened, with Major Warlby, dad rang up the headmaster to complain."

"To complain?"

"Yes sir. That I wasn't being stretched."

"Stretched? You'll find yourself being stretched by your classmates if you start putting in pleas for extra work. They're going to be afraid I might give it to everybody."

This is an observation based upon a background swell of hissing and muted catcalls. It seems to me that the anxious fourth-former would be better off facing the wrath of his over-concerned father than the outrage of his peers. I have no fear of a carpeting at the hands of George Pointer, the great appeaser of parents. "We must, Mr Davies, remember our customers." Whom I, by contrast, take not to be Mr and Mrs Mum and Dad, nor even their sometimes-deserving offspring, but rather those among my anonymous paymasters who are sensibly concerned with the passing on of man's accumulated knowledge. Thus, I largely see my responsibility as being to 'my' subject, and to those who have taught it before me, a perspective owing much to aping Major Warlby. The Major has the excuse of age in his dislike of the child-centred approach, whereas I, by virtue of my more tender years, ought to be more fashionable.

So, having dispensed one week's dose of information and theory, I collect notes and briefcase and turn into the corridor. Raybould walks purposefully towards me, skipping from side to side to avoid the onrushing wave of released internees.

"Hey, Bernard. Must be your lucky day. There's a cracking looking bit of stuff waiting to see you. She's back in the staffroom."

The hesitant Raybould has acquired a defensive and unendearing cockiness. Though both surprised and curious at the news, I choose, therefore, to remain casually indifferent. "No kidding. Well, if you want to rush back, tell her I'll be along in a few minutes." Raybould, mouth gaping, does as he is told. Now, I can be openly inquisitive. I collar Marion, who has obviously just left the staffroom herself.

"Hi Bernard. Had a good week?" A reasonable question since her daily entombment in the depths of the science block tends to isolate her from the manoeuvrings and trials of her working colleagues in other departments. She only ever sees me within our shared resistance to morning service.

"Yeh, so, so. Listen, Raybould tells me there's someone to see me along there. You didn't see who it was?"

"Well, no. Not as such. Woman in her mid to late twenties I'd say. Surrounded by men offering tea. Get there quickly and you can have one of the surplus cups."

"Okay. Thanks. Have a good weekend Marion. Anything planned?"

"Oh God. Fred and I have opted for Christmas shopping. Get it done before December strikes. God how I hate it. Roll on Monday!"

"Well, not my sentiments! See you then."

I step up my pace, overtaking a pensive-looking Warren, and make my entry into a staffroom, already emptying at a furious pace. I side-step a departing posse off in search of relaxation, and squeeze alongside a bank of wooden lockers, doors bulging open in the face of their contents; discarded vacuum flasks, jars of instant coffee, defunct teaching notes and unmarked essays. It's a gloomy rendezvous: a dark, cloudy, late-afternoon light failing to penetrate the twisted and grubby venetian blinds, which earlier that day, have been let down against the glare of the low November sun, now disappeared. The overhead fluorescent tubes flicker disconcertingly. The air has something about it of the petrol station, the result of inadequate ventilation in the printing room which lies directly alongside, and which sends out powerful whiffs of duplicating fluid through the inefficient seal of the linking door.

I can hear Major Warlby's voice. "Yes, Bernard will be along any second. It would be unlike him to stay longer than absolutely necessary."

It comes from behind a peninsular bookcase which juts out halfway across the centre of the room.

"Fine." The replying voice says too little to be of help in identifying itself.

I walk around the protruding end of the shelves. Major Warlby has now stood up, and his back obscures the woman sat opposite him. There is no sign of the lustful tea waiters to whom Marion had alluded. Only the military mind has recognized chivalry as something demanding a less than prompt uptake of the weekend ahead.

"Ah, Bernard. Someone here for you …"

The Major's words, uttered as he turns around in response to the sound of a presence behind, are lost to me amid my surprise at seeing Deborah. She smiles a nervous hello.

*

It has been with astonishment that I have learned of Sarah's suing for divorce.

"Hell, Bill, Warren's his normal self at work. You'd at least expect that something like this would have had some visible effect on him."

"I think that's the essential problem." Bill is always keen to analyse. "Nothing could ever change him. Sarah perhaps was somehow deluded at the outset. Now she has realised her predicament, she's decided to call it a day."

"But hell, whoever would have thought she had the guts. What's happened? She's moved out or what?"

"God, no. She's really come of age. Stayed put. Warren's camped out at some seafront boarding house in an unheated bedroom."

But it is an even greater shock that Deborah's flight to Steynmouth has similarly been occasioned by disaffection with what marriage has come to offer.

She looks incongruously fresh and lively, quite out of keeping with the dismal time of year and the circumstances of her visit. Her coy opening smile quickly becomes more relaxed and ambitious, the pure white of her teeth lightening the year-round tan of her face, her large eyes wide open in happy recognition of having reached her goal. Standing up, she leans across and plants a polite kiss on my right cheek. Major Warlby clears his throat and walks briskly away in a diplomatic puff of pipe smoke.

"Deb. Hell. What are you doing here?"

"Oh, I'll explain later … Oh, sorry, that's assuming you've nothing planned. If you have, then perhaps I could see you tomorrow."

"You're on your own?"

"Yes."

"And not just passing through?"

"I don't know."

"You don't know. Well, I'm sure I know less. Look, let me just gather my things, and we'll go back to my place. You can spill the beans over something to eat."

"Could I stay the night? Or would the Reverend So-and-So and his wife object?"

"Keith. The Reverend Keith. Don't worry. You can stay. My God! This was going to be a normal weekend."

"Shall I follow you then? I've driven down."

"In which case, you can take me home. I'm foot slogging these days."

We walk out to her car. On the rear seat is a large blue suitcase.

*

It has often occurred to me that environment must impact strongly on the manner of courtship and mating. Thus, the warm blue skies of the tropics must lend themselves to a certain degree of easy promiscuity, not least of all, because of the invitation to wear few clothes, so removing a barrier that the hungry adolescents of more temperate regions find irksome and inconvenient. I have wondered, by contrast, how the inhabitants of the tundra ever procreated, since enthusiasm for the act would need to maintain itself through peeling off multiple layers of oilskin and furs. Yet aside from these broad climatic distinctions, no doubt quite invalid, I recognize divisions of even finer detail, one being that between town and country. The paradox is that while the deluded urban young of London see themselves as pioneers in the sexual revolution recently inherited from the sixties, their adventures are small fry compared with the far less self-conscious and traditional activities of their rural equivalents in the fields around Byschurch. To the sons and daughters of farmers, agricultural labourers, village people generally, sex has no more status than is deserving of something whose results are encountered annually at lambing and calving times. It is part of the pattern of things, lots of it, but nothing to fuss about. As with the difference between the African and the Eskimo, it is all down to environment: green fields and haystacks being more inviting than tarmac and concrete.

Although my immediate schoolfriends and I were creamed off by the educational process as the potential elite of Byschurch society - and likely therefore, to abandon it at some future date - our membership of a small market town and its school presented us with the sort of initiation into the world that was more country than city. Teenage handfuls in the hedgerows, willingness in the woods. But in the case of me and Deborah, it had been reasonably selective. We had liked each other at times other than those spent horizontally, and in the process, had had little time for anyone else. So much so, that our eventually separate reintegration into the mainstream of young Byschurch life had had something about it of the begging.

*

In spurts, in the car and over the first few hours back at the bungalow, Deborah explains her presence, sometimes calmly, sometimes threatening tears. But never appearing desperate enough to have undertaken a journey which was unprecedented, unannounced, and to a person whose allegiance ought in theory to be equally divided between both her and Philip.

No, Philip didn't know she was here. No, she hadn't abandoned the children. She was, in fact, visiting an ailing aunt in Hampshire. Philip had agreed it was a good idea: There was the possibility of of a bequest. No, it was okay, the aunt wasn't on the phone. No, no time limit had been set. It was all open-ended.

I throw some chicken pieces, rice, sweet corn, and chopped peppers into a frying pan. In retrospect, it would have been better to have eaten after talking, rather than during, for questioning and answering intruded so much into the lifting of forks and the need to chew that the warm appeal of the dish, inexorably faded. For the remainder of the evening, the table plays host to cold and congealing leftovers.

"Honestly, Bernard, I can't cite the classic reasons. No physical cruelty, no infidelity. Admittedly I'm taken for granted, and not allowed great independence of mind. As you no doubt noticed last time you called on us. But to a degree, that's not unusual in a marriage, and in any event, it's something over which I've some control. I mean, I could make an effort to assert myself."

"Deb, you've just fallen out of love. Perhaps, you won't fall back in, but you might slowly work your way back. It must be worth the effort, surely, if only to avoid any sense of hasty mistake if you part for no sound reason?"

"That's the problem. I don't think the world at large would ever judge my reasons to be sufficiently well based to justify a family split and all that."

"Try me. I'm not that atypical."

"Well … I … oh, he's so indifferent to his own physical appearance. I mean, I know he's well-tailored, but it strikes me that he owes it to me, to look after what's beneath the clothes."

"Deb! Philip was always going to be, well … big!"

"Fat! Not big. He drives everywhere. drinks more than he ought. I just get turned off by his increasing bulk. He's only twenty-eight, yet bodily he's God knows what. There's no vitality about him. You know what - no, of course you don't - he rarely cleans his teeth these days. All smart suits, gilded specs, after-shave, but tobacco and plaque on his breath. I just don't think I can take his lack of physical appeal. I'm not ready to abdicate from that side of it all, but I've lost almost all desire. Bernard, his distinguished whatever it is, it's just a facade."

"I don't see myself, Deb, that he's too different to the man you married."

"Oh, please Bernard," she began to cry, "please see what I mean. The man, maybe, the outer frame, no. Hell, this makes me seem like someone whose concerns are entirely carnal. But it's important Bernard, it is." Her hands shake nervously. She lifts them up to her strong black hair and twists its strands into a loose ill-formed plait.

I rise from the chair opposite, sit alongside her on the sofa, and scoop her sideways towards me, comforting her within the arc of my left arm. "Hey Deb, look. We'll have to talk more about it, I know. But for now, it's quite a pleasant evening outside. Get your coat on and we'll take a walk along the quay.

Then, tomorrow, or whenever, after a good night's sleep, we can get back to it all."

She plucks her handbag from its imprisonment between our adjacent thighs and removes a tissue to wipe her face.

*

Breakfast is eaten with genuine appetite, conversation surfacing irregularly between mouthfuls of toast spread with thick-cut marmalade. Deborah is, as yet, without make-up. She looks very little different from the girl of old, more mature but not really more aged. The past few years of marriage and parenthood have had a differential effect upon the physical appearances of her and Philip, hence her current predicament, although no-one could sensibly attribute Philip's decline to the married state. Indeed, it might have been even more pronounced had he remained single and thus less prone to the expectation that he spend time at home. Nonetheless, the Byschurch Luncheon Club, drinking sessions with fellow legal practitioners, and the general lack of any exercise other than the depressing of clutch, brake, and accelerator pedals, have taken their toll. And far too prematurely for Deb who, although not one to cultivate the sense of self, is nevertheless aware of her own attractiveness, not meticulously maintained but neither abused through neglect.

"Could I stay the week, Bernard?"

I finish swallowing my orange juice and put down the dimpled amber-tinted glass.

"At how intense a level? I don't think we want days of heart-searching and remember, I'm back at work Monday. But you're welcome, if it's of help." I smile across the white lacquered top of the kitchen table. "Yes of course you can, Deb."

"It's alright now. I feel more relaxed, more of the opinion that while a brief and complete break won't solve things in any way, it'll help in the short term. Just to breath some different air. I've not had such an uneventful breakfast for some time now."

"Really? Well let's compensate for it and make it a more eventful day. We could, perhaps, take a drive inland onto the moors. It looks a bit bleak this time of year, but there's a lovely old pub out at Cross Bridges. Log fire, good beer, plenty to eat. Then, perhaps this evening, we could take in a film?"

"Thanks Bernard. Sounds, well, just right."

"Okay. Well, before we escape, didn't you ought to ring home? You know, have arrived safely and all that. A progress report on aunt what's her name."

Her face tightens. She looks down at her coffee, still too hot to drink and says loudly into the cup...

"It's not necessary. He wouldn't expect me to."

"Nor the kids?"

"I'll ring them Monday."

*

Deb is still in bed. I knock on the door.

"Yes. Come in, Bernard." It's the strong response of someone who has been awake a while.

She's sat propped up, hair already brushed, blue-black, shining against a large yellow pillow, white towelling dressing gown wrapped tightly around her and disappearing beneath the bedclothes. Evidence that she'd been on her feet, as are the half-opened curtains.

"A good book?" I inquire, nodding towards the paperback on her lap.

"I've only just started it." She lifts it up, pointing the front cover towards me.

"You didn't ought to compound your problems by reading Iris Murdoch!"

"Bernard, whatever my problems, they're not on this scale. Could be, I'll end up realising what a mountain I've made out of a molehill."

"You could be right. Look, I'm off out to buy the papers. Any requests or will you share mine?"

"Oh, *The Observer* please. Apart from the main bit, I'm collecting a pull-out series from the colour supplement."

"Okay."

Deborah's reading for the day is going to be on the serious side. It would not test her intelligence. Basically, I think she is more intelligent than Philip. For some reason or other, she had chosen not to continue with formal education after school. She'd worked for a short time on the continent, waitressing, au-pairing. She'd been contemplating occupational therapy, when her ministrations were suddenly demanded closer at hand, the unexpected death of her father leaving her mother alone in Byschurch. Her hometown return, coincided with that of the newly degreed Philip, then still something of a recently lively student. They married three months later. The less than exciting solicitor was to follow.

Some half-way to the newsagents, I enter a telephone kiosk. The morning mist hangs damply to its door handle. Inside is dripping with condensation.

"Hello Amy ... I haven't got you out of bed, I hope... Yes, it's a call box. Only I couldn't say what I want from home ... Well, because I was wondering what your reaction might be if I were to bring along an extra person this afternoon. Someone from Byschurch. She's staying for a few days. Yes, she! Actually, it's the wife of a friend. Look, to put you briefly in the picture, there's some sort of marriage crisis going on, and I'm not sure I want the 'her and me' bit to get too claustrophobic. So, if we could both join you and Liz for the Sunday tea you usually have... What? ... Okay, so two weeks running doesn't make it usual ... But I'd be grateful anyway. No, no, I don't resent her coming at all. I mean she's an old friend, and good company when in the mood ... Okay, that's great of you, Amy. Assuming she's agreeable, we'll see you later. Otherwise, I'll come on my own. She wouldn't expect that I do nothing weekends. Bye ... Oh, while I think about it, you'd better put Liz in the picture, will you? I don't want her dropping any clangers, deliberate or otherwise ... Amy! ... you still there? ... I tell you what, if you see Bill before I do - which won't be till Thursday - ask him to get in touch with me. Only Deb, that's her name by the way, is possibly staying the week, and Bill might be his gentlemanly self and occupy some of her time while I'm at work ... Yes, I know he's elusive, but he might just call in on you. Okay, that's finally it ... see you later."

*

Amy is her expected welcoming self. So that Deb quickly relaxes. She seems not to notice Liz's staged indifference to her presence.

Liz stations herself away from the pine table where the other three of us are seated. Instead, she sits cross-legged on the floor, amid the forest of cane and indoor foliage that sprouts from the rush matting divide between business beneath and living above. She puts out a hand, speculatively and successfully, towards a stoneware mug of tea, her eyes firmly fixed on one of Amy's trade magazines which is opened across her lap. She looks admiringly at the photographs of German wax reliefs, intricate miniatures, solid and ivory-like in appearance, but each with a future dependent on delicate handling. The teasing flat gloss of the magazine denies her this experience. In frustration, she breaks her silence.

"Can't you get any of these, Amy? I wouldn't mind a row of them, tell you the truth." She lifts the magazine towards the table.

Amy peers across and pours instant cold water on the idea. Talks about them being out of character. Tells her that, to be credible, a craft shop must mirror its locality, display a strong regional affinity and that anyway, goods couldn't normally be ordered in the very small quantity that Liz would want.

"But a lot of your stuff isn't local! Not West Country but made in some Lancashire factory. Mock rustic! Or in Kuala Lumpur or somewhere."

"Yes, but it's what people want or expect of me. Black Forest cuckoo clocks or Swiss cowbells wouldn't do."

Liz flicks over the page in undisguised annoyance and returns to her isolation.

By now, Deb is sufficiently at ease to be moderately perceptive. She recognizes that Liz's contribution to proceedings is likely to become even more minimal than it has been already. "Can I help you wash up, Amy?"

"Oh please, if you would. I don't think I could face it later."

Liz shows no inclination to follow them through to the kitchen. Nor did I, as I'm now determined to prize her out of her afternoon's silence.

"Look, you've never told me how you got on round at old Le Bryce's place on Guy Fawkes night. Did you meet his wife? Does she exist even?"

"She exists, but she didn't appear. At least, I assume she exists. Talking of third parties, by the way, are our arrangements for Tuesday night affected by latest developments?"

"Well yes, they are, unfortunately. I took Deb to see the film last night. It's good, you ought to catch it. She'll probably be staying until the weekend. So maybe we could meet one evening next week instead."

"Yes … mmm, tell me. Isn't it all a bit heavy, even dangerous, having the disillusioned wife of a friend staying with you?"

"Drop it, Liz! Once those taps stop running, you'll be heard through there. Besides which, don't make me deny my fondness for her so as to reaffirm my ambition for you."

"Bernard! Do you always have to be so bloody blunt?"

*

Dear Violet,

My problem is that my husband's physique disgusts me. He was never slim, but now his waist demands Y-fronts of such hefty circumference that at groin level, the garment flaps loosely in grotesque contrast to the obscene tightness of fit above. Even that most vital of parts seems inconsequential beneath his belly. His mouth emits the scent of a smoke-filled lounge bar. He treats me reasonably well. We have two children. A nice home. Two cars. A gravel drive with separate in and out gateways. A dog. A cat. I have gone for help to a friend. No, a former lover: well, not that exactly, but rather the first person with whom I ever made love. The only person other than my husband. (Sorry; except that is for the doctor to whom I was once au pair in Switzerland, and whose Vermouth we drank one night.) This person is helpful and understanding. He is the same age as my husband, but looks so much younger, seeming only recently, a boy. Tall, upright, flaxen-haired. Inviting dark-brown eyes. He has re-awakened my desire. Should I leave my husband and children? I can hardly resist.

> *Yours,*
> *A worried reader*

Dear Reader,

You are in a pickle and must ask yourself why. Has your husband got fat because you have selfishly fed him mountains of potato, while you have indulgently nibbled away at wafer-thin rye biscuits? Have you created the object of your disgust via an orgy of pastries and puddings? Think carefully. Perhaps your subconscious prefers the porcine form. Why prevent it surfacing? In short, are you abusing the counselling services of this magazine purely to enact some silly personal debate to whose resolution only you have the key. My advice, for what it's worth in the face of your dishonesty, is that you get yourself screwed by your friend and enjoy it. As for the problem with your husband, well, that's it; your problem,

    Violet

*

What time is it? I grope for the alarm clock. Only a luminous six o'clock. I wake in a sweat quite incongruous with my exclusive occupation of the bed and the chilly feel of the still dark morning. Dropping my head back on the pillow, I still have the dream magazine correspondence firmly in my mind. It fortifies the habitual wakening stirrings, and I determine to walk across to where Deborah will be waiting. I drift back into and out of sleep. She folds back the bedsheets, pulling me quickly against her naked body, still the same as I had once known it. We both cry loudly in almost instant climax, her fingertips digging tightly into the back of my shoulders. Thus released, I press at my eyes with my right hand, focus more clearly on the walls around me and with the squeeze of my left hand serving to contain what little is left of the bolted horse, I tiptoe swiftly to the bathroom, my heart beating quickly lest my house-guest should awake and poke an inquisitive head around her bedroom door.

*

Through to Wednesday goes smoothly, crisis free. Amy is her Samaritan self, meeting Deb for lunch on Monday, and inviting her back to the shop for the afternoon. Monday and Tuesday evenings, Deb and I talk together over a drink, watch T.V., listen to music. We avoid direct discussion on the issue at hand. Deb spends Tuesday and Wednesday daytimes window shopping and counter browsing in town, finishing Iris Murdoch, strolling by the harbour.

"Deb, I usually play squash Wednesday evenings. The court's booked for later. I could cancel, but … well, I'd forgotten about it until now, and it's a bit short notice for the other person."

I get back about nine thirty, flesh still tingling, body sparklingly clean from the shower. She's sitting alongside a dim corner light in the lounge, sad, introspective, not the free spirit of the last couple of days.

"Hi! I need a drink. There's one in the fridge. Can I get you one, Deb?"

"Bernard, I know you've been dreading this - or probably have - but could I talk to you again?"

I make to sit down but she manages a half-smile. "No, get your drink first. Maybe, I'll have one later."

She speaks at length, quietly and firmly, her head face down to her knees, occasionally looking up to display her determination. She must go back and tell Philip that she intends to leave him. Her main anguish is the children. If leaving Philip were a means to liberation, then the children, too young ever to be left alone - and even Philip did some baby-minding - would render that liberation almost without worth. She loves them beyond words: they must be hers, but they have considerable potential for sabotaging her future. No, she doesn't know how Philip will react. Yes, she accepts it might be fair to point out his physical decay, to give him the chance to rejuvenate. But she has finally to admit that there is more to it than just his waistline: the unfathomable descent from love. It might be capable of pragmatic solution, but in reality, it's probably irreparable. Then the new practicalities: the need for a home, necessarily away from the introversion of Byschurch, yet nothing improvised, something offering reassurance to uprooted children. It is perhaps their fate, rather than her own, that promotes the sudden onrush of tears that indicate to me that I should get up from my seat opposite, accept her arms around my neck, and offer my chest as a cushion for her head.

I coax her gently alongside me on the sofa, put my hand to her chin and turn her eyes directly to mine.

"Deb, love, look ... you're going to hate me saying this, if I've not said it already, but why not give reconciliation a try? Hell, not even reconciliation since Philip knows nothing of this yet. Why not go back and issue a friendly ultimatum, make known your expectations? Perhaps contribute more yourself. Don't get me wrong but make yourself enjoy his company and see what the response is. You don't know that you couldn't make it work again. Deb, you honestly don't, because this visit is perhaps the first time you've even argued it all out within yourself."

She makes no response. Her eyes redden further, and she sobs quietly, her head on my lap for five minutes or more. I stroke the palm of my right hand across her hair. Eventually, she straightens.

"I'll think on what you've said." Her voice has an uncharacteristic tremolo. "I'm sorry, Bernard, but if you don't mind, I'll go off to bed now."

"It's only quarter past ten. Sure, you wouldn't like a supper drink or anything?"

"No. no. But thanks. I'll see you in the morning."

"What about tomorrow by the way? Any plans?"

"Oh, I don't know. Give me a knock well before you leave for work. I'll have breakfast with you."

I smile. "Lovely. You're better company than the cereal packet."

"Thanks! For more than just the compliment." As she leaves the room, she turns back to face me, residual tears on her cheeks. She places her hand to her lips and blows a kiss.

*

At breakfast, she feels that she owes me something, most especially the prospect of less tension during the remainder of her stay.

"I've decided to drive back home Saturday morning. Aunt Megan is making good progress!"

"So, no reading of the will then. Bad news for the acquisitive Philip!"

"On that score, yes."

"And on the other score?"

"I still don't know, Bernard. But you've helped me a lot. I realise a decision has to be made, but I'm uncertain as to how soon. Yet I do know that it didn't ought to be made with me down here. It's funny, I'm no clearer in my own mind, but crazily, I'm more confident that I'll do what's right."

"I'm not sure, after all that, that I have helped you."

"I am." She stretches across and squeezes my hand.

"You realise, Deb, that it's Christmas soon. At the risk of sounding trite, it is a family occasion. Why not use it as a healing time? I loathe thinking of you being unhappy."

"And that, Bernard, is your help to me. It doesn't have to be advice on tactics, just the assurance of your concern. As for Christmas, well I mustn't forget that more mundane months exist outside of December's presents and plum pudding."

There's a pause as we deploy the toast rack, milk jug and other paraphernalia of breakfast to our mutual advantage.

"Lunchtime, Bernard, could I buy you something?"

I laugh. "Well, it's like this. I usually meet Bill, Thursdays. A friend. There's no way of forestalling him really. Come along and buy all three of us lunch. He'll have no money anyway."

"Is he worth the expense?"

"Yes, in his way. But not to worry, it's pretty cheap grub where we meet."

"Okay. And this evening. I owe you something more pleasurable than yesterday's scene. Could we go out somewhere? I'm the stranger in town. The suggestion will have to be yours."

"Excellent. I'll think of something."

*

But what I think of, as much the fault of Steynmouth out of season as my own lack of imagination, is simply a drive to another country pub. A few drinks. Updates on life in Byschurch. Idle, yet happy chatter. Caught up with by closing time.

Coffee and music back at the bungalow.

"Do you like living here?"

"Yes. It's better than a bed-sit, and the rent's reasonable."

"Does it inhibit you?"

"Inhibit me?"

"Yes. I mean living under a Reverend's roof. Do you feel obliged to behave in a way of which he would approve? When you're indoors that is."

"It's not a bloody church, Deb! What are you on about?"

We both speak with the lightness of an evening delightfully spent.

"What I mean is, could I sleep with you tonight?" She's sitting on the floor across from where I'm kneeling to change a record. She says nothing more. Looks straight at me with wide open eyes, darker than the midnight blackness outside. She tilts her head sideways, so that her hair falls across her right cheek. Her hands tap at her kneecaps.

I stare back, saying nothing for a full half-minute … "I … umm … I don't know what to say, Deb."

"You don't have to say anything."

So, I don't. For a further minute or so, during which time neither of us move. Until my kneeling becomes difficult to maintain.

Then, from the edge of the armchair next to her, I begin to respond, sometimes looking her in the face, sometimes, a hopefully furtive glance down to what is really on offer. "I don't know, Deb. I mean, yes, it's an irresistible invitation! But is it all to stick needles into Philip?"

"No. I just want you. Tonight, as always."

"Always? For Christ's sake, Deb! You can't say that. It was you, remember, who gave me the push."

"Bernard, I was seventeen then! Don't ask me to explain my teenage mistakes."

"You can't pretend Philip's nothing to do with this. Can't pretend that he hasn't supplanted me in the meantime."

"He's never excited me like you did. I just feel like a reminder, that's all. For its own sake. I promise."

"Oh, c'mon, Deb! The excitement way back then was that of your setting foot on unexplored territory. I was just lucky to be involved. Your exhilaration would perhaps have been the same if Philip had been the initiating agent."

"No. Again! I'm the only person who can compare you with Philip on that score. I mean you've never been to bed with him."

"True. Not even as boy scouts."

"So, I'm asking you for myself, you for yourself, for our own pleasure."

"I just feel we'd do it, then walk out of the sunshine to find ourselves under some black cloud of guilt. Over Philip."

"He ought to be my burden, not yours. Stick to your own problem person."

"Meaning?"

"Meaning that if I can forget Philip, you can forget Liz."

"What do you know about that, for God's sake?"

"Oh, reading between the lines around at Amy's place."

"Well, anyway, I may bloody well have to forget her. Not much progress being made in that direction, I can tell you."

"Then she's in need of advice."

"Maybe. But she's not the only one."

"Well?"

"Well, mine to you ought to be that you should iron out what you're already wearing before you add a further crease."

"So, you're not turning me down flat? Just suggesting a postponement!" She smiles. Not offended at the failure of her advance.

"Christ, Deb. I don't know."

"Trouble is, Bernard, that many a postponed fixture ends up never being played at all. Didn't we ought to get on the field of play while we've the chance. While it's clear."

"You want my reaction?"

"Please."

"There already are other players on the pitch. But let's take the field anyway. Maybe, we can avoid them?"

Which proves delightfully easy. Though twenty-four hours later, we both seem wary of a rematch. The following day, her last day, ends with perhaps the most antiseptic goodnight of the week.

*

Saturday morning, she is the inevitable victim of emotion.

"You ought really to dry your eyes thoroughly before driving off." I shelter her in the fold of my arms. "No sense in generating your own impediment to forward vision. I want to think of you travelling in safety."

"God, Bernard. I don't know what to do. All my bravado of the last few days is evaporating."

"Go home, Deb. Cuddle the kids. They're more part of your decision-making process than I am."

"Just don't write me out, Bernard. Your support's important."

"Deb, you're assured of it. Look, just call on me when you like, irrespective of what I've been doing in the meantime."

"Maybe, but that's not really fair. I might stumble in on your wedding day. Like Dustin Hoffman in *The Graduate*." It's meant to be said as a loosening of the knot that she perhaps feels she'd wrongly tightened around me, but what she begins with a smile she finishes with another sob. I dab at her tears, ineffectively. My fingers have no absorbency.

We peer curiously at one another. Then close our eyes and place mouth to mouth. Neither of us pulls back, the kiss eventually succumbing only to our need to breath. I usher her into the car. She winds down the window. Starts up. "I'll call you when I've decided something. I won't ask you to participate in the debate anymore." She pauses, as if waiting for a reply. And when it doesn't come within the second or so demanded by her racing pulse, she lets out her farewell over the generous roar of a departing engine exhaust. "Take care, darling!"

I walk back limply to the bungalow.

Chapter 8

Christmas

When I was three years old, I had a wooden dog on a string. As you pulled it along, the hinged lower jaw snapped upwards to give a flat noisy slap, and the sprung metal tail waved gloriously backwards and forwards.

"You mean you don't do anything like that at all?"

"I'm afraid not, sir. The nearest thing we've got is a noiseless wooden dog that doesn't move, or, failing that, a very noisy plastic caterpillar that does."

"Then perhaps you could recommend me something for a boy of three. Oh, and since I'm here, for his eighteen-month-old sister as well."

"Do you want to spend a lot, sir? I mean, are they your children?"

"Look, even if they were, I wouldn't want to spend a lot, but they're not and I don't intend to. No, something reasonably priced. Or, if you've got it, something cheap that looks reasonable."

The shop assistant is anxious that his time yields maximum commission. He looks at the more promising customers awaiting his attention. "There's a help-yourself counter behind you, sir."

It is weighed down with the offerings of the play industry, all nicely rounded up in price for this the first decimal-coined Christmas. I pick up a flimsy cardboard box. Out of its clear plastic window, stares *Tommy Gunn*, a miniature paratrooper in search of a home barracks, looking beggingly at the potential buyer. I open the box above his camouflaged helmet, and grab at his green-jacketed torso, pulling him sharply into the brightly fluorescent air. Every conceivable joint is quickly put to the test, shoulder, elbow, hip, knee, ankle. Maybe, life is less attractive for him outside the box, after all, a case of better left on the shelf. Then, he finds himself back inside, only stuffed in upside down with his left arm wrapped suicidally around his plastic neck, and his now detached back-pack pressing hard against his rubber stomach. He is put down to a foreign posting, away from his fellow fighting men, *Cradle Land*. His box leans Pisa-like against *Tiny Trisha* with her fully functioning urinary tract.

I discount them both, *Tommy* by virtue of price and his objectionable bulldog face, and *Trisha*, on the basis that young Emily, not yet two years old herself, would not have the manual dexterity to detach a scaled-down diaper from its wearer. On top of which, Deborah might make some ungratefully modern observation about the harmful effects of gender stereotyping her children at too early an age. Choosing suitable gifts, ones that would gain approval from both children and parents, is proving tiresome. But it has to be done without further delay. The twenty days before Christmas is barely enough for the packaged presents to reach their destination in time for the event itself. I am not without experience of the inefficiency of the Byschurch end of the post office system when it finds itself under pressure. As a temporary employee at the parcel sorting office during my student holidays, I had myself once strongly contributed to it.

*

The Christmas in question might have been thought of as promotion. Previous sessions of helping with the holiday post had had me pushing mail through ice-cold letter boxes, cycling back red-nosed to the depot. But now, the big-time, parcel sorting at Byschurch Baptist Hall. Tough on Philip. He was still out on the streets.

I followed the postmaster into a large room with a central aisle between opposing rows of sacks slung from metal frames.

"In, to your left. Out, to your right. Otherwise, it's more or less self-explanatory. Any problems and Maldwyn there will show you the ropes." I glanced towards a fearsome six-footer with a round, shaved head. "And by the way, any parcels needing repair, well, there's string and scissors up on the stage. Oh, and if the fire gets too low, then there's a scuttle of coal in the corner there. That's your job. The hours are eight to five, with forty minutes for lunch."

Which was usually fifty minutes sat huddled around the fire, a small, black cast-iron grate whose paltry heat output was irrelevant to anyone at work and a marked insult to the needs of seated sandwich eaters.

"What do you make of all this Christmas business then, Bernard, you being an educated man and all that? LONDON UNIVERSITY! Are we to believe in it or what?" It wasn't that big Maldwyn resented what he saw as an intellectual presence, just that he resented any speaking presence beside his own. He was much practised at inviting opinions, and then immediately putting them down.

"I don't know."

"What do you mean, you don't know? You must have an opinion. Come on now."

"Maldwyn, I don't know if we're celebrating the birth of a boy to a virgin mother or not. It takes some believing. You've got to admit."

"Well what are we celebrating then, c'mon!"

"Well, it's an on-going celebration, I suppose. Part of the folklore by now. That perhaps it did happen, with God involved somewhere along the line."

"I tell you, if you college kids haven't got the answers, what about the rest of us? It strikes me we're not so dumb after all. My opinion - and at least I've bloody well got one - is that Christ was actually a Roman spy, trained by Mary and Joseph, then other Roman undercover men, John the Baptist and all that lot, would put it about that he was the Messiah. The idea was that he would then infiltrate the Jewish top-dogs and feed through information that would do for them for good, only it all went wrong. Firstly, only the underdogs in society would have anything to do with him and the Romans didn't need to learn much about them anyway. Secondly, Christ himself started to get above his station. He actually came to see himself as the Saviour of the Jews, so, the Romans saw him off because he sort of let them down."

"Sounds improbable to me, Maldwyn."

"Improbable! Any more than the accepted version then?"

"Well, perhaps not at surface level."

"Exactly. Trouble with you bloody college boys is that you never think. Just read and accept."

Maldwyn, thirty-two years in the postal service, was a fountain of unsolicited advice.

"See here, Bernard. What you do if it says 'Ealing, London' with no district number, is say 'sod it', and chuck

it in any of the London sacks. Let them sort it out down there, eh? Or up there, as you clever types would have it."

"Okay, okay." I aimed for the nearest London sack. The parcel bounced off the metal hanging rail and nestled elsewhere.

"What the hell are you doing, Bernard? Just stay put. Leave it where it landed. It's going to take us till New Year to clear this bloody lot if you start ferreting around correcting mistakes."

"Whatever you say."

Not for one moment did I contemplate disputing Maldwyn's authority, no matter what the consequence for myself or the customer.

"Here, Bernard. Go up on the stage and give Dave a hand in re-wrapping this bloody lot."

"Aw, why me?" It was a whispered protest. I was unenthusiastic not because of the nature of the task itself, but because of Dave's notorious flatulence, the reason why Dave had been put out of harm's way in the first instance.

There were ten or so parcels, spewing out their contents through flimsy wrapping paper optimistically held down with tiny strips of sticking tape. With some, repair was a gesture of no practical use. Just new paper and string around already cracked glassware. As Dave indifferently pointed out, it was the customers' fault. If they insisted on writing FRAGILE on everything from a bathroom sponge to Dresden china, then who the hell would take any notice. Only a year off retirement, and he'd never known it any different. *"After all, you'd think that with all these polystyrene balls around these days, you could protect things properly. I mean just look at some of this stuff."* He kicked something my way. *"Here, you can deal with that bugger!"*

I bent over, picked it up gingerly by the only corner of the brown paper cover which hadn't partly disintegrated through the seepage of moisture from within. The smell was unpleasant; no, revolting, though just how much of it could be attributed to the carp was difficult to assess, since Dave's intestinal blow-outs were a constant accompaniment to repair operations. The post mark was dated 'Nov. 28'. Alongside it was a sticker, saying 'Fresh Fish'.

"Do we actually deliver this, Dave?"

"Depends."

"Depends on what?"

"Who it's addressed to."

"Why?"

"Well, if it's going out, we'll sling it, but if it's coming in, then maybe not."

"Maybe not?"

"Is there a Polish name on it?"

I eased out the express delivery address label from within the putrefying mass which I had by now dropped back to the floor.

"Yes. It says 'Boniek'."

"Then wrap it up."

"Why? What's so special?"

"God. Maldwyn's bloody well right. You so-called brainboxes don't know everything. Not all cultures are the same, mate. About time you respected that. Poles, if you must know, have a big fish dinner on Christmas Eve. We've been delivering the Bonieks their carp for years now."

"What! In this state?"

"Yeh, well what the hell do they know? Bloody Polaks. Always gets to them nicely packaged with a new date stamp."

"Yes, but what about the actual fish?"
"Look mate, fish is fish."

*

Just a little further along the shelves is the games section. Snob games for the coffee table, with playboard in up-market mahogany, and moveable pieces inlaid with mother of pearl. Intellectual games, allowing mental agility gained unfairly through intimate knowledge of the rule book and hours of unremitting practice to be nonchalantly displayed before a novice opponent. Inexpensive games, whose hardware would last no longer than a quick pillow fight and would probably provide less than a tenth of the enjoyment. Infant games, supposedly suitable for all two-to-five-year olds, but whose ultra-simplicity would soon prove insufficient for even the most pedestrian of young minds.

'GAMES FOR ALL THE FAMILY'. This looks more promising. I pick up a six-inch cubed box: *Catch a Carrot. Hours of Fun for Mum, Dad and the Kids.* Inside, is a short wooden rod, to which is attached a plastic carrot on a string, a yellow carrot, and six plastic rabbits, in six different colours, which are somehow to grab at this vegetable prey. Exactly how they will do this isn't immediately obvious. The rules, in small print, cover an entire side of a stout piece of folded pink card. This might be a game for some family somewhere, but not for the occupants of Elm Court, Byschurch. Philip wouldn't chase carrots on all fours. Presumably, it would be on all fours. Adults usually knelt or crouched for this sort of thing.

I decide not to give up. The games section has one obvious merit. Most games demand an opponent, and one present will, therefore, serve both kids. Unfortunately, toy manufacturers world-wide have evidently concluded that Emily's eighteen months do not make her a likely recipient of their products. Perhaps it wouldn't matter too much. Most kids are over-provided for at Christmas in any case. And Uncle Bernie's offering can be put aside for the proverbial rainy day. The shop is crowded. A noisy, red-haired boy, about eight years old perhaps, has been getting in my way for some ten minutes now, stretching across me, disobeying an angry mother. "I shan't ask you again, Donald. We can't stay any longer!" But she does ask, again and again, finally pulling him aside with such force that the defiant Donald drops the latest object of his enquiry across my feet. I pick it up.

FUN ON ELDERFLOWER FARM. The latest in recreational concepts for the young and not so young. From the makers of 'BUILD IT UP'. A multi-purpose farmyard complex to match your children's moods. A simple world of rural fantasy with life-like model animals. Just play and say 'moo'. Or a challenging game as these same animals compete for pasture. As shepherd or herdsman, you control their destiny in the great 'FIGHT OVER FODDER.''

Donald has come up trumps. Buy it. Parcel it up and trust that the post office will do its bit in time.

*

This will be the first time since leaving Byschurch that I won't be going home for Christmas.

"But Bernard, Dick and Sybil will be so disappointed. Just as we are."

"Yes, I know, Mum. But, as I've explained, it's nothing to do with not wanting to be with the family." Which isn't entirely true. Even as a child - especially as an only child - I'd come to begrudge the predictability of the twenty-fifth of December. The inexcusable morning absence of church-going Elspeth, the post-dinner snoozing of Harold and his brother, the televised monarchical mouthings at three o'clock in the afternoon, the battle to dragoon adults into doing what I wanted to do. The resentful retreat into the pages of some new Comic Annual. Boxing Day around at Philip's was better.

More recently I had effected some change in the proceedings. Most spectacularly, I'd shamed Harold and Dick into conquering the sleep barrier and lending a hand with the washing up.

"C'mon, Harold. It looks bad for us to sit here with your Bernard doing his bit out there."

"It's never been our bit in the past."

"No, but in the past, he wasn't of the age and inclination to embarrass his elders."

"I don't understand it. What's wrong with lethargy, for heaven's sake?"

*

"I tell you what, Mum. I'll be up in February without fail. Make a long weekend of it over half term. Only, well, I need to stay here in Steynmouth this Christmas."

"What? The whole two weeks, Bernard?"

"Mum, you know it must be important for me to let you down like this."

"Well, yes I do, Bernard, but it'll seem so strange without you here."

"You'll tell dad I've telephoned and that I'm sorry to have missed him."

"Yes, yes."

"And I'll call again soon. Christmas morning too."

"Make sure you do."

"I will."

"And if you were to change your mind …"

There will be no change of mind. Being in Byschurch would mean calling in on Deb and Philip. Unavoidably. It is too soon to intrude. Going to Byschurch at all is avoidable. Steynmouth is a necessity this year. Yes, Liz would love to have Christmas dinner with me.

"Unless you've anything else planned, Liz?"

"No, no. I'd half thought of going to Anne's in London."

"Anne?"

"Sorry. My cousin. She and her husband are good friends. They've invited me over. But if you're staying, I'll stay too. I can pop across and see them around New Year."

*

I tuck *Elderflower Farm* under my arm and make for the cash register. It has been a mistake to do all this of a Saturday morning. The place is busier than Wimbledon on Finals Day. I join a long queue of parents and kids. It fails to move forward, and I decide to leave the toy floor, opting instead to pay downstairs where the books and stationary department might be less crowded.

The escalator trundles noisily downwards. At the bottom, annoyed, I push my way past four or five twelve-year-old boys who are attempting to mount the steps against the direction of movement.

It's a quieter world on the ground floor. Not quiet, but certainly less noisy. The piped music now makes itself obvious and becomes more irritating by the second. This Christmas' musical offering from the entertainment industry is a pretty-pretty little tune, with a sugary chorus sung by a children's choir. If there'd been no divinely inspired event, real or supposed, on that 'first' twenty-fifth of December, then Tin Pan Alley would have commissioned some major festival or other, something to give that once-a-year boost to flagging record sales. Joining a queue only barely shorter than that which I have just left, I start humming to myself a quiet medley of Christmas songs past, deliberately searching out the most absurd. The type which elevates Rudolph to sit alongside Christ, and donkey worship, and the old ones; *All I want for Christmas is My Two Front Teeth, I Saw Mommy Kissing Santa Claus.* It's not the same these days. Rock groups really ought to lay off this sort of thing.

The queue moves slowly forwards. The till rings loudly. Books are forced into undersized paper bags, which split in protest but aren't replaced. Do-it-Yourself manuals, recipe collections, photographic guides to beautiful places; all are good, solid presents. *Elderflower Farm* seems conspicuously out of place. There is now only one person ahead of me before the cash desk. A large woman, or possibly, a medium-sized woman in a large fur coat, obscuring what's in front. Suddenly, she moves to one side, out of the queue altogether. I step gratefully forward and move my left forefinger around inside my shirt collar. It is ridiculously hot. Time the store manager checked the air thermostat. The customer at the till is making a meal of his transaction, flicking clumsily through his wallet in search of a note of appropriate value. He places the wallet flat open on the desk as the cashier taps impatiently at the till. I might not have noticed the bus ticket but for its colour. A bright self-declaring pink, with the word 'CRAGGS' written boldly across its face. It occupies the window where the cheque guarantee card ought to be. And then, and only then, do I recognise Clive. Undeliberately disguised by a large Sherlock Holmes hat and new, more delicate spectacle frames. Now, I feel cold, frighteningly chilled. For 'Craggs Omnibus Co.' gives out pink tickets only on its local bus services into and out of Byschurch.

*

On the last afternoon of term, with pupils sent home early, George Pointer throws a Christmas sherry party for his staff. An Oxbridge gesture to be found at no other Steynmouth school.

"Ladies and gentlemen. This has been a long and tiring term for us all. It's no doubt something to do with the length of day: photoperiodism I believe it's called, Mr Kirkby." He nods ingratiatingly towards the head of his biology department. "The prospect of an earlier gloom with each succeeding twenty-four hours serves to dampen the spirit. But come the Spring, we shall all feel newly invigorated. In the meantime, we have before us that most hallowed of festivals. It means, or unfortunately has come to mean, different things to different men, but there seems to me to be no real reason why it should effect anything but a spirit of reconciliation between otherwise opposing factions of the human family. If carols could be sung across World War One trenches, then even Bernard and Warren might swallow their mutual antipathy along with the Bristol Cream they have in their hands."

A silly laugh, silly use of Christian names. Damned silly observation full stop. But typical of him to single out one or two people for no good reason.

"But on a more serious note, and begging the indulgence of our two colleagues, I do make a plea for a greater sense of unity among the staff. We all work equally hard - and I like to think of this little occasion as a gesture of thanks for your unceasing efforts on behalf of the pupils - though we do sometimes seem to pull in opposing directions. Christmas is perhaps an appropriate time to question this disharmony. So, enjoy the holidays by all means, but do come back next term prepared, if you will, to build a common launchpad for our New Year programme. I shall chair the working party myself. These are difficult times, with society subject to marked centrifugal pressures, and it is up to us, more than most, to show a disciplined and united front to the world outside. Worthwhile values cannot be imparted by a body of persons unsure of its own priorities. Thank you again, ladies and gentlemen, and a happy Christmas."

After five or six sherries, I am willing to speak even to Warren. "Seems like you and I, Warren, need to buckle down and set the tone."

"Bloody Pointer. What the hell does he think he's getting at? I would have thought that any thinking person would welcome a diversity of views. You're not trying to goad me are you, Bernard?"

"No, not trying to. Actually, I'm offering a Christmas pipe of peace."

"Well thanks, but, pardon me if I don't inhale."

"You're so damned suspicious, Warren."

"I've learned to be."

But the truth is, he has less reason to react harshly to my contrived taunting, which can be harmful only via exaggerated response, than to Major Warlby's innocence which comes to follow.

The Major rolls joyously across the room, a sherry in each hand. "How are you two young men then? Looking forward to the break I'll bet? ... You're staying here this year, Bernard? ... Well, good luck. But away from home, Christmas Day is no fun. You'll be envying Warren here, handed his gift stocking by Sarah."

Warren isn't at all thankful for the reminder that the only communication he might have with

Sarah will be through the offices of her legal counsel. He transfers his hostility away from me, and like a coward, I withdraw.

*

The crowded Christmas Day tables in the dining room of *The Green Man* would be seen by Elspeth Davies as a sorry sign of sad times. The decline of the family Christmas - even though, Liz and I excepted - every table is in fact occupied by a family. Her objection, essentially, would be that these families were not at home, like her and Sybil, in the kitchen.

It's this question of not being at home that Liz queries. "Why the 'give Byschurch a miss' this year?"

"What if I said it was because of you?"

"Umm ... I'd wonder at your doggedness. All this determination, and no proper reward yet. But I suppose I ought to be flattered."

"Are you?"

Well, I'm here with you now."

"Maybe just because you couldn't stomach dad and stepmother."

"Maybe. But on the other hand, I could stomach Steynmouth on my own. Have done before. So, it could be that your company's something after all."

"Good." I finish the beer which I've taken with me to the table. "But I'm still hoping for something more than just company!"

"Well, let me add that I'm delighted to be seen in your company. Which means that you look good to me. Always have. But I'll melt fully in my own time. Because I've a feeling that the consequences might be beyond my control."

"You sound fearful."

"No. Just cautious. And mistrustful of myself."

"Well, here's to whatever! Happy Christmas, Liz."

"Cheers!" She lifts her empty wine glass. Waiter service is slow.

Also, out to dinner, is the family to which the inadvertently helpful Donald belongs. I explain to Liz how *Elderflower Farm* had fallen across my feet like manna from heaven and its deliverer is now sat at the next table with mum, dad and three grandparents. But this time, he delivers the awkwardness of Deborah into my tableside conversation.

"So, this will be the first time you've not delivered her children's presents in person. Why Bernard? Are you afraid of seeing her again?"

"Well, first of all, I don't know if it's fear or what. Probably just sensible precaution."

"Against what?"

"Against heightening *her* problems, Liz."

"And she's not *your* problem in any way at all then?"

"Well, yes, she is, in the sense that she's a very close friend married to a very close friend."

"Yes, but … well, to come down all this way from Byschurch, as Deb did, means something. A woman's journey to a man."

"Perhaps. But perhaps it was really a girl's journey to a boy. We happened a long time ago."

"And nothing happened last month?"

I hesitate and lie. "Not in the sense I presume you mean." My guess is that she suspects my appetite and Deb's frustration will have combined and achieved a temporary solution, pleasantly acceptable to both sides at the time.

"Then you presume wrongly ... I don't attach great significance to *how* you may or may not have comforted her. Not quite strangers in the night, I admit, but something of that. I'm asking instead about the possible effect upon your strength of resolve regarding me."

"Meaning?"

"Meaning, is your continuing keenness now an escape from confusion?"

"Liz. If you will pardon me saying so, my confusion regarding you and me is generated almost entirely by *you!* There's no third-party complication as far as I'm aware."

"Yes, I'm sorry."

"Well, don't be. Take your time. Decisions long in the making are often the best. Or so I'm told. Here! Open it now before the turkey arrives."

I pass across a small package wrapped in unassuming blue striped paper. She pushes aside her soup bowl to make room.

"I'll wear it now." A thin gold neck-chain of simple design. Her hands disappear behind her neck as she fastens the clasp, then return to straighten it at the front. It lies delicately against the soft, still summery skin displayed within the not over generous scoop in the neckline of her fawn winter's dress. "Thank you. Thank you so very much. I got you a book. Back at my place. You can collect it later. It's too cumbersome for me to carry here."

"Oh, a big book!"

"Well, quite big. A collection of arty photographs, mostly black and white. Matches one of your hobbies."

"That's good of you. But you've spoiled the surprise."

"No, I haven't. Important not to open it until you're back at your place."

"Donald! How many times do I have to tell you to stop either slurping or dribbling that soup? If you were to eat it more quickly, it would be half the battle."

"I don't like it Mum. I said I didn't want any."

"Look Donald. Dinner out, especially Christmas dinner when all's said and done, means that bit extra than beans on toast at home."

"Why? Why do we have to have a first course?"

"Because that's what people do when they eat out. I've just told you. And what about your bread roll? You've hardly touched it yet."

"It's stale."

(He's right, laughs Liz, quietly)

"Nonsense Donald. It's a crispy roll."

"Yes, but it's crispy all the way through."

"Oh, my goodness! Just put it all to one side and let's see you make a better job of the main course."

"I'm not hungry, Mum."

"What? Of course, you are. You know you love turkey."

"I didn't like it last Christmas."

"Well, that's because it was too dry. Blame your father. He was in charge of the basting. Anyway, the chef here knows his job."

"Did he bake the bread rolls then?"

"When did you say you were going across to your cousin and her husband in London?"

"Well, I can go any time I like as far as they're concerned. In fact, I'm half thinking of going tomorrow. Because if I leave it until say New Year's Eve or whatever, then it's all a bit hectic to get back to work for the fourth."

"Oh, that's disappointing Liz. I mean, hasn't Amy invited you over to her place tomorrow? Along with Bill and me."

"Well yes she has. But it's all very flexible. Really, I've more or less made up my mind to leave tomorrow morning. There's a train from Exeter at ten, if I drive across."

"Would you like me to take you? It'll save you from leaving your car there unattended."

"What, you'll take *my* car and bring it back? You told me yours has some problem right now."

"Precisely."

"Okay, that's fine."

"Why don't you think of driving all the way to London by the way?"

"I don't like driving. You ought to know that, the number of times I've had you ferry me around. Anyway, train journeys are potentially more interesting."

"Councillor Le Bryce?"

"Leave off Bernard. Actually, funny you should mention him, but the great man sent me a Christmas bouquet and a greetings card."

"My God. With what message?"

"Well, odd in fact, decidedly odd. It said, 'To Elizabeth III, my Queen'."

"Jesus! The guy must have lost his marbles."

"Well thanks!"

"No, no. God, you could destroy his public life with that."

"You're not jealous?"

"Do me a favour."

"Donald! You really are infuriating at times. If you don't want the sprouts, just put them to one side. There's no need to prod at them like some frightened soldier crossing a minefield."

"But Mum, I said I didn't want any in the first place."

"Nonsense. Your dad eats his sprouts and look at him."

("Boy, who needs encouragement?" Liz nods discreetly sideways towards the nondescript Donald Senior, the perfect foil against which to test memory. Close your eyes and his image disappears beyond all possible recall.)

"Talking of Amy's place tomorrow, what is she doing today?"

"Oh, going to her parents' place, I think. It's only a fifteen-minute journey out of town after all. She'd be silly not to. After all, if they can set her up in business, they can provide a pretty good Christmas dinner. I'm sorry I'll not see her really. What with disappearing tomorrow up to London and all that."

"One thing about tomorrow is that she'll not be serving today's turkey. As a kid, I used to hate Boxing Day meals. Repeat performances always seem to me to be cheating."

"As with Deborah?"

I feel my cheeks flush slightly, but she appears not to notice. "Aw, c'mon. That's not fair!"

"No. Nor serious. Do carry on."

I hopefully disguise my relief. "Well that's it! Boxing Day food shouldn't be Christmas Day all over again. Like life in general, each day ought to bring some new experience."

"In which case, Amy won't disappoint you."

"Be careful. This conversation is becoming ripe with lines that invite misinterpretation."

"Oh no, I'm not wildly off the mark. I mean you do know she dotes on you, don't you? So maybe, if we're being open and all that, then perhaps we ought to talk about her."

"I'd rather not, Liz. Not now anyway. Anyway, she's just so decent and honest, and I'm trying to think of three-way implications here. If she lost out to you, with me I mean, she wouldn't be stupidly jealous. Wouldn't overthrow you as a friend, nor me for that matter. But if she won out, she'd feel stupidly guilty. Too self-scolding to stay close to you."

"I think you're wrong. I don't think that Amy and I function around you and me. We have our own space."

"Well, even so, it's potentially more complicated than I'd like it to be, especially since I'm fully preoccupied by *you*, and don't need distractions."

She looks me full in the eye, setting the record straight. "I'm not trying to come out top in some competition here. I'm not on an ego trip at Amy's expense."

"Well fortunately, I see that the whole thing hangs together best – that is the three of us – if I don't register her entry, nor yours for that matter, into any contest in the first instance."

"Umm … that's a good way to look at it, but if you're ever tempted to think differently, then I warn you, don't ever pin numbers on our backs, Bernard. Because if you were to do so, I'd tear mine off and retire and that would be a shame with me in the lead!"

Not that this comment makes much sense to me. How can she think herself ahead of some sort of pack, if she objects to the very notion and I don't even recognise it? Though I'm quietly pleased that she seems content with her ranking.

"Donald! Will you stop picking the fruit out of your Christmas pudding?"

"But Mum, I don't like the taste of the rest of it."

"What do you mean?"

"It'll be the brandy, dear" whispered Donald Senior.

"Yes, it's the brandy." Donald Junior is quick of hearing.

"How do you know? Whenever have you tasted brandy before?"

"I don't know, but it's a nasty taste."

"Well, put some more cream on then, and you won't taste is so much."

"I don't like cream. Not this stuff." He pokes at it with his spoon. *"Can you ask for some custard?"*

"Oh, for goodness sake. Why can't you just be grateful? I don't know why we bother at all. Now unless you're going to be cheerful, then this will be the last Christmas treat you ever have."

Some treat! He hates soup, dried up turkey, and plum pudding. Poor little bastard. But he's a welcome side-tracking from the heavy conversation that Liz and I have just endured.

"You could count on one hand the number of times I've been back here since the Wednesday evening sessions folded up." Liz's observation bears no mark of regret, neither physical at being denied *The Green Man's* weekly visual fix of mock Tudor architecture, nor social, at having lost a circle of friends.

"Well tell me, how come you ever became part of it all in the first place? I mean whatever made you want to join Clive for a drink?"

She looks a little resentful at the inquisition. "Oh, I don't know. Just really that he's such an Aunt Sally for the women at work. In a way, I just couldn't add a further slap to his face by refusing an offer to join him for a drink along with an old university friend with whom he'd suddenly become re-acquainted. I wasn't aware then, that it was going to be a semi-regular Wednesday thing. Anyway, I took Amy along for peace of mind, like an insurance policy against boredom. Then you were there, and I immediately looked forward to the next Wednesday".

"Nice of you to say so."

"I think Clive's gone to Folkestone to see his mother."

"Good!"

"I'd almost say you sound relieved."

"Look, I haven't told you about this before, bearing in mind the way in which you played down his shadowing of me ... but this whole thing is getting out of hand..."

"Okay, Bernard. I admit that the bus ticket elevates the stakes somewhat. But I still feel that all you can do is to wait for things to burn themselves out. I tell you what's crucial here, and that's the attitude of the police. Their files are probably full of case notes on harassments that came to nothing. Which is why they're less worried than you and why you, therefore, should be as little worried as them."

"Well maybe. You know this whole thing makes you get down to real basics."

"In what way?"

"In that if it were, well anybody else but Clive, I might have hit him hard by now, even though it would be massively out of character."

"In which case, for what my opinion's worth, you've acted, or rather not re-acted, correctly."

"Yeh, but at whose expense in the long term?"

"Not at the expense of your conscience, Bernard, that's for sure. And that's important. Don't brandish your fist at an oddball. Besides, as I say, it'll eventually go down in your personal history as the great non-event. Finished your coffee?"

"Yes."

"Then come around to my place. I've some new music we can listen to."

"Okay. Lead on."

As Liz rises to her feet, eyes stray away from tabletops. Furtive and not so furtive stares from various husbands. Donald Senior's admiration of this graceful, honey-haired girl is cut short by his graceless wife.

"Come along dear. It's time to give Donald his surprise present."

"But Mum, I thought I had all my presents."

"No Donald. This is something extra. Something special from daddy and me."

"Why, Mum?"

"Well, for being such a darling boy and giving us such pleasure. Here!!"

Tommy Gunn finds a home.

*

"Hello Dad."

"Bernard. We were expecting a call this morning. No problems?"

"No, only technical ones on the line. Happy Christmas. Is Mum there?"

"Yes, she's right here with me. I'll pass you over in a minute. Have you had a good day?"

"Yes, fine. Had dinner with a friend, Liz. You'll have heard me mention her from last summer."

"Yes, I expect so. Only your mother's got a better memory for names than I have."

"Did you have a good day yourself?"

"Oh, yes, yes. Dick and Sybil have been here, of course. Left for home half an hour ago. They'll be sorry to have missed your call. Actually, we'd almost given up on you. We're just off to bed."

"Yes, well I've just got in. Put Mum on a second and I'll get back to you afterwards eh …"

*

One minute into Boxing Day. I open the present from Liz. A large hard-backed volume full of monochrome photographs of some people having fun, and others having anything but fun. Nineteen-twenties flappers, then big-band jamborees, nineteen-sixties supergroups playing in the open air. But also, society's unfortunates, queuing for New Deal handouts, fleeing lines of refugees, sad-eyed long-stay prisoners. I feel rather uncomfortable. And inside the front cover, a message, 'Bernard, from Liz. Life can be good for some, but only if you're both sharing it'. I'm not sure I fully understand how the book plays to this idea, and I enter sleep, perhaps a little annoyed.

*

The whole of the day at Amy's.

"What did you do yesterday, Bill?"

"I walked along the cliffs to Blisscombe in the morning."

"And?"

"And walked back in the afternoon!"

"What, after Christmas dinner?"

"No Bernard, I had a drink at *The Old Masons*. A chat with the landlord, that's all."

"So, no dinner?"

"No. (a) I don't *need* to feast, (b) can't *afford* to feast, and (c) I don't think that given the state of the world, people *ought* to feast."

"So, you'll feast today instead!"

I had been right. I didn't get any Christmas Day leftovers brought back from Amy's parents. Instead, a hot casserole thoughtfully meeting Bill's declared but not impeccably observed vegetarian preference.

"Is this from the recipe I gave you, Amy?"

"Yes, but tell me Bill, you didn't recommend it from any experience of its preparation I would guess."

"Well, no. It just sounded good. What about its preparation?"

"Yes, well not so much the preparation actually, but more the difficulty in procuring some of the ingredients. Steynmouth's greengrocers are not overflowing with okra pods at any time of year."

"No, no. I suppose they wouldn't be." He smiles. "And how do you tackle them once you've got hold of them?"

"To quote your recipe: Okra pods, stalked but not pierced."

"That's not a peculiarity of vegetarian food, of course," I interject. "I mean a meat eater could encounter a somewhat similar instruction."

"How do you mean?"

"Venison. Stalked, but not shot."

Neither of them groan, but I do, quietly, in embarrassment.

A pleasant day. Not a laugh a minute, but plenty of good humour and plenty to eat and drink.

As we are about to leave, Amy gives me a present. "I'd have preferred to give it to him without you being here Bill, but with you both arriving and departing more or less simultaneously, well I'm genuinely sorry to say that I've nothing for you at this moment, but …"

"Don't worry, Amy." Bill looks massively disappointed.

"No, wait, let me finish. I'd hoped to have it ready in time, but my knitting isn't what it used to be. There's a new sweater on the way."

Bill glances down at his woolly self. "Oh, well thanks Amy. Colour?

"The obligatory!"

"Great … umm … I've nothing … well, how should I put it … nothing … "

"To give, in return. I'm not expecting anything. Please drop the subject. I'm just glad you could both come around today."

"Perhaps you would like a painting I've just completed? Nobody seems to want to buy it."

"That would be smashing, Bill."

Her selfless acceptance of Bill's brushwork causes me to change my plan. Some hours ago, I'd decided to keep my gift to her to one side, until such time as the impecunious Bill was elsewhere. "Well, if we're all being so honest, I needn't keep this till later." I fish a small packet out of my anorak pocket. Amy smiles and moves to open it. Bill turns away and whistles.

"No wait!" I shout. "Perhaps open it when I've gone. I'll do the same with yours."

"Good idea." She realises, like Bill, that this gift to her is not the afterthought that his was. And he's squirmed enough.

*

She slips the wide silver-plated bangle on to her wrist.

I flip through the pages of the compact, tightly printed A-Z of current music to be found in most good record shops. On the inner title page is a message whose clarity Liz might do well to ape.

"To Bernard. Love Amy. xxx"

Chapter 9

A Toe in the Water

The holiday is far too long. Not this holiday in particular, but every such holiday celebrated south of the Scottish border. New Year's Eve in Steynmouth is not New Year's Eve in Glasgow. There's no need for a good slice of January in which to recover. All is quiet after the Christmas pud. For me, it's a week of lie-ins, television, books, and half-hearted attempts at keeping in trim.

With Liz away and with me here, I feel I've somehow miscalculated. Maybe I could have managed Byschurch after all, somewhere in between the vacuum between Boxing day and the start of the Spring term. I could have engineered things so as to see Deb only in Philip's company. A face-to-face just with Philip, by contrast, would have been even safer. I'm sure that Deb would have bitten her lip upon her return home, and that Philip's mental turmoil would still be limited to wondering how soon he might be able to plunder the estate of his ailing Aunt Megan to whom his wife had unfortunately ministered all too successfully.

As it is, there's now the glum prospect of a dreary mid-February drive back home. I've promised mum. Maybe something will crop up to cause its postponement. I didn't ought to hope.

*

I reflect that it takes a remarkably free and confident spirit to thrust two fingers at the employing hand that feeds it (notwithstanding the odd occasion when a weak-kneed but well-heeled someone, with no cause for caution, might have a full enough wallet to walk out on his job without the need for courage). But Liz isn't affluent, at least not in the sense of having a cushion against self-inflicted and potentially lengthy unemployment. Thus, her decision to take a perhaps prolonged solo trip to mainland Europe is a little baffling. Okay, it is all part and parcel of her personal liberty and self-assurance but to a very large extent, she's been persuaded and it's all down to her irritating cousin. I suppose it's better for me to scapegoat someone than to think about my obvious inability to keep her in Steynmouth.

The whole irksome interference is as much as you'd expect from a cousin anyway. If there's one thing for which I have to thank Sybil and Dick, it's their infertility. Other aunts and uncles have selfishly provided me with a grand total of thirteen first cousins. All of whom I was expected to like. With my play-together obligations in the extended family now long since over, I see cousin X or Y these days only when Elspeth and Harold insist that I attend the latest clan wedding. There are now only two of these left to happen. And mine is one.

One good thing about the twentieth century has been its playing host to the erosion of wider family links. I welcome the shrinking down to the nuclear scale. Mum, dad, offspring and the dog is all I can reasonably handle. At a ludicrous extreme, one of the most insane things anyone can ever do is to succumb to the advances of a cousin and marry her because paradoxically, this would enlarge one's family responsibilities by combining hitherto almost separate segments into a new and barely manageable whole. By contrast, the more normal marriage to an outsider reduces the expectations placed upon you by virtue of their unacceptable number. No one can reasonably demand that you smilingly acquaint yourself with every thread and sub-thread within a newly spun web of in-laws and their extensions, the more so when, as is often the case, the two component parts are geographically separate.

So, the big surprise to me then is that Liz, having cut herself off completely from almost all outside influences, even that of her father, now sacrifices her normal independence of mind to accept the advice of a cousin, of all people. Someone whose coincidental possession of a shared biological heritage gives her no validity as a life-coach. And, although I've no evidence for thinking this, someone who might even be trying to realise her own frustrated ambitions through Liz.

"And you really think that Bernard? You don't know her. She not the sort to live her life through other people." Liz looks not incredulous, not annoyed. Perhaps a little of both but combining into some indistinct attitude of its own: one difficult for me to react to with advantage to myself. I feel more than a little stupid. It's not really about her cousin, but more about me wanting her to stay here in Steynmouth when she is, from her perspective, legitimately thinking of some time out.

*

"You've closeted yourself away for long enough, Liz. Don't you think so, David?"

"No, Anne. I mean, no, I don't see it's really our business."

He'd replies without looking at his wife. She had once been a young, lively Lancastrian, confidently bolder than the London to which she had recently moved. Now, she is large, less than lively, but still loud and she loves playing at being a metropolitan somebody to her provincial cousin.

"Well, Liz **is** my business and I'm sure she appreciates being so. Correct Liz?"

"What exactly are you getting at?"

"Okay, okay. You're twenty-six, twenty-seven, attractive, intelligent. But you waste your life."

"How come? I don't see it that way."

"Look, David and I were saying only the day before you arrived, how much more deserving you are of the spotlight. I mean, come on Liz, a Steynmouth civil servant for God's sake!"

"Go on!"

"Surely you don't intend to stay, there do you?"

"Actually, I'm happy to stay, for the medium term, at least"

"Why now all of a sudden? You've always voiced disenchantment previously."

"Simple. I'm about to move in with a man! Though I've not told him yet."

"What? For good? I mean he's the man, is he?"

"My business. It's a New Year thing. I've decided."

"Oh Liz, hell. That'll tie you to rustic oblivion for ever. Don't!"

"What if I were to be in love with him?"

"Tell her not to, David."

David, whom marriage has seriously let down, prepares himself for the onslaught against life together. "I wouldn't really presume to, Anne."

"Looks like it's up to me then! It's awkward in a way Liz. I don't want what I say to reflect upon David and myself. It's simply an academic point I want to make."

"Well, why pertinent to me but not to you?"

"Because I've experienced problems thrown up by marriage, or by a long-term relationship if you like and okay, David and I have conquered them. But that's not to say that I'd recommend it all to someone else. After all, some people survived Auschwitz, but subsequently they didn't proudly display their photo snaps to valued friends, or cousins!"

"Christ, what a parallel!" groans David. "You have a never-ending capacity to astound, Anne dear, you know that. See, don't listen to her, Liz. One thing I can say is that living with someone can offer a **new** experience every day. She's proof!!!"

"Yes" interjects Anne hurriedly, "but that new experience might be something like unexpectedly encountering the sudden presence of halitosis. The long-term lacks romance with a capital 'R'. A short-term affair and you'll smell only the sweetest of breath. Go with him for a short while Liz, and then take off somewhere."

"I'm not sure if you're warning me off the man or the place?"

"They're probably inseparable dear. He's the key bearer to your West Country dungeon."

"She's probably right in some ways, Liz. I mean, who knows, he might turn to fat."

"Nice of you to agree, dear." Anne's love affair with
the mirror had ended years ago.

*

"Liz! Over here! … Hi, had a good time? Come
on. Your car's just around the corner. Let's get in out
of the cold."

"It's great to see you again, Bernard." She
nudges her elbow into my forearm.

Some halfway between Exeter and Steynmouth,
she lets out the good news.

"God. It's been cold these last few days. London
can seem so Arctic after Steynmouth."

"Well it's been pretty unpleasant here too.
Hardly the winter Riviera touch. You could do with a
steering wheel glove on this machine of yours!
Though maybe that's a bit precious."

"Hell, if the car's still cold well into its return
journey, then what's my flat going to be like?"

"Even colder?"

"That'll do as an excuse. Though I don't need
one."

"Liz?"

"The Reverend and Mrs Keith, Bernard. They
bought a bungalow for two?"

"Just *what* are you saying, Liz?"

"That I'm moving in for a while. You'll have
had some heating on!"

"Moving in *for a while*?"

"Yes. Maybe for quite a while."

"Liz … I …"

"Oh, one other thing. The Reverend and his wife. You know you've always remarked on their foresight."

"Yes."

"On the way they've stocked the place with everything needed for their eventual take-over."

"Yes ... oh come on!"

"They've a double bed, right?"

She leans across, folds back the upturned collar of my now well-worn and smooth napped suede jacket, and plants a kiss on the side of my neck. It's the first of seven nights.

*

"I'm okay for overnight stuff. Perhaps we could go round to my place tomorrow and collect a few more things."

"Sure. Would you like another coffee?"

"What. No Ovaltine?"

"Err ... no. Did you ever drink the stuff?"

"Well actually, yes. Before mum died. She used to convert it into this sickly elixir. Added mountains of sugar. Was always way too hot to drink immediately. I was usually falling asleep by the time it had cooled down. What about you?"

"No. Hot milk on its own. In a tall brown mug. I used to push the skin to the far side and let it hang down over the rim. Annoyed dad, it did. Almost every night, 'for goodness sake Bernard, it won't harm you'. Trouble was, I thought it probably would. I imagined it remaining intact and forming some sort of impenetrable membrane in the gut. Funny really, I used to see death threats everywhere. Would listen with inquisitive alarm at my heartbeat thumping in my ear against the bed pillow. Had a feeling that it didn't ought to be happening like that. People's pulses didn't exist outside of their wrists. Was always concerned too with appendicitis. My grandfather had gone under when his burst at home, and I could never console myself that this was in the final days before an ambulance would speed you towards a healing hand. I dreaded twinges in the abdomen."

"You've outgrown this hypochondria then? I mean I'm not moving in to play nurse!"

"Oh yes, I've outgrown it alright. Quite amusing really. I could tell you."

"Okay. Go ahead. You've aroused my curiosity."

"Well, I'd have been, what, fourteen maybe fifteen. And I started getting a bit concerned about this dark blue-black staining in my groin area. I'd wash it off at nights, and hell it was back a day or two later. God, I thought it was gangrene or something. Or the pox, a word that figured often in schoolboy jokes. I knew something horrible was wrong. Was petrified. Tried to disguise it with talc. After what was probably a couple of months or more, mum sent me to the doctor with an eye infection – talking of which I had vivid fears of a white stick for my birthday – and while in the surgery, I plucked up courage to mention the unmentionable. By this time, I was worried that my manhood and its dual appendages might even drop off or something. In the event, the greyish dye used in my school trousers was the culprit. It just wasn't very colourfast. The doctor was rather scornful. From that day on, I abandoned self-diagnosis and embarked upon a life of deafness to the protests of my body."

Liz smiles … "So, everything's in working order then?"

"What?"

"You know!"

"Yes, well yes."

"Shall we test you out?"

"I'd love to."

"Me too."

"Great. It's been a long wait!"

"Look, you fly through the bathroom first. I'll get rid of these coffee cups, ferret around in my case, and join you in a second or so. By the way, it's Sunday tomorrow."

"It is."

"No need to get up early then."

"No, so you can really test me out."

"I'll rise to the challenge."

"No. That's my privilege!"

*

"I saw Amy today."

"By design or accident?"

"I went to her place at lunchtime. She's been calling me these three days since I came back from London. Wondered where I'd got to."

"Now she knows then?"

"Yes. I thought she should learn of it from one of us. Actually, she said very little."

"Hell, what could she *say*? Thing is, how did she *look*?"

"I don't know really. I think I didn't turn full face until I'd manoeuvred on to something else."

"I suppose I'd better pay her a visit."

"If you like, but I don't know that you wouldn't be better advised to wait a while."

"I'll think about it."

"She said one thing about it though."

"What was that?"

"She said, selflessly, sarcastically or what, that she hopes it proved enjoyable."

"Well, let's raise a glass to realised hopes, ours I mean!"

"It's late. Shall we realise them some more?"

Night Four. Liz flops to one side, her head encountering a displaced pillow and her hair wild across the left-hand side of her face. She stretches her left arm towards her knees, looking half-heartedly for the sheets which lie heaped somewhere in that direction. Failing in her quest, she diverts her hand sideways towards me. "Careful where you go!" I exclaim. "It's in rest mode."

"No problem. When it's ready again, I'm sure it'll find its own way back."

"Mmm … I'm not so sure that's entirely a good thing. I rather like it with the guiding hand of a female pilot."

"Okay, but I have in mind something different when you're ready!" She moves slowly from her back to her side, places her left thigh across my midriff and her cheek against my chest. "See you later. Soon?"

I lift myself forward with her attached and pull the bedclothes up over both of us. January's assertive chill won't allow itself to be denied.

I meander across the asleep-awake boundary and back again. In and out of dreamworld. But unlike the fantasy nights to which I have long become accustomed, reality now lies alongside me. It's twirling its forefinger in increasing circles across my chest, poking playfully almost everywhere and whispering laughingly in my ear.

"God Liz. Is it morning?"

"No, just a few hours on, I think"

"Really? Something wake you?"

"Mmm … you!"

"What did I do?"

"You invaded my mind."

"I did?"

"And now you should complete the invasion."

"Should I?"

"You must!"

She's more alert than me. Rolls on top of me. Kisses my forehead. "Would you mind if I put the bedside light on?"

"What?"

"I want to see you this time, to *look* at you."

"You can't."

"Why not?"

"Because light or no light it's cold enough to demand the cover over us."

"Nonsense."

She kneels bolt upright, straddled across me, and then dismounts to hurl back the multi-layered cocoon of cotton, wool and eiderdown. Turning sideways, she stretches to the far side of the bed, bringing one knee over me. Her other leg is perilously close to the flex of the old angle-poise lamp that lies towards the very front edge of the neighbouring white faced chest of drawers. She touches it, and it falls noisily to the floor. Her head and shoulders follow it in retrieval, leaving me a shadowy glimpse of her back from head-to-toe, flecked by highlights of crisp frosty moonlight through the flimsy cream curtains.

"Here. Let me." I raise myself in her direction, enveloping both her and the lamp within my right arm and pull them firmly into the bed. She disentangles herself and replaces the rickety light in its home and quickly makes good her intention that all is to be illuminated.

"Amazing it's not broken." She's genuinely surprised. "Where shall I point it?"

"Anywhere but at my knees."

"Why not? They're not so bad as you often make out."

"I tell you what. Just reflect the damn thing off the ceiling and come here."

"You ready then?"

"Most definitely." I look at her. She is completely flawless. And so wonderfully scented.

Her hands reach behind my neck and pull my face down towards her breasts. My right hand moves slowly downwards.

"No, Bernard. I want something more … oh, you know, more fit for purpose!"

"Should you inspect it closely first? It may like some prior grooming."

"Of course!"

When it was all over, it took us some time to re-orientate to the flickering lamp and the missing bedclothes. Then, some short while after the covers had been raised, "It's five -thirty, Bernard. I thought maybe you'd want to know."

I smile. "Are you seriously choosing now to remind me that I'm at work today? That I've got to be up in about two hours' time?"

Well, not exactly. I thought that if we made it two and a half hours, we could do something nice together in the shower before you leave."

*

"Amy."

"Yes."

"It's Bernard. Look I usually leave work for a quick lunch out Thursdays, with Bill for the most part. Only he's not in town this week. Do you fancy a drink and a bite to eat by any chance? On me of course."

"I ... uh ... "

"Please Amy. I'd like it. You can spare the time. Just leave your sandwiches or whatever under the counter and shut up shop."

"Oh yes, well okay. Only you must ... sorry, look I'll have to hang up now. A customer. See you tomorrow then. Oh where? What time? Fine. Okay Bernard, ciao."

*

"You don't have to talk about it, Bernard, you know. I mean, Liz has told me."

"Yes, but Liz is Liz. I'm sure it was all very matter of fact."

"But that's how I want to hear it. Any other way and I'd feel, oh, damaged perhaps."

"I'd hate that. I mean you're ..."

"Look, Bernard. Don't say anything that flatters yourself. Just remember that I've only ever kissed you once and then I was a drunken American gangster."

"Well, not so drunk as not to know what you were doing or more importantly, not to remember it afterwards."

"You're doing it again. Flattering yourself. Every word of comfort you intend to pour out is going to help you more than me. Just accept that you've won out and keep quiet about it."

"It's funny that."

"What?"

"Well ... 'won out'. Liz too got annoyed over the *contest* idea, but you both know it was never like that."

"Okay, I'm sorry. But I would really prefer not to discuss it, Bernard. Just ask yourself what possible purpose it might serve. Much better to simply eat, drink and smile." And she displays a proud smile that changes her from offended to determined.

We remark on the beer, the wine, the cheese, the Christmas decorations that should long since have been taken down. Conversation without conversing. Except for her final declaration ...

"Thanks for the meal. See you again soon. Oh, and by the way, you are right, of course. I wasn't drunk the night I kissed you."

Which helps her more than it helps me. Hers is not the confusion of a small plurality of suitors.

*

"Bernard. I thought with it being Sunday tomorrow, you know, a leisurely day and all that, I could move back to the flat in less of a rush than on a weekday." She says it in the same tone of voice as that she has just used when asking if there was a clean tea-towel to dry the breakfast things. This neutral, even indifferent, air makes her remark less easy to accept than if it were uttered as part of some emotional maelstrom. Instead, it is casually inserted between putting one cereal bowl on the table and picking up another one from the draining board.

"What do you mean?" My reply is permeated with quiet, almost frightened anxiety.

"I mean that a week's been long enough for me to discover what I needed to know."

"Agreed. But pardon my naivety, I was under the impression that everything was more than okay here."

And her cheerful smile perplexes me further.

"Everything has been okay; dare I say perfect. I now know that living with you appeals to me very much. What I next need to find out is whether, after this, living without you is worse."

"But Christ, Liz, you must know the answer to that already. You've lived without me for far too long, well, from my point of view anyway."

"Yes, but living without you now, afterwards, is bound to be different from living without you before. I need to discover how unbearable, how prolonged, will be the withdrawal symptoms. If it doesn't hurt, and carry on hurting, there'll be no need to return. I do want it to hurt, so that next time, we get together, it'll be, well, more of a commitment, rather than an experiment."

"And I'm to passively acquiesce in all this?"

"You've no choice as such. I've made my mind up. If you're not here, not available, when and if I return, then that's just an unfortunate part of the equation. The part that counts me out."

"And when, pardon me asking, might you return? I mean how long do you need to unravel your emotions while I restrain the hands of the clock?"

"Actually, since you ask, I've thought about that in some detail. It seems to me that circumstances mustn't be such that I can easily fly to you whenever I feel the need to repeat this week's delights. There'll have to be geographic distance between us."

"Well moving back, the half mile or so to your place hardly fits the bill."

"Exactly. That's why I've done what I've done."

"God Liz, don't be so damn mysterious." I'm now sat dolefully at the breakfast table, with no further interest in the mechanics of clearing up.

"Sorry. I'm not meaning to be. I've given up my job at the tax office. Or rather, I've handed my notice in. Mid-February, I'm taking a Channel crossing to

Europe. I'll visit some friends in Germany and probably Italy, and then … well, I've not thought on much further than that."

"Mid-February? That's three or four weeks off. So why move out tomorrow?"

"Because of how good it's been. If I were to take any more of this, I'd never resolve to leave it."

"I suppose it would be too much to hope that the woman I fall in love with be not only beautiful but uncomplicated!"

"Beautiful, but boring. You'd not want that."

"No, but there must be a happy medium somewhere along the line. Predictability isn't you for sure. Where did all this business spring from? I mean there's been no wind of it in the air at all."

"Umm … I had a long talk with Anne up in London. She made me feel I ought to weigh things carefully in the balance before coming to any real decision. So, this week I've tested out the weights on one side, and now there's the other to deal with."

"Look Liz, from what you've told me of this cousin of yours, she's not a person whose opinions are to be valued. She strikes me as someone whose …" and I stop because I see that she is tearfully resentful of my words.

"Bernard stop it! Why be so … well, like you're being? You should know that I'm within an inch of using the 'L' word with you."

I rise from the chair into which I have just sunk in disappointment. I lift her chin with my right hand and sweep her golden hair behind her ears. "Yes, I can see that you must be … after all, I've never seen you cry before. Nor, I suppose has anyone else." I press her tightly to my chest. "Oh shit!"

*

The day though still has to be lived. "Let's lunch out," she suggests.

It leads to an out-of-town pub meal, drowned in the uncertain and ambiguous atmosphere which we import with us. Boy meets girl, boy maybe loses girl, all in the flash of an eye. Something verging on a declaration of love, reduced to nothing by a nonsensical loving goodbye. It feels to me like a full-frontal assault on my self-esteem. I push half my meal aside.

"Have you finished, sir?"

"Yes thanks."

"Anything else?

"Not for me. Liz?"

"Umm... Well I'd not thought."

"We have a lovely apple pie madam, piping hot with rum custard."

"Okay. A very small slice. You sure you won't Bernard?"

"I'm sure."

Eventually, we move from the table and seem loath to leave. It seems safer to cling to the bar side and avoid any type of emotive conversation which might lead us to raise our voices, even marginally, and elicit curiosity among other customers. So, we calmly delve into her projected European adventure whilst avoiding the whys and wherefores. We observe other diners, their sometimes-peculiar physical shapes, the seemingly unlikely man and woman combinations. I try not to be resentful that every other man is at least viewing his Saturday simply as part of an enjoyable interlude between Friday and Monday.

"Excuse me, sir. Could I have your glasses? We close for a couple of hours between four and six."

"Really? Isn't that unusual?"

"It's a winter thing, sir. Not in the summer season, of course. We hope to see you both here again sometime."

"I hope so too." I look across at Liz. The second whisky seems to have calmed my stomach.

*

Next morning, what ought not to matter is what is held to matter by the world outside. We really don't *need* the Sunday newspapers. To attach any importance to events on the greater stage is somehow to demean our own crisis which almost insists on occupying our attention completely. It destroys all appetite for breakfast. We simply drink coffee.

In mid cup, she asks, "Shall I walk around and buy the papers?"

"I guess so. I'll come with you."

"No, don't worry. You take a shower or something. I'll not be long. And then, when I get back, we can sort things out".

"Sort things out?"

"Get my stuff together."

*

At the third attempt, she closes the front door behind her. The energy conscious Reverend and Mrs Keith have so securely draught-proofed it that to engage latch and receiver demands the most hefty and determined of pulls. The short five yard crazy-paved walk to the wrought iron front gate is distance enough for tears to appear and flow conspicuously down both cheeks. She deceitfully attributes them in equal part to both the cold mid-morning air and the self-induced distress of leaving her lover. She is herself, perhaps responsible for the activity of only one eye. She brushes away the offending droplets with the rear of her leather-gloved right hand. Turning left, she picks her way gingerly through the sodden leaves whose decomposing wish to return to Mother Earth has, for three months now, been frustrated by the barrier of concrete paving slabs. Between the footpath and the road, the now bare trees stand starkly at regular fifteen-yard intervals in the middle of a grassy strip muddied by the oily spray hurled sideways by-passing motor vehicles. In the fullness of summer, the lush greenery would provide a beckoning setting for people just to walk by. But now, on a harsh Sunday morning, the stripped branches give an atmosphere of emptiness that serves only to highlight the incongruous human presence that she catches staring straight at her. More chilling than the air itself.

"Clive! What the hell is going on here?"

There's no attempt at concealment, no discreet peeping from behind trees, no repetition of the shadowing techniques he has long since mastered. Instead simply a brazen being there.

"Going on?"

"Yes! You know what I mean, God! This isn't your patch at all. Just what are you doing standing here as I come out?"

"Out from where?"

"Oh, stop farting around, Clive. You know from where. God, you look colder than Titus Oates must have done. How long have you been here? C'mon, just how long?"

"I was just passing."

"Look, this is too weird for words. I don't think I know what to say, other than to swear at you. Which would achieve just what? Please, whatever this is all about, just cut it out, eh?"

"I tell you. I was just passing."

"Well, do it then. Do it! Pass on!"

"Where are you going?"

"This way. Newspaper hunting."

"I'll join you."

"No! If you're just *passing*, then even my few yards walk from the gate before seeing you must mean you're off in the opposite direction. Mustn't it? Mustn't it?"

"You're suggesting I'm lying. You don't believe that I was just passing."

"Don't believe it? Had better believe it, so as to send you off that way while I go this!" She walks away quickly, not looking back. But her ears can't evade what her eyes can. It's shouted loudly, billowing after her down the street, probably causing a curious pulling back of various front curtains.

"I tell you; I WAS JUST FUCKING WELL PASSING!"

Not a word of his protests does she believe. She now shares in the anxiety over Clive's recently reported activities. But she determines to make no mention of this conversion. No further words can be afforded, save the regretted goodbyes from whose clutches she cannot afford to let herself escape. Sticking with her decision is going to be difficult enough anyway.

Chapter 10

A Promise Delivered

According to the previous evening's TV documentary on hibernation, some seventy percent of dormice fail to survive their winter's sleep. It's a pity that the mechanism is so imperfect. The poor creatures might be better advised to stay awake and chance their luck. But even this sad revelation on rodent mortality fails to make me think again about my own wish to see off the rest of the winter in a state of suspended animation. In the three weeks since Liz arrived back with the Sunday newspaper and left with her suitcase, I've voluntarily imprisoned myself in the bungalow, notwithstanding the reflex nine-to-four, Monday to Friday, attendance at work. I've subsisted off a stock of now largely depleted food which I purchased in one of the most stupendous spending sprees ever stayed at the Steynmouth Superstore. My long checkout receipt had billowed spectacularly from the overflowing trolley as I'd wheeled it to the car, after which I've bothered nobody but myself. Liz had insisted that she needed time to prepare for Europe, undisturbed by the attractions of what she was leaving behind.

As at Khartoum, food is now running short, but I've one advantage over General Gordon in that I can lift my own siege. Not when my belly starts to distend, but considerably before that, when the Weetabix packet gets low and the tomato sauce bottle assumes a hint of transparency. How on earth had my grandmother sorted out all this sort of stuff? She lived fifteen miles beyond Byschurch in a remote hill farm, never once, as far as my child's eye view of things could tell, venturing out to buy the wherewithal to survive. Yet, she had more on her table than could ever be accounted for by the paltry output of her sheep and fern-covered domain. There were bountiful breakfasts of crusty bread and smoked bacon; lunches of thick vegetable soup and more crusty bread as appetisers to hot cheese flowing like candle grease over the edge of yet more crusty bread; and an evening meal of stew, huge, generous pieces of lamb with their turnip and potato escorts amid a light-coloured oily sauce, to be mopped up by even further slices of the by now, not so crusty bread. A pudding – hot, steaming – of winberry pie, in season, or fruit preserve pie at other times, with stiff and deep yellow custard. A supper drink of hot chocolate, with the offer of the end of the day's loaf, spread with golden honey. I relished my weekend visits, made initially, once every two months or so, but subsequently more often at my own insistence. It eventually took Deborah to convince me that there was something worth staying home for at weekends, something better than home cooking in the hills. I was unable to resist and in retrospect, just as well. Further gluttony and I might eventually have gone the way of my over-indulged grandfather, who was lowered prematurely into his grave with far too full a stomach for a man who daily had to carry his weight up thirty- and forty-degree slopes. Though maybe, the path to such a fate would be preferable to the dwindling supply of fast and junk food that is currently my daily diet and which, without early restocking with something more wholesome, will soon exhaust itself. Beef burgers, instant this, dehydrated that, and canned beans. Better perhaps to forgo food altogether even, like a dormouse, at the risk of non-awakening.

My lethargy and moroseness are not easily budged. What comes along causes not their elimination, but their sublimation. For looking in on a hospitalised Clive, is hardly the sort of expedition which is likely to be curingly therapeutic for any visitor's problems. Nor is it something I would do anyway were it not for Amy's articulating my supposed responsibilities. Over the phone. Had I heard the news? Yes, I had. Briefly, off Warren at work. It had needed something drastic for Warren to surpass his normal condescendingly grunted, hello. And indeed, there'd been a hint that I was not without blame. That my calling time on the Wednesday night group had served only to heighten Clive's sense of alienation and to drive him to a state of despair. Even Amy comes on a little too strong with this, less purposely stated but still citing Clive's lack of real friendship as a factor in the whole mess.

"You really ought to see him you know!"

"Why?"

"Well, because you've known him for far longer than any of the rest of us."

"Which is precisely why I don't want to see him, and why I suspect, he wouldn't want to see me."

"I'll come with you."

"You'd have to. Or somebody would. I wouldn't know what to say."

"Well, he needs genuine sympathy. It's going to be a major repair job. He can't be left on his own."

"What about his mother?"

"Apparently – or so I hear from Bill who called in on him yesterday – she's said she's not coming over."

"Perhaps she's just about had enough. I could understand that."

"Oh, I don't think so. In fact, it was her prompt action that saved the day. Have you heard the details? … No? … Oh well, seemingly, he rang her from his office desk to say what he'd just done. At the end of his usual meagre lunch. The aspirins were dissolved in the glass of milk that he normally drinks at the same time. No one noticed. Nor did any ears pick up on what he was saying over the phone. It was a bad line – or so it had seemed to others who were there, Liz included – and he was almost shouting down the mouthpiece. Only in German, and his final goodbyes just drifted over the heads of those present. Fortunately, his mother had the presence of mind to quickly call the Steynmouth police and that was it, ambulance at the office, stomach pump at the district hospital. Poor Liz, it was more or less her last day at work and she had to witness all this."

"She can't have been too upset. Your call and Warren's scolding represent all I've heard of it."

"Come off it, Bernard, she can't afford to fly into your arms at this stage. Let's not complicate things. Please come with me to see him. He's been transferred to the psychiatric unit over at Titherley. How about tomorrow evening?"

"I was planning to go to the supermarket. I'm very low on food."

"Oh, don't be obstructive. Come on. I know you don't like him, but ..."

"I loathe him"

"I know, I know. But, you're part of the life he's got to return to."

"Not True. I've no such intention to be."

"Well, you know what I mean. He has to adjust to all sorts of things and the fact that you're living, and breathing is one of them. Might be good if he could form a more amiable image of you. I don't expect you to be bosom pals. Anyway, without one or two of *us*, he'll have no visitors at all."

"Oh, alright. But don't expect me to be anything other than helplessly awkward."

"Bernard, you're a better sort than you're pretending to be. You'll not let yourself down."

"We'll see."

*

Like many other a psychiatric hospital, the Titherley site is out of town. A former isolation clinic now extended and converted to cater for one of the twentieth century's major growth areas in medical practice. I think to myself that the 'cordon sanitaire' between it and the urban populace is more important when it comes to separating off Clive than it ever was in the days of scarlet fever and diphtheria.

We park the car amid the usual confounding morass of blue-background, white-worded signs. Reception. Physiotherapy. Pathology. Day Care

Centre, Outpatients. At least, the last two give an element of hope, there's nothing saying, 'Long Stay Wing' or 'Life Patients'. I look for the theme for the ward names. I've joked with Amy about this on the drive here. I used to be slightly amused in the past by the names I'd encountered above the ward doors of Byschurch Cottage Hospital where I'd worked as a porter during university holidays. 'Warren Ward', 'Nest Ward' came readily to mind, depriving patients of human status, although as Amy amusingly pointed out, not so insensitively as to house them in a 'Kennel Ward' or 'Hutch Ward'. But Titherley proves to be more pedestrian. Clive is being tended to somewhere within a ward structure whose labels owe everything to local topography, 'Steyn Valley Ward', 'Blisscombe Hill Ward'. 'Angel Wood Ward'. Perhaps slightly bizarrely in that the wards have windows that afford views of none of them. Their names are too alike for even the normally alert Amy to remember just where Clive is to be found. "Sorry Bernard, I ought to have written it down."

"That's okay, we'll sort it out at admissions."

But before we can get around to this, she does what I would never do. She consults an elderly and rotund porter, who ought to suggest admissions but predictably doesn't.

"What did you say your friend's name is? … Lyon? … Clive Lyon? … Does that mean anything to you, Ernest?" He turns behind him to face one of four languid accomplices sat untidily on plastic stack away chairs inside the cramped porters' lodge. There's much indifference and token shaking of heads.

"Sorry dear. I think one of us *might* 'ave carried his case for 'im. Well, let's see now. 'E'll be in the men's wing, that's for sure. Less of course 'e's elsewhere."

"Elsewhere?"

"Yes luv. Could be anywhere at this minute. X-ray, group therapy or just wandrin' around the garden."

"What, in a dressing gown at this time of year?"

"Might not be in no dressing gown luv. Depends just what's up with 'im. You know, 'ow safe 'e is and all that – to 'isself and to others. 'E might be allowed to do as 'e likes, or maybe not. Now, if you could give me some sort of clue as to what's up with 'im, maybe I could guess where to point you both."

"Well, not to beat around the bush, he's here after a suicide attempt."

"Oh well, there's lots like 'im. 'Ow long ago?"

"Only last week."

"Oh well, e'll still be a bit dodgy eh. They'll probably be keeping a close eye on 'im still."

"So, you know where he'll be then?"

"Ah well, 'ang on now. It ain't so simple as that. Depends on other things about 'im. Like 'e's obviously disturbed, right, but is 'e simple as well? Or, like 'im being a friend of your's luv, is 'e clever and well brought up?"

"I don't see how his being well brought up would have anything to do with his being basically simple or not!"

"Well, it's like this luv: When you've been 'ere as long as I 'ave, you get to know things. Like the well-off, and I can see you're a well-dressed young lady and all that, well, they eat different and so on. Their brains is better fed. There ain't so much simple mindedness around in their class of person. Mind you, that ain't to say that the odd one or two can't go dotty like the rest of us."

"Sorry, but I don't follow your logic. But you are right in supposing that our friend is intelligent enough. Just that, as you very quickly point out, he's rather disturbed right now."

"Ah, exactly! When they're clever see, they can get *disturbed*. When they're simple they're just plain *crackers!* One lots 'ere for the ride, the other lot are 'ere for ever. Mind you, I 'ave known the odd genius never leave the place. What do you reckon your friend's chances are then? Cos that's what the docs will 'ave in mind when they sent 'im to wherever is 'is."

"Look!" I decide it's time to intervene. "We don't know what his chances are, as you put it. We're just visitors. Let's leave forecasts to the doctors, shall we? Now, if you could tell us where the admissions desk is, then whoever's manning it can tell us where to find him." I know from my own past fleeting experience of being a hospital porter just how the holder of that job often likes to think of himself as administrator, doctor, catering officer: anything but the portering role for which he is paid. Thus, the medical staff, doctors and nursing sister alike would occasionally have almost to beg, not instruct, that patients' files be brought across from central records, that daily drug supplies be ferried in from the pharmacy, even that the sick be accorded the treat of having their institutional meals wheeled in on time.

I used to find the job challenging. It was a major feat of self-discipline and motivation to prevent my brain from dying when on duty. Unlike the often, slothful response of my colleagues to the arrival of a task that wouldn't go away, I seized on every boredom-banishing demand as soon as it came along. Only once did I regret my hurry to volunteer, when Percy, the mortuary porter, asked for assistance in tidying up his empire. The 'dungeon of the dead' as it was affectionately known, was a semi-basement pair of rooms whose prominent central location within the Byschurch hospital site suggested an intensity of use frightening to incoming patients. Percy had looked after the set-up there for thirty years, but incongruously, had an infectious jollity which led me to banish from my mind any suspicion that what was being asked of me might involve anything even vaguely distressing. It hadn't been a good fortnight on the wards. There was much flu among the geriatric community. Insufficient drawer space to allow Percy to properly conceal the deceased. Would I help re-arrange the white shrouded overflow on the floor? To give more order to what might soon give offence as simply a pile. It was quickly and sensitively achieved.

"Oh, Bernard, before you go. One more thing. Through here. If you could just help me lift an old fella on to the slab? Don't look so confused. Preparation for a post-mortem. You ought to stay and watch."

"Okay. There's a half hour or so before the lunch trolleys need moving." It was an invitation taken up on the basis that what I'd had to do so far had left no sensory perception other than the feel of white cotton cleanliness. However, this antiseptic notion of death was soon dispelled when I grabbed seemingly frozen feet and felt the almost creaking stiffness of the corpse as it was raised from floor to

an operating table, too late to be of help other than to an inquisitive pathologist.

"What do you mean by prepare?"

"Well, it's like this. I do the dirty work, then the chief man comes in and looks at what I've exposed."

"You mean you're going to cut him open?"

"You don't have to stay."

I stepped back and leaned against the cold plastered wall. I looked down along the length of the body from head to foot. Facing me was a tousled mass of hair with no sign of thinning.

"What did he die of?"

"Old age mate. But unexpectedly, so there's all this to be done."

Percy donned gloves and made a large incision, running down from mid-ribs to groin. Almost like cutting into and separating a refrigerated sheet of expanded polystyrene. No flow of blood. Within what seemed like microseconds, he removed yards of curled intestine and hung it, as a butcher would sausages, on a wall hook to his rear. When the episode returned to me that night in a dream, Percy's green apron had metamorphosed into a garment of blue and white stripes.

So far so 'good' or perhaps, so far, so so. Not nice, but not massively disturbing. It was only when hospital implements were forsaken for what I regarded as out-of-place DIY tools that things took a turn for the worse. Percy brandished a red-bodied knife that looked suspiciously like the type I had used the evening before to fit a new lounge carpet at the Davies home. He grabbed hold of the sod mass of grey hair with one hand and tilted the dead man forwards, almost immediately opening a deep slit across the back of the head from one ear to the other. I shuffled sideways, rubbing my back nervously against the wall.

Percy dropped the head back down, none too gently, put the knife to one side, and then returned to pull forward the scalp towards the face, exposing the hummocky bone of the top and rear of the skull. The face was now contorted out of all recognition. A man who only a moment ago appeared happily resigned to death was now a grotesque mish-mashed victim of those who wouldn't leave him in peace. I felt great hiccups of guilt welling up from my oesophagus. Percy continued with the task in hand, but with a further inappropriate and insensitive piece of machinery that was now being put to a use presumably never imagined by its makers. A workshop-sized power drill with a vicious saw attachment that quickly cut a reasonably neat round hole whereby those alive could peak in at the brain of he who was dead. I felt the blood drain from my head, felt my own brain to go in the same numbed direction as that whose display caused me such misgiving ... I was sat on the stone doorstep to the mortuary. Nauseous. Alternately green and ashen in colour. With Percy's arm on my shoulder, and an offer of a reviving drink of water, I returned to the ribald laughter of my card-playing colleagues. I seized the chance to take food to those still breathing in their beds.

*

Angel Wood Ward is an architectural disaster or at least, it has become one through the cavalier partitioning of what clearly had once been a much larger room. This means that an over warm patient in one cubicle can't open his window without inflicting a blast of cold air on to some less hardy, more chill-prone patient in the cubicle next door. Equally, light switches are now positioned in sub-rooms other than those whose illumination they control, so that Amy and I arrive as witnesses to a discordant to-ing and fro-ing of people annoyed at the sudden extinguishing of brightness from their own fibre-boarded corners. Electric light bulbs flash on and off in a disconcerting display of individual patient power.

The charge nurse, a man whose face suggests he has been quarried rather than born, directs us to Clive, to a point, some halfway down the ward, on the right. Just before reaching our destination, we walk past a noisy, black-and-white television which is pouring out some Wagnerian shrieking to the seeming indifference of anybody in the vicinity.

"Out of the bloody screen you two." Sat back on his bed against a vertically positioned pillow, Clive is peering out through a flimsy open door at a programme that only he had wanted to see. At his insistence, his fellow patients are being denied their majority viewing preference. No-one in a supervisory capacity has sought to intervene. It is for the good of all that social relationships on the ward are left to the patients themselves. The lack of control ends only when violence threatens, at which point, nursing muscle comes into play.

"It didn't take long for the vultures to arrive! What do you both want?"

"How are you Clive?" Amy flashes a brave smile that would melt the hearts of ninety nine percent of the country's male population.

"I was watching opera!"

"So, life does have its interesting points after all?" She sits side-saddle at the foot of the bed, obscuring his view even more completely than before.

"Look, if you're here to delve into my personal anxieties, then you're not welcome. If you're here to bring me gifts – reading material, whisky or whatever – then I'll tolerate you. I mean I've been through the whole bit already – with the shrinks – and I'm damned if I'm talking my way through it again. Apart from which, if they're right and reliving the whole experience is to exorcise it, then I'd rather say nothing and leave the options open for a repeat performance."

"Sounds like you're successfully rehabilitated then!" I make a blundering entry into the conversation.

"You needn't look so bloody smug, Bernard. From what I heard from Bill yesterday, you're up to your rotten eyeballs in your own problems…" He turns almost furiously towards Amy… "So, one lady love is gone then. What's it feel like to come on as a substitute?"

"If you're going to be so thoroughly unpleasant Clive, then we'll leave. This is a charitable and well-meant visit after all. You should think yourself lucky to receive it."

"Well, well. The world is with me after all! Let me tell you that this unpleasantness, as you call it, is by courtesy of Largactil. I've been calmed down good and proper. Get rid of this chemical interference with my workings and I would regress to my normal self. Bolting the door in your faces!"

I move to stand behind Amy, placing a hand on her left shoulder. "You're going to prove one hell of a challenge, Clive. I'll bet your case notes are bulging."

"I should bloody well hope so. It would be something of a slight if they weren't … Hey! What the hell do you think you're doing?" He cranes his neck sideways, peering angrily towards a pyjama-clad pensioner who is 'impertinently' switching TV channels. "What do want that stuff on for, Grandad? Just leave things as they were, will you!"

But the old man is deaf. He just like to watch the legs of the mini-skirted dancers on *Top of the Pops*. "Christ Almighty! I've made it clear all sodding day that I want the opera this evening come hell or high water."

He makes to climb from his bed to exact revenge, but with a push of my foot, I slam the door to. "Leave him be Clive. He's doing no earth-shattering harm."

"Damn you Bernard! Look, he's in just next door." He thumps hard against the thin partition behind his bedhead. "Too much excitement on that TV and he'll be groaning away in his own imaginary orgy."

"Why don't you join him? Two's company."

"Don't be so bloody disgusting."

"Look you two, why don't all three of us go and sit in the lounge area? We're a bit like caged tigers in here and getting equally as fraught. Clive? Bernard?"

"Yes alright. Whatever suits you!" He shuffles into his slippers, draws to his dressing gown, and follows us out.

We sit well to the rear of the television, with the old man impervious to the looks of vicious disapproval which Clive is signalling through the co-axial cable and onto the screen.

"Well, what do you both want to talk about? You Amy, you're good at conjuring worthless conversation out of nothing."

"Okay but pardon me for pointing out that it is just absurd to purposefully avoid talking about you. It would deny any sense to our visit."

"Oh, look. What do you want me to say? That I saw the romantic allure of death, but that I now regret having been so silly? I'll tell you this, I'm neither sorry that I tried, nor sorry that I failed. I just couldn't care a toss! From now on, everybody else can do the worrying. With me, it's going to be complete self-indulgence. Sod work! Sod everyone!" Suddenly, his eyes widen. "And sod him!"

He leaps violently to his feet, and dashes across the short distance to where the elderly TV viewer has just demonstrated either his complete absorption in the programme or his habitual incontinence. He grabs him by the striped lapels of his fading flannelette pyjamas and shakes him as if were a human dice. "My God! What you need, old man, is a blast of E.C.T to the bladder. You disgusting old git!"

"Let go of me!! Geroff, geroff!"

"CLIII … IIVE!" The charge nurse bellows his way down the ward, clawing after his voice, as it precedes him in huge disciplinary waves. Within seconds, he separates the two mismatched combatants. The freed victim sinks to the floor, into the offending puddle and plays with much dismay at his torn pyjama jacket.

"Are you alright?" Amy bends over him.

"Leave him be. I'll get both him and the floor cleaned up in a minute." The charge nurse clearly feels that the old man can wait. More immediately pressing, is whether or not he can safely release the assailant from his iron grip. Clive's resentment at being manhandled quickly takes over from the unbridled anger that had preceded it. A determined jerk of the arm and he's loose to carry his hurt pride back to his room. He leaps on to the bed, sits bolt upright and stares at nothing in particular.

Amy looks at him through the open door. "Do you know who he reminds me of, Bernard? Not to look at exactly – except perhaps for the hollow cheeks and the hairline – but indefinably."

"Who?"

"Rudolf Hess."

"Christ! He'll be incarcerated for about as long as him if this is how he behaves. Shall we go?"

But our departure is twice interrupted.

Firstly, by the charge nurse. "Oh, before you go. Do you think I could have a word?"

"Surely." Amy's rush to leave is less than mine.

"Well it's like this. A major problem in our treatment for Clive is the absence of any real information, except for the small amount volunteered by him, about his day-to-day environment, his working and social life. We need some sort of picture of this. I've been asked to see if I can persuade visitors such as yourselves to call in for conversation with the doctor in charge of his case. At your convenience, of course. We've no family input at all."

"I'm sure we'd like to help. Bernard?"

"Umm … well, okay. I suppose that what helps Clive, helps me." I don't explain this.

"Good. Perhaps you could drop in within the next few days. A phone call in advance and we can arrange a mutually convenient time. Thank you both, and safe journey home; the roads are very slippery tonight."

We leave the ward and turn into the corridor. It's busy with wandering patients, regular purposeful visitors, lost first-time visitors, occasional porters and clipboard carrying medics. I set a respectable pace, with a more contemplative Amy, a few steps behind. I suddenly feel a soft-fingered hand play across the back of my neck, instantly followed by arms tightly around my waist.

"Amy! What are you?"

"Hi, handsome!"

My assailant does her best to twist me around and aims her moist lips at the side of my neck, sucking determinedly at my uncooperative skin.

"Hey. Leave off will you!"

I tear her away, then gently force her a yard or two in front of me. I'm glad of Amy's hastening steps to the rescue. She positions herself as a barrier. The attacker, rebuffed and loudly tearful, disappears as quickly as she had come.

"Wow. I might have known it wasn't you."

"True. My behaviour is never that strange, Bernard."

"Strange she was, but no stranger!"

"Heh?"

"You didn't recognise her?"

"No. Should I have done?"

"It was the Marilyn Monroe look-alike from Warren's party of last summer. Seems like rampant nymphomania has taken complete hold."

*

The nameplate on the door makes the simple statement that somewhere behind it an entering person will find Dr J.I. Davidson. At least, I think to myself, a consultant psychiatrist does not paradoxically seem to divest himself of all obviously medical qualifications by calling himself 'mister.'

The door is opened, not by a secretary or nursing sister, but by the man himself. An elderly but still physically imposing Scot. A refugee from the Western Isles where lives don't disintegrate nearly often enough to demand the soothing skills that he is trained to offer.

"Come in. Do come in. Very good of you to come of an evening like this. Good of you both to come. Take a seat. Yes, please sit down."

He places himself behind a huge mahogany desk, an item of furniture obviously older and more substantial than the new prefabricated hospital wing in one of whose rooms it now resides. It has about it, the sort of solidity demanded by the huge white-sleeved forearms that descend on it with the confident assurance that even an earthquake would not trouble its sturdy rigidity. The shock wave sends a pencil rolling off the central green leather writing pad. Davidson picks it up, and true to his heritage, tosses it like some mini caber back to where it had first lain.

"Now, I've already spoken to one other person, a mutual friend of yours and Mr Lyon."

"Bill? He wears a huge sweater." Amy senses that more precise identification is not going to be offered.

"He talked a lot, mainly about the depth of his own concern but actually, told me very little of value. Perhaps one or both of you could be of greater help."

"Well. I think Bernard here, might be the better one to start. He's known Clive since university days."

"Fine, if you'd like to fire away then. Mr Davies isn't it?"

I do my bit. Detail what I know. The circumstances of Clive's upbringing, the eccentricities which it's been mine to witness, and recently to feel a little threatened by.

"Good. Well thank you Mr Davies." Davidson picks up the pencil and works its pointed end inside his right ear, removing it to tap off a block of dark brown wax on to the desktop. Maybe, I think to myself, that it's this exercise, carried out intermittently, that has contributed to the magnificent sheen of the mahogany. "I feel however that – no doubt subconsciously – you're tending to place undue emphasis on the strangeness of Mr Lyon's behaviour. It's easy to do this, to retrospectively embellish when confronted with present-day mental disturbance. If I, for example, were to confront you with your own past brainstorms, then you'd question your own normality. Episodes of aberrant or unusual behaviour need not be all that important in themselves. In a sense, it's of more value to me to learn more of what is unspectacular in Mr Lyon's past."

"Well, I've told you all I know of that too."

"Yes."

"So, if you'll pardon my asking, has it been of any help at all?"

There's a pause in the conversation as Davidson takes the pencil to his teeth, dislodging some pith of an orange that has been annoyingly stuck in his mouth since lunchtime, but leaving a prominent smear of graphite across much of the white enamel of his top incisors.

"Helpful? Yes, to a degree. You see, some would argue that there's no such thing as mental illness. Only problems in living and that consequently, the concept of mental illness is unhelpful in therapy, even counterproductive. A rather extreme view admittedly – less fashionable these last few years too – but you'll find few people willing to entirely discount the importance of environment. We now tend to see most mental illness as medical and social in varying degrees, and our treatment reflects this."

"Well, what's the mix in Clive's case? I mean, how does all this affect his treatment?"

"Hah … umm … well, if you – or anybody else known to him – are seeking to entirely absolve yourselves from blame, then I have to disappoint you. You mustn't walk away from here consoled that his problems are one hundred percent biochemical. Mr Lyon is, in my opinion, a schizophrenic. Now, to put you in the picture, to dispel popular myths if you like, this doesn't denote a single disease process, but rather a number of somewhat similar patterns of psychological reactions to life situations. Horrible expression that! So, it's difficult to understand. In terms of incidence, schizophrenia is the most important of the major psychoses, yet still holds many mysteries for us."

"Is it so mysterious that it doesn't give out early warning signals? Prevention much better than cure and all that." I'm clutching at straws. It's already too late to pretend that Clive hasn't been shadowing me from behind trees. "Signals? Yes, but it's the horse and the stable door all over again. Certain recommendations for prevention centre largely on the provision of warm understanding relationships in the family, particularly with the mother. On this basis then, withdrawn children should perhaps be given early guidance directed towards improving socialisation. But personal difficulties of this type are all too often only recognised – or admitted – retrospectively and retrospection, as you'll recall me saying some moments ago, is a hazardous insight at the best of times."

Amy looks at him in mild disagreement. "Not so here, though. I mean all of us have noted Clive's difficulties in relating to other people. Noted them as they've happened!"

"Mmm … but you've never alerted anybody who might have helped. And I don't mean this in an accusatory way. It's almost always the case."

"I'm sorry. I wasn't meaning to be over-sensitive. One other thing. You mentioned the mother-figure. I was always under the impression that Clive was very close to his mother."

"Possibly like the cow is close to the farmer. She was the only one available to offer him food and shelter. But my having to talk to you rather than to her must say something."

"Yes, I suppose so. But again, what about treatment? Because we are where we are now."

There's a further hesitation before Davidson replies. This time, the pencil ferrets up both nostrils, coming away with nothing solid, but gliding out easily in a silvery sheen.

"Treatment? Well, you have to understand that there's no cure on offer. In many cases of this type, provision of a protected environment seems important, somewhere in which the patient can gradually work through periods of confusion."

I think of the old man in front of the TV who had needed protection from Clive. One man's barricade from reality is another's frightening encounter with life at its most menacing. "Can you provide that here?"

"Oh yes, we think so. But preferably only in the short term, via carefully structured programmes. Based on our experiences with other patients, but hopefully tailored to the individual."

"But he's not here compulsorily?"

"True."

"So, he could reject all your overtures. I mean, I don't suppose he even accepts that he's got problems."

"Again true, Mr Davies, but you must remember that I'm trained to overcome non-cooperation, to a degree at least. I've spoken to Mr

Lyon, Clive, three times now, at length. He admits to nothing but tells me a lot, so to speak."

"So, you are able to embark on treatment from a platform of understanding what's wrong?"

"I think so, yes."

"And it's to be this protective shield and nothing else?"

"No no, not at all. There are numerous special forms of treatment which use physical means as an adjunct to psychotherapy ... "

I think that this has a nice ring to it, but the sort of punch which a regrettable part of me has sometimes felt inclined to throw Clive's way is clearly not what Davidson has in mind.

"... for instance, although increasingly less favoured, it's not unknown to use ECT in cases of this sort. However, this is not so effective in this disorder, as it sometimes is in other psychotic conditions, or, if I'm honest, was thought to be, until recently. So, I'm essentially proposing continued psychiatric therapy coupled with a carefully monitored programme of tranquillisers. Which, you understand, act by relieving symptoms. They are not a specific remedy."

"And with them, you hope for successful reintegration?"

"Yes, at least for some time. He ought for instance, to be able to regain the ability to concentrate on work, to rekindle some basic career enthusiasms. I've spoken to his office head and it seems he's been out of sorts in this direction for some time now. Not to mention, according to office gossip, that a female colleague has paid no heed to his seemingly ham-fisted infatuation and has now rubbed salt into the wound by announcing her intention to leave Steynmouth for some indeterminate period. Not that I personally feel that this episode, in itself, will have tipped the balance."

My unspoken reaction is that I don't see why not. I know the impact on myself of Liz's departure.

Amy still has questions it seems. "And the long-term prognosis? Good or what?"

"It's difficult to say, but there is one sign that may point to a reasonably promising outcome. And that's the mixture which we seem to have in Mr Lyon's case of schizophrenic symptoms with those of manic-depressive psychosis."

"What?" I'm hugely puzzled. "You're saying that the more complicated the jigsaw, the easier its solution?"

"Yes, in a way. Again, we've no real understanding of this, but past precedent leads us to this conclusion. It means, perhaps, there's a master key somewhere."

Five hours later, lying awake in bed, I relate this observation to the triple life complication of Liz, Amy and Deborah and console myself that the ultimate resolution might ironically, be more easily achieved than if Liz were the single undiluted source of this mayhem.

Amy is persisting. "So, how soon will we be seeing him again?"

"You mean out of here?"

"Yes."

"Oh, sooner rather than later but of course, he'll remain on our books, as it were. And you, his friends, will be an important element in his rehabilitation.

Thank you for your help, and perhaps if I need to see you again?"

"Yes, of course. Bernard?"

"Oh yes, anytime!" I jump to my feet, cursorily shaking Davidson's outstretched hand, almost pushing Amy before me out of the door.

"Heh, what's the rush? Not as if we've a bus to catch"

"No. Sorry. It's just that he was about to pick up that pencil again."

"So?"

"Well, he's run out of polite orifices."

On the way out, I keep open a careful eye for Marilyn Monroe. But it's someone altogether less precocious who catches my attention.

"Amy, was that Sarah disappearing to the left there?"

She goes off in curious pursuit and returns a full five minutes later to confirm my sighting.

"She's not, well, here as a result of the trauma over Warren?"

"God, Bernard, no! She's a hospital volunteer two evenings a week. Library service on the wards."

"Ah ha. Makes sense. After all, if living with Warren didn't drive her nuts, then the release of not living with him certainly wouldn't."

*

It's three days until Liz leaves. I'm meeting her this evening for dinner. I get home from work around four-thirty and then spend a torturous three hours occupying time in unhelpful thought. I dab on some aftershave, coat up for the cold, and shut the door behind me.

I step out briskly along the intermittently icy pavement, sometimes lifting my arms from my sides to secure better balance. The roads look even more treacherous. This, plus the spectre of the breathalyser, has led to my decision to walk. A hostile side wind gusts bitingly against my left cheek and ear. It's funny how often weather seems to match the nature of the occasion. Californian love stories full of cinema screen sunshine. Conan Doyle characters wrapped in sinister mists and now a numbness of the skin to match that inside me.

I quicken my pace, but no amount of limb movement seems able to counter the refrigerating effect of the evening air whose temperature is falling at a rate faster than that of my own plummeting morale. Thinking about it afterwards, it was probably this complete engrossment with self, plus the anaesthetising effect of the cold, that had combined to render me insensible to the thrusting of a knife into my back, until just a few steps on, nausea and a swirling head had seen me fall in a rapid faint to the ground.

Chapter 11

Crisis of Conscience

Liz has been stood up only once in her life. When eight-year-old Tommy Egglestone didn't show up in the tree house by the river.

Eventually, after fruitless door knocking and telephone calls, she obeys an inexplicable self-instruction to visit the Police Station. Enquiries on her behalf locate me at the District Hospital.

"Don't you worry miss," says the reassuring Sgt Hilda Livermore. "But seems like your friend has been attacked".

"Attacked?"

"Stabbed in the back it would seem. The hospital authorities are trying to contact his parents. Seems like he had a letter from them in his wallet."

"But … but … is he okay?"

"I'm sure he will be, miss. Would you like to sit down until the shock passes? A cup of tea maybe?"

"No, no! Tell me exactly what they said, will you? Tell me!"

"Well, he's received a deep stab wound, which miraculously caused a lot of tissue damage and bleeding, but somehow missed anything vital."

"And that's it?"

"No, the main problem is that he hit his head as he fell. He's being kept very heavily sedated because of this injury, and there's some concern about the overall stability of his condition. But he's in good hands, miss. I'm sure he'll be alright."

"Oh God! Look, can I use your phone? I promised Amy I'd call her … sorry, a friend of ours, to let her know if anything is wrong. I … I'd troubled her earlier thinking she might have some idea where he was."

"Yes, of course."

"And perhaps first, I could have that drink after all. Water please. Water will do."

Hilda Livermore leaves the room. It's only during her brief absence that the thought dawns on Liz that the weapon which injured Bernard hadn't done so of its own accord. She waits impatiently for the Sergeant to return.

"Here's your water, dear."

"Yes, yes. Put it there will you. Look, who did it? You don't know do you? Otherwise, you wouldn't have had to ring the hospital. You'd know what I was on about the moment I walked in."

"I'm sure, miss, that we'll apprehend the culprit fairly quickly. Most incidents of this sort involve a member of the family or an offended friend. Something like that."

"Too true! It's Clive damn him. It must be. I'll give you his goddam address and this time, tell the bloody doctors to keep him locked up!"

"You know who might have done it then, miss? I don't know why people don't voice their fears over this kind of thing *before* it happens."

Sgt Livermore is either weak on memory or selectively dishonest in what she chooses not to recall.

*

The ease with which hospital rules are broken proves to be related to the condition of the patient. 'No more than two visitors per bed', seems not to apply when the object of interest is unconscious. The greater number of visitors now speak in whispered tones lest the bedridden Bernard surreptitiously comes to and hears something not meant for his ears.

Amy murmurs quietly to Liz, "He looks so amazingly contented. *Peaceful* seems a word best not used; I think."

He has the appearance of a poorly shaven, young, fortune seeking prospector from Klondike days. No gold yet, so instead, lying back in happy inebriation.

Liz says nothing in reply. Amy looks instead to Harold and Elspeth Davies who are sat on a foam-covered metal bench on the other side of the bed. "Mr and Mrs Davies, why don't we go along to the canteen? I'm sure you wouldn't say no to a cup of tea. Liz and Bill can stay with Bernard. They'll let us know if anything happens, I'm sure."

"Yes, Elspeth dear. Amy's right. We can spare a minute or two."

Elspeth slowly rises to her feet. She'd arrived as a shocked fifty-year-old, but in twenty-four hours, her brow has become progressively entrenched with the furrows of someone much older. Her physical mannerisms, normally barely noticeable, have exaggerated themselves to the level of preposterous nervous ticks: both hands lifting alternately to squeeze tightly at her earlobes before patting drum like across her thighs.

Amy shepherds them both out of the small side-ward which Bernard is sharing with two other patients. One, an elderly farmer whose two gangrenous feet had thoughtlessly demanded removal at one and the same time, and who is the object of much scolding for playing with his reddened bandages. The other, a jaundiced and even more elderly seafarer, whose yellowing complexion is not yielding to treatment. Neither of them ever receives a visitor, a further reason perhaps, why Bernard is treated so generously in this respect. There's plenty of space available.

*

The hospital canteen has the smell of an unholy alliance, the activity of the cooks failing to entirely dispel the leftover aroma from disinfectant which the previous evening had been spread liberally over the green thermo-plastic tiles floor. The yellow walls too, have a smooth scrubbed look, perhaps defence against salmonella, but offering no cosiness as somewhere to enjoy a comforting warm drink. Even supposing that on this occasion enjoyment were otherwise possible.

Elspeth sips slowly at her over-sweetened tea.

"It's very reassuring for us to find that Bernard has such close friends here. Isn't it Harold? He's always kept this sort of thing to himself. We never really knew all your names until now."

"I'm just sorry to have met you under such circumstances, Mrs Davies."

"Yes ... tell me Amy ..." She embarks unenthusiastically on a conversation which she somehow knows to be preferable to quiet disconsolation ... "What do you do for a living? Not teach with Bernard, I presume?"

"Why would you presume that?"

"Oh, I don't know. Just that teaching seems to roughen the edges on people. You seem, well ... more *presentable*."

"Thank you!"

"And on top of that, you've spent much of yesterday and today here at the hospital. Which seems to suggest you're more your own master."

"Mistress! Although, maybe not the right word." She laughs.

"Of course."

"Actually, I run a small craft and souvenir shop. Things are very slack at this time of year anyway."

"Yes, I suppose so. What about Bill and Liz? What do they do with themselves?"

"Oh, Bill, well, he doesn't have a job as such. He occupies himself worrying, helping life's unfortunates, sometimes constructively but usually only aspirationally."

Elspeth is very much a subscriber to the Protestant work ethic and isn't impressed with altruism when its activist is supported by unemployment benefits. She raises her eyebrows, as if in disapproval, then realises the incompleteness of Amy's reply.

"And Liz?"

"Oh Liz, well, she's just finished work at the local office of the Inland Revenue."

"To do what?"

"Well, it's not to a new job or anything. She's about to go off to Europe, on an extended holiday, you might say."

Elspeth is beginning to fear that the more she learns of Bernard's friends, the more it becomes apparent that he's associating with the work shy of this world.

"When does she leave?"

"Well, tomorrow, in fact."

"But, wouldn't she want to …"

"What? Wait for good news about Bernard, you mean?"

"Oh no, I shouldn't presume too much."

Amy offers no response. She says nothing about the fact that Liz is to leave in sixteen hours' time amid a crisis of conscience that threatens to add further to the emotional trauma of her departure. If she were to stay until Bernard regains full consciousness, then she'd never go. But if she leaves on time – once scheduled but now almost cruelly premature – he might never want her back. In the end, but with no great certainty, since the final mealtime rendezvous had never taken place, she's decided that optimistic au revoirs should remain just that. It's no time to change plans. Amy has feigned to understand but finds it all unfathomable.

"Would you like another cup, dear?" Harold breaks his silence.

"No. No thank you."

"What about you, Amy?"

"Umm … yes, Yes I would." The tea is disgusting, treacle-like in appearance and only lukewarm. But she feels she'd like to defer Elspeth's return to the bedside.

Harold returns from the counter with his and Amy's teas. He sits down and pushes her cup across the incongruously grubby Formica surface.

"How long have you known Bernard?"

"Oh, since very soon after he first came to Steynmouth. I like him very much."

"Yes, of course. You both had that enjoyable holiday together in France last summer."

Amy looks at him. To see if his eyes are shut and he's not seeing exactly who he's talking to. But no, it's the semi-ignorant comment of a father starved of detail by a less than forthcoming son. Elspeth, whose delving into her son's affairs has always been more forensic, senses the error immediately.

"I think you're mistaken Harold, dear. Though I've no doubt at all that Amy here *is* a very good friend of Bernard's."

Amy saves them both from adding embarrassment to today's sadness. "Well, I'd have to be, wouldn't I? I was the one left at home!" She offers her usual infectious and disarming smile and Harold, unhooked, joins her. But her non-blushing display leaves her exposed to further interrogation from Elspeth who sees that here is someone willing to swallow pride for the sake of honesty. With Bernard hopefully, surely, bound to recover, it will be as well for his mother to know what awaits him when he wakes up.

"Then pardon me asking Amy, the thought hadn't occurred to me until now. So much on my mind, I suppose. But if it was Liz who went with him to France, and who's sitting with him right now, then why is …"

Amy cuts her short. "If you're asking me *again* about her leaving him at this time, then that's for her to tell you. If she wants to. And if you feel you really *ought* to ask her."

"Do *you* think I ought? I mean if she's playing with Bernard's affections, then that's hardly likely to aid his recovery, mentally at least."

Harold pushes in. "Elspeth, come on now, dear. The whole thing is getting on top of you. I think perhaps we might pray for his physical recovery before we start worrying about his love life." He looks at Amy. "Sorry to put it like that. But first things first."

"Yes, obviously, dear. I'm sorry." She roots deep in her handbag for a paper tissue.

It needs someone to alter the whole drift of the conversation.

"May I join you?" Bill has been asked to leave by Liz. Politely, but unwilling to take no for an answer.

*

The problem is that whereas Bill can walk to the canteen and leave Liz behind, the farmer and the seaman can barely move an inch. Whatever the respective failings of their circulation and liver, there's nothing wrong with their hearing, nor do they show any reluctance to intrude into the private world of the former tax inspector and her formerly conscious boyfriend. The farmer's observations smack of senility. Silly but bearable but those of the seafarer are full of ill-humoured bile.

Liz takes hold of Bernard's right hand, carefully avoiding the plastic drip-tube. She leans slowly across him and flattens his hair.

"For God's sake Bernard. Recover." She allows herself the privilege of watery eyes in place of what Elspeth is now regarding as cold dispassion from someone who will be up and off before the sick man comes to. The only person who *might* understand her is he who at present can understand nothing.

"You'll have to speak louder than that if he's to hear you," volunteers the liverish one. "Have you tried shouting? Maybe his ears need a lot of extra stimulation?"

"Please keep your suggestions to yourself. Doesn't it occur to you that what I'm saying to him is confidential? Not for *your* ears. Please!"

"Oh, suit yourself, my dear. Suit yourself."

"He's right though, missus. I had an old sow once. Went into some sort of trance. Wouldn't grunt for nobody. Vet, 'e said I should 'ave 'er put down. But in the end, I bloody well bellowed her back to life. Told 'er to knuckle to. Saved 'er bacon you might say. Your friend there, 'e needs some sort of shock, I reckon."

"Spot on! Maybe if she smiled at him. Instead of looking so bloody miserable."

Liz fixes them both with a stare that changes from tolerance to disapproval, as she shifts her eyes from farmer to seafarer. "Look. If you can't occupy yourselves with your own problems and not push your way into a private conversation, then I shall have to fetch Sister Samworth."

"Conversation! How can you have a conversation with someone who hasn't said a bloody word since he was brought in here? Just my luck to have a cabbage one side of me and a turnip head beyond him."

Liz lets go of Bernard's hand and pulls the curtain along its noisy metal tracking, to create a barrier to sight, if not sound, between them both and the unwelcome neighbours. Within a microsecond, the help which she has threatened to summon, appears. A white capped head through the central join of the curtain material.

"Yes, Sister?"

"I wonder if you would leave the curtains pulled back please? Only they now obscure our view of Mr McDermott from the corridor. We usually look in the door as we pass. With his condition, very severely jaundiced, there could be a sudden deterioration."

"But Sister, he's just so rude that I'm unable to concentrate on Bernard. I feel I'll explode if I don't shut him out."

"Yes, yes. I know he's a bit cantankerous. Aren't you, Mr McDermott? But he could possibly lapse into a crisis state, and we do need to keep an eye on him. Now, I must insist and anyway, unpleasant as he is, he is someone for *Mr Smith* to talk to."

"Yes, but their talk is across us. I mean, couldn't the beds be re-arranged? Or Bernard moved to a single room?"

"I'm afraid not. Firstly, we've no single rooms. And secondly, circumstances change so quickly on this type of ward, It's simply not worth entering into supposedly better arrangements just to overcome what may be very temporary problems. We don't have a stable pattern of bed occupancy, if you'll pardon the jargon."

The shrew-like Sister switches back the curtains even more loudly than Liz had pulled them across and marches out to return to her business.

Aesthetically, the curtains deserve concealing. A mish-mashed pattern of gaudy apricot-coloured flowers within a maze of lime-green creepers. Neither does the room beyond deserve revealing even when a visitor doesn't desire privacy. Victorian in age and décor, glossy green, above waist high brown with the odd patch of flaking plaster.

On reaching the door, Sister Samworth turns around, perhaps regretful at having implied that the sickly trio might soon be a twosome. "I'm sorry, dear. If it were just the patients and their beds, but it's all the paraphernalia of tubes and monitoring equipment as well. I'm sure you understand."

"Yes, I understand." Liz sounds sour.

"She understands now that she isn't the boss around here." The sailor sounds even sourer. Too grumpy even to gloat.

*

Elspeth has changed her mind about the tea. With talking still preferable to silence, she's now embarking on a programme of reminiscence which needs an intake of caffeine as fuel. Bernard is alternately portrayed as having been mischievous but angelic, helpful but uncooperative, cowardly but adventurous, admirable but reprehensible. It's a sort of word picture of universal application – recognizing the inconsistency of human behaviour – but a sad comment from a mother who is chattering without thinking.

Amy thinks it best to be quietly receptive, but Bill pitches in here and there with questions which confirm to Elspeth that her son has often been difficult to read.

"I'll bet you've never known what he was going to do next, Mrs Davies. He's still unpredictable, now isn't he, Amy?"

Amy nods but disagrees. Bernard's changes of mood, brief flirtations with new directions in life, are one thing. But they don't imply inconsistency of character. In fact, she feels she truly *knows* him. And not knowing him, how he works, would long ago have frightened her out of her frustrated affection for him.

Elspeth and Bill plough on with their verbal equivalent of a foray through the photograph album. Amy occasionally catches Harold's eye. He's sitting quietly, revolving his empty cup and saucer between the forefingers of both hands. She feels a more intense level of communication with him, through saying nothing, than is being achieved between the busy tongues sat next to them. He's a likeable man, through being so much like his son. An *old block off the chip*, for that's the order in which she's met them. Whereas, Elspeth might often reproach Harold for frivolity and lack of seriousness, at least he knows when to say nothing and doesn't despise quiet contemplation. Amy knows Bernard to have that same sensible balance. She feels she'd make a far better partner for Davies Junior than Elspeth has made for Davies Senior. She immediately hates herself for her conceit and then quickly, for her mental betrayal of Liz. But it's getting increasingly difficult to accept being second in the queue, especially so when the person at its head is leaving and might not return before the bus arrives, though this is a problem of her own making; she's never actually promised to keep Liz's place, nor been asked.

Bill and Elspeth have, by now, passed through Bernard's childhood and are into his adolescence. It's at the mention of his former schoolfriends that Amy asks the question.

"And how is Deborah now?"

Elspeth looks puzzled. "You know Deborah?"

"Well, we met once. When she visited Steynmouth last November or whenever."

"Visited Bernard? What, here in Steynmouth?"

Amy hesitates, but is now trapped in her indiscretion. "Yes."

"But not with Philip and the children, surely? I mean Bernard doesn't have the room to put them up." Elspeth has never been able to accept that sleeping arrangements are something ripe for improvisation.

"No. But Mrs Davies, she came only for sympathy and advice. Because of her problems at home. She hoped that Bernard might have some words to help."

"Problems at home? Do you know anything about this, Harold?"

"Nothing at all, dear."

"And she stayed with Bernard at the bungalow, Amy?"

"I … I believe so. But really Mrs Davies, you shouldn't worry."

"Shouldn't worry! I really don't know what to think." Elspeth is clearly of the opinion that women don't cry on other men's shoulders unless they prefer their feel to those from which they are fleeing. Besides, she's always associated Deborah with the sexual awakening of her son, something difficult to ignore when you're responsible for an adolescent's laundry. Now, here she is again, only this time threatening a genuinely catastrophic intervention into Bernard's life. "Do you know what sort of problems, Amy?"

"Oh, some minor marital hiccup, I suspect. I'm sure it's all smoothed over. You should feel proud that Bernard was able to help. Too many people elevate themselves above their old hometown acquaintances."

But Elspeth looks troubled It's now a crisis of many facets. Should Bernard recover, he'll re-enter the dubious company of the voluntarily unemployed Bill, will find himself deserted by Liz in favour of the Grand Tour and added to which, he is now exposed as a party to the disintegration of a marriage between two of his long standing friends.

"I … I think we should get back to the ward, Harold."

Bill rises first and takes the back of Elspeth's chair. "Look, you two go ahead and send Liz down here to join Amy and myself. Tell her to hurry. We'll get a coffee in."

"Yes, we'll do that. Come along Harold, dear."

Bill fumbles in his pockets. "Anybody got any change for Liz's coffee?"

*

"Could I see you both before you return to Bernard?"

Sister Samworth intercepts the Davies's and ushers them into her office. A cluttered desktop, quite out of keeping with her ordered and insensitive oversight of the ward.

"Take a seat." There's only one available. It looks like a former piano stool. Harold indicates that he'll stand.

"Now, what exactly has doctor told you about Bernard's condition?"

This is a question which serves only to exacerbate the worry of his two parents but asked necessarily, in order that the extent of information she might convey, does not exceed that which a more senior authority has already thought appropriate. In which case, there is really little point in their meeting. In any event, her role as a potential source of comfort is effectively ruined by the abrasiveness of her manner and the harshness of her unsmiling appearance. She is somewhat wizened, with thinning hair and cold blue-tinted glasses, as if drained of both physical energy and compassion.

"Well Sister, my wife and I are both very concerned. The doctor's told us really what we can see for ourselves. That Bernard's out of immediate physical danger, in terms of his life, but beyond that, it's difficult to say"

"And that's all you've been told?"

"Well, not in so many words, of course. Or rather in more words. More detail, but that's the gist of it."

Which is true. There's been some discussion as to whether Bernard's unconsciousness could be entirely related to a brain injury deriving from impact to his skull, or some more indefinable causation linked to the physical consequences of the stabbing itself. But in the end, all that has come through to Harold and Elspeth, is that Bernard has not died and does not seem likely to but is fast asleep. The point and manner of his awakening is left without forecast. "Impossible to say at this stage, although it's complicated by the fact that he's under quite heavy sedation right now."

It's Harold's concise reporting of this conversation with the doctor that causes Sister Samworth to overstep the mark. 'More detail, but that's the gist of it', she takes to mean that mention has already been made of possible mental impairment in Bernard if and when he is aroused. And she quickly alludes to this. The following day, she's reprimanded for causing premature and possibly unnecessary distress. Hence, the grudge whose venom the Davies's have to bear for the rest of the time that they wait upon their son. No permanent bedside vigil is to be allowed. "Rules are rules, and I have already made too many exceptions in this case."

*

Bill fetches Liz the coffee whose purchase cost he has borrowed.

"Any change while we've been away?"

"No, no. Of course not!" Liz's reply is curt and irritated. Though her annoyance is not with Amy for asking the question, but with Bernard for his unknowing part in the current emotional blackmail pressing her to stay. In this, he proves not to be without allies, with both Amy and Bill now combining their last-minute voices in a plea for her not to go. Easy for Bill, perhaps less easy for Amy. Liz quickly expands her annoyance to encompass everyone who is now pushing her into overturning what she sees to be a decision sensibly taken and potentially of enduring benefit to the quality of her remaining life and one in which she sees even Bernard himself as having acquiesced. She doesn't recognise that she's given him no choice but to accept what was on offer.

"Oh please, both of you! I shouldn't have to tell you again that Bernard understands. He knows just where my return would place him in relation to whatever else the world might offer. *He'd* not expect me to be steamrollered by all this mess. If I stayed now, he'd come to, as we hope he will, to find someone with less spirit than she once had."

"Damn your spirit!" Bill is uncharacteristically reproachful, but characteristically on the side of the physically sick as opposed to the blatantly healthy.

Amy says nothing, out of discomfort at the open airing being given to the idea of 'Bernard and Liz'. She thinks that Bill in his innocence knows little of the whole romantic melodrama, but his quick-fire admonition of Liz is not the reaction of someone surprised at what lies beneath Liz's self-created problems. She wonders to what extent her own role has been discussed by one and all and whether it's generally agreed that she is never likely to be anything other than the runner-up.

"I'm sorry. I didn't mean to be … oh, nasty or tiresome or whatever." Liz looks wearied. Her hair seems lank. Yellow rather than honey-blonde. The harsh fluorescent light of the canteen offers her face no flattering shadow, no hiding of her misery.

"No, forget it. We're all on edge. Let Bill here buy you another coffee."

"Okay. Black this time."

Bill walks to the counter but comes back for Amy again to finance his errand.

Liz plays nervously with a strip of loose Formica along the table edge. "I don't think I'll go back to the ward again. I really ought to get back and catch up on some sleep before I leave tomorrow."

"I'll miss you, Liz." Amy looks bewildered. "Look, what if Bernard revives before you go? I mean do you want that I should contact you? What would you do then?"

"Oh, there's no need to plan or decide in advance. It'll all be down to reflex in the end. I gave you the address in Koblenz, didn't I?"

"Yes, I have it somewhere. Perhaps I'll write to you first."

"Say something for me to Bernard's parents."

"I'll try."

"Thanks. I don't like drinking on my own. What about coffee for you two?"

"Oh, that's okay. Amy and I had a start on you." Bill sits down, rubs his hands together, and fiddles with the cuffs of his sweater. "I've been bothered about Clive through all this." For a moment, it's as if a member of Churchill's war cabinet has voiced concern over Hitler having an upset stomach. Liz takes a deep breath. Amy prepares herself for the unpleasant turn which she suspects their conversation might now take. But Bill continues to push the line that in the end, Clive should leave all of them no option but to regard him as an object of sympathy and very reluctant compassion. Sgt Hilda Livermore had finally done her duty, and with male reinforcements had made none too dignified an entry into his bed-sit. He is now remanded in the psychiatric wing of Devwall County Prison. There is little doubt that the expert voice of Dr Davidson will be ready to suggest that all will be well in the future, and clearly no admission from him that Clive's discharge might have been premature, even ill-advised.

*

"Mr Lyon?"

"A bit bloody polite, aren't you? Considering how you've pushed open my door!"

"You are Mr, Lyon?" Sgt Livermore deepens her voice an octave or two.

"Yes." Clive replies almost nonchalantly, his untroubled eyes searching for the strong coffee which he put down when the door ball rang. He strokes his black-speckled chin in irritation.

"Do you know a Mr Bernard Davies?" Sgt Livermore is now flanked by two heavy police constables. One of them looks curiously around the grubby room, with its unswept carpet, its litter of open books and scattered record sleeves, its collection of unwashed crockery. He then steps back to block the line of path to the doorway.

"Bernard Davies. Yes, I know him."

"Mr Lyon. Were you at ..."

"I did it!"

"I see. As simple as that?"

"Oh, even simpler. It was no crime you see. It was all agreed."

"Agreed?" Sgt Livermore looks spectacularly confused. But Clive hasn't forgotten the request he'd long ago made at South Kensington tube station for Bernard to acquiesce in his own injury. Though he's ignored Bernard's unenthusiastic response.

"Yes, he knew it was coming ... well ... Something like it anyway. It was all arranged you see."

"Perhaps you'd like to come down to the station and explain all this, Mr Lyon?"

"Explain? God, you people! Look, nothing to bloody well explain. I've just told you. It was all agreed."

*

"What will happen to him?" asks Amy.

"Well, let's hope he can be rehabilitated poor chap." Bill can't appreciate the need to moderate his concern.

Liz looks both quizzical and unconcerned, not understanding that someone could so equivocally accept a murder attempt involving two of his own friends. She is so wrapped up with Bernard, and even more so with herself, as not to be too worried over Clive's malevolent brain waves and what they might hold in store for him.

"But, I mean, can he be rehabilitated do you think?" Amy frowns.

"Yes!" Bill has splendid confidence. "After all, he's not actually killed anybody," and then, less confidently, "well, not yet."

"I would have thought that it was intent that mattered. Surely?"

"No Amy, no, mattered at the time, but not as a shadow over the rest of his life. I'm very sure that a spell of caring hospitalisation will sort things out for him. It's not punishment he needs."

Liz drops her cup loudly on to its saucer. "Spoken like someone whose back remains unpierced. Get through to Bernard, if you can, and see what he thinks!"

Bill is spirited in his retort. "Much the same as you obviously do, I suppose. But whether you'll be demanding retribution with quite so much passion when the dust has settled, remains to be seen. I doubt it."

"Yes, yes, You're right. Okay. But … oh, never mind!" About to embark upon the risks of releasing the criminally 'ill' back into society, she stops short. Gives no voice to her mistrust of the trusting. Is tired of it all. "Look, I'll go now if you don't mind. I'll give you a call in the morning, Amy. Look after yourself Bill." She gets up, punches him in the left shoulder, and kisses his forehead. "See you sometime."

He looks up at her. "For fuck's sake, Liz. You're not *real*. How *can* you allege to care for Bernard, yet callously leave him like this? If I were him, if I were able to speak out of unconsciousness, I'd tell you to go to hell."

She stares coldly at him and walks quickly out of the now, almost empty canteen. Bill taps his fingers on the side of the chair seat. "*Some* people might say she's heartless." On quick reflection, he doesn't want to be guilty of so uncharitable a thought.

"Come off it, Bill! You don't get many people kissing you." Amy's response might have been less cruelly phrased had she too received a goodbye more physical in its nature that the promise of tomorrow's telephone chat. She'd not balk at a kiss of her own.

*

"Mr Smith, I'm sure you didn't really ought to be doing that."

The farmer's bandages are dangling like limp streamers over the bedside and on to the floor with patches of blood-stained lint scattered nearby like confetti at some Transylvanian wedding. The culprit looks up but takes no heed of Elspeth's reproachful observations. He returns with enthusiasm to the task of confirming that thin air now exists where his feet had once been.

"Harold, didn't we ought to call Sister?"

"No, no. She wasn't too concerned about it last time. Except perhaps that he might exhaust the dressings cupboard. No, just turn away dear, for now."

"It really isn't good enough putting Bernard in here with these two." She starts to cry.

"Hey, hey. Look. Barnacle Bill there's asleep now and Mr Smith here, well he's harming nobody but himself. C'mon dear, cheer up."

"Cheer up? Oh Harold. Really!" Being upset gives way to irritation. "That's just not possible. Not while everything with Bernard is just, well, so much the same. If we could only see some gradual change."

"I don't suppose things happen like that dear. I expect he'll come to quickly. Just you wait and see." Harold is churning up inside, but on the outside, he steadfastly maintains the placid stance needed to counter Elspeth's more violent swings of mood.

"Oh, I don't know. I really don't. If only we could do something. Even if it were helping him sip some water, or somehow letting him know we're here."

"Maybe he does know, dear."

"No. He doesn't. His eyes tell you that." She looks at them in much the same way as she had anxiously searched for the first glimpse of filial recognition, twenty-six years previously.

"You can't say that, dear. To me, his eyelids seem more open at times than others, and for longer. And in any case …" he lowers his voice … "shouldn't we confine our remarks to a more positive tack. We've no real idea of what he might be taking in."

"I tell you Harold, his eyes would tell us. I'll be the first to encourage him when the time arrives."

"As you say dear … but it we talk more positively it might help us too."

"It's not you and I that matter, Harold."

He places his elbows on his knees and cups his forehead in the palms of his hands, staring down silently towards the beige tiled floor. By the time, barely thirty seconds later, that he raises himself up, he has subtly wiped away the tears which had trickled towards each side of his nose. But wanting too to hide their salty tracks, he turns sideways towards the window. Then, as his eyes are making their return journey back to Elspeth and Bernard, he notices Mr McDermott.

"Elspeth, fetch Sister, will you?"

"Why Harold, what's the matter?"

"I … I think our sailor friend has died."

*

It's while Elspeth and Harold are out of the room – talking to Bill and Amy, now back from the canteen – that Bernard flickeringly comes to. He's propped up against a gently inclined pillow, the perfect vantage point from which to be welcomed back to the world. Straight ahead of him, Mr McDermott's corpse is being wheeled out. Just to his right, lies a fully unbandaged pair of footless ankle bones, only partly healed.

Chapter 12

A Very Smooth Move

"… and then suddenly, I felt as if I were away from my body. I was separated from everyone. Alone in space, but not drifting around. I was floating on the same level, looking down on my body from above, but still feeling as though I had a complete body form. And yet, I was like a balloon or a feather. So light, that it's difficult to put into words. I could see my friends and relatives around the bed. I remained strangely unaffected by their distress. Then, what seemed like a gust – a warm gust – of wind swept me into a blackness. I was almost tumbled, still floating, through a long dark tunnel, at the far end of which, eventually, there appeared, a brightness, initially almost blinding. As I left the tunnel, my eyes slowly adapted to the light. It had its own identity, but no recognizable shape. I felt as though I were surrounded by overwhelming love and compassion. I looked back down the tunnel, trying to catch a glimpse of what I'd left behind. By then, I was feeling some sadness at the thought of never seeing my parents again. But the light suggested – in words, though not in sounds – that I turn away and instead, step across some sort of line that was shrouded in mist before me. I followed the light and almost immediately, all these people were hovering around me including my grandparents, other relatives and friends who had died years previously. They all seemed pleased to see me. It was a happy occasion. They acted as my protectors. Then, the light started to question me, picking out certain items from my past and asking me to recall them. All through this, it kept emphasizing the importance of love. It wasn't at all accusatory of my former shortcomings. The whole experience seemed to last no time

at all, and yet we had covered my entire life. Then, it was as if I were picked up by the light. I didn't have time to think, to work out why, but I knew I was being sucked back into my body. I can't recall getting back inside. It was just as if I woke up and I was lying back on the bed. All the people were standing around looking at me, in the same places as before. I brought back the most wonderful feelings, indescribable really. I still feel them now and again. In a way, I look forward to it happening properly ..."

I put the book aside. It was only three days since I came to, but already, I'm the subject of Bill's obsession with the paranormal.

"No Bill, honestly, it wasn't at all like that."

"Are you sure? Look, read some more. All the reports are very similar."

"Well, if so, no need. I felt nothing like that. I remember nothing between leaving home and being introduced to Mr Smith's stumps."

"But Bernard, you were near death, on the point of it, for a while, maybe temporarily beyond it. You're the only person I've ever known whose been through one of these near-death experiences. How come you can't provide a testimony like these other people?" He points to the now well-fingered paperback whose pages he has already devoured avidly, in readiness for this conversation.

"What is this? Some new area of interest of yours?"

"Oh no. I've always been fascinated by the idea of life beyond the grave and this seemed a chance to get first-hand evidence."

"Well, sorry to disappoint you Bill, old boy."

"Look, maybe if you were to think carefully enough, it might all come back."

"Oh, you mean I might just regurgitate what I've just read. What I wonder is, how many of the witnesses in your book had themselves, read the pages of others like it, at some time or other?"

"No, that's where you're wrong, Bernard. Apparently, all this stuff pre-dates the written word. It's the same story among people where there's just the oral tradition."

"I don't see how that proves the myth isn't contagious, like being able to describe what malaria's like without having actually had to suffer from it. Except that in this case, some conman in the past, fabricated the lot when he came to after a severe blow on the head."

"If you ask me, Bernard, your own bump has strengthened your already horrible scepticism."

"Well, I'm sorry again, Bill. But that's the way I saw it, or rather, didn't see it. And anyway, why this interest in death? Don't tell me you're now extending the range of your concern to encompass the afterlife."

"Flippancy apart Bernard, it seems to me that proof of the afterlife might be of some help to those unfortunates for whom this life is sheer hell."

"Isn't that an unfortunate way to put it?"

"You know what I mean."

"Yes. So, you think it exists then? The afterlife?"

"Yes, though not that I think you necessarily need to carry a Christian ticket to get there."

"So, it's for all people?"

"I expect so."

"Umm … I can't think very highly of something that so lacks discrimination."

"But then you're a bloody elitist, Bernard, and what's more …" He smiles … "You're having me on. Glad to have you back with us anyway, whether you've been anywhere else or not!"

"Cheers. And by the way, the heavenly welcoming party …"

"Eh?"

"They were all wearing red sweaters."

*

"Your parents are here to see you, Bernard. I've asked Staff Nurse Clarke to tell them to stand outside for a moment." Sister Samworth, still annoyed with them after the official reprimand for her earlier mistaken candour, feels that the least she can do is to keep them waiting. "While I check your dressing. Turn over a second, will you? … Fine! They'll be a couple of minutes. You can tell them, by the way, that you can leave hospital the day after tomorrow, other things being equal." She no longer communicates directly with Elspeth and Harold.

In the five days since I regained consciousness, I've been slowly reintroduced to food, have been the subject of a battery of tests and further X-rays, and have reactivated my brain by asking innumerable questions about my own condition, the identity and fate of my attacker, and most importantly, the whereabouts of Liz. This interrogation is not yet the product of a perfectly clear mind. In particular, regarding the timescale of events. I discover later that

I'd re-gained consciousness just before, rather than after, Liz's ferry had sailed. Amy, untypically dishonest, had impulsively sought to take personal advantage of my initially hazy grip on reality by keeping me and Liz less than accurately informed on this. I come to reflect that perhaps she'd *also* thought it to be partly for my own good.

"Amy. I said I'd call you before I left"

"Yes. You're all ready then?"

"Well. I'm all packed. But I've no energy. Hardly slept really, needless to say. Dare I ask? ... how's Bernard?"

"He's ... umm ... "

"Why are you hesitating? Please don't say there's been a deterioration?"

"No, no. He's comfortably still stable. There's no change, Liz, none worth the mention."

"I see. Amy, you know why I have to go, don't you?"

"I think so, Liz."

"I expect I'll be back."

"I thought you didn't know that and couldn't say for certain."

"Oh, I expect I will be. Medium term. There's a lot for me to lose otherwise. I'll see you then. Look after yourself."

"Will do. You too."

It was the shortest phone conversation they'd had in years. There'd been no time for Liz to sense that although she was talking to a friend, it was to a *friend* who had now opted to foster her own interests. The final instruction to 'look after yourself' added an ironic reinforcement to what its recipient had already decided on her own behalf. When Amy shamefully told Bill the extent of her deception, whilst striving to play it down as probably unconvincing, he being Bill, and thinking her still to be what she'd always appeared to him to be, impugned no deceitful motive. He never for a moment imagined that even a hint of scheming had taken over from a lifetime of her just being consistently nice to others.

Whether I feel less deserted through thinking I was asleep rather than awake when Liz left, I can't say. In a way, it's no worse a situation than that in which I'd found myself before I was stabbed. All that are missing are the formal goodbyes and Bill has done a good PR job on Liz's behalf, getting across to me that her distraught conscience-ridden exit is, if anything, a measure of her feelings for me. Amy has said much the same thing, though not so strongly as to redraw old images on what, perhaps, she now sees as a relatively clean slate. My state of mind is thus one in which my delight at being alive is mixed with boredom at my hospitalisation, and recurring, though not persistent, invasions of melancholy over 'my' missing woman. It's this latter self-pity that my mother decides needs purging. No-one who has, on some whim or other, turned her back on both a good job and a good man is worth fretting over. I am to be prodded back to sense.

"Sister says you can go in now." Staff Nurse Clarke holds open the door for Harold and Elspeth. They walk around to the far side of my bed where there is, as yet, nobody to replace the departed Mr McDermott.

"Hello Bernard, dear." Elspeth leans across to kiss me. "You look better again today."

"Yes, I've been up and about most of the morning. They've put me back between the sheets to observe protocol for visiting."

"Just like back in Byschurch. Rules for everything!" Harold thinks it more important to amuse me than not to offend his wife.

"Too true, Dad. Remember Mum's lavatory regulations?"

"I don't know what you're both talking about. I really don't." Elspeth speaks with the indignant fear of where this reminiscence might lead.

"Oh, come off it, Mum. When you were trying to install in little me some independence in toilet going. A fifteen second flush for a wee but at least forty-five seconds for anything more substantial. That was the instruction. I used to feel that if I hung on to the chain for much longer, I'd be catapulted up into the overhead cistern."

"All right, Bernard, all right. You'd have been the first to complain if you'd have had to use an insanitary facility."

"Well, how come when I visited Gran up in the hills, I came through unscathed, because there you had to ..."

"Bernard! I don't wish to be reminded. Can't you talk about something more wholesome?"

"Okay, mother dear. I've some good news for you. They're letting me out in about two days' time, Thursday probably."

"Oh, that's marvellous. We'll have to sort out exactly what's happening. Obviously, Dad and I will stay on at your bungalow for a short while and then, well, I could stay that bit longer again, until you are completely back to normal."

"I'm not sure that's a good idea, Mum."

"What?"

"Oh, don't get me wrong! I appreciate your concern. But why not both just stay to the weekend? Clearly, they wouldn't let me out if there were any physical problem still but if you're going to sit and watch me in other ways, then you might be around a while."

"What do you mean, Bernard?"

"Mum! I can tell by your face that you've got things on your mind. Still! Look, we talked about her the other day and I'm telling you again that I can't sort myself out overnight on that score."

"But I don't understand it at all. Do you Harold? Put yourself in Bernard's shoes. Would **you** let her walk out on you with only the vaguest of suggestions that she might come back?"

"Possibly dear. Who knows? Liz is a very attractive young lady, and we must admit to Bernard here having the advantage of knowing her far better than we do. If he's willing to take a chance on a possibly fruitless wait, then that's it."

But my mother is one for rigid judgments and hers of Liz is not favourable. "I don't see it, both of you. I just don't."

"Let me work it out on my own then, Mum, eh?"

"Nobody works out anything on their own, Bernard. Nobody! Too many people today think they can. That's what's the trouble half the time. We've shut our ears not only to the voice of God, but also to any advice offered by our friends and loved ones."

"But I've friends here who can help me, mother. Just through being around, being themselves. You must know that. You've met Bill and Amy."

She sighs. "Look, even after so short an acquaintance, I know that Bill's Samaritan intentions will always exceed his ability to deliver."

"Aren't you being a bit harsh?"

"As for Amy, well, there's little to be said for a second woman interfering in problems caused by a first."

I suspect that mum might be even more worried if she were privy to a building suspicion of mine, the likelihood that any help Amy will offer me might now be via helping herself.

*

"A visitor for you Bernard."

It's George Pointer. Reluctantly, through a sense of duty, he's anxious to discover for how long he might be short-staffed.

"Hello, Bernard. I thought I'd better call in. Nasty business all this. Very nasty."

"Yes, indeed. Good of you to come, Mr Pointer."

He surrenders to the hospital heat and takes off his vicuna overcoat. He looks at me as if in disapproval of my lying on top of the bed with pyjama jacket unbuttoned to a depth which Florence Nightingale might have regarded as grossly indecent, but whose opening, in fact, descends barely half way to navel level and has failed to offend even the fastidious Sister Samworth. If George were in my place himself, he would be donned in a silk dressing gown from Noel Coward's wardrobe.

"Must have been a great shock to your parents all this?"

"Of course."

"Something of this sort of leaves a scar other than the physical." His platitudes are giving little useful prospect to our conversation.

"How are things at school, Mr Pointer?" It's a question I hate to ask.

"Fine Bernard. Fine. A very successful term so far." George knows that no headmaster jealous of his reputation dare answer otherwise to one of his hirelings. Unfortunately, he then amplifies his own commendation into a full-blown bulletin. I'm no more interested than I would have been had fate not deprived me of the excitement of being there myself. At work, I seem to have a peculiar talent – in an environment where all are supposed to be pulling together – to be able to operate as an independent entity, unaware of the to-ings and fro-ings of my colleagues. It's always been my approach to the job.

Inevitably, George's report ends with the enquiry as to when Steynmouth High School, despite what has clearly been its best term to date, might expect my return.

"Oh soon, I expect."

"We needn't make a temporary arrangement to engage a supply teacher then, for the rest of term?"

"I don't expect so, Mr Pointer."

"Good, good. In which case, I'll simply maintain the day to day cover for your classes for the time being. But obviously, the sooner you're back the better. All this tends to impact unfairly upon those members of staff whose timetables happen to dovetail with yours. Warren Metcalfe, for instance, has lost most of his free periods. Added to which, of course, he's an historian, so poor chap, he knows his way through time but not through an atlas. Perhaps, if you're not going to be back for a week or two, you might send some work for him to set to your younger pupils. As for those in the public examination year, well you'll obviously have to make up for lost ground with them yourself. Fine, fine. Well, look after yourself then. And we hope to see you back soon. The staff send their best wishes of course."

"Thank them for me, will you? Goodbye, Mr Pointer."

"Goodbye, Bernard."

Soon it will be 'welcome back, Mr Davies.' Surnames are his norm.

He picks up his coat, turns to leave but after two steps finds his leather-brogued feet entangled in the grubby coil of Mr Smith's bandages. His disdainfully shakes his legs, one after the other, but this proves insufficient to free them from the liana-like grip of the offending objects. He thrusts angrily into his pockets, bringing out a pair of tan kid gloves whose shield he's always thought of as a protection against the English winter, but which now have to be unwelcomely employed as a barrier against whatever ugly collection of bacteria the old farmer has infused into his lint and muslin wrappings.

George Pointer hasn't been the only unexpected visitor I've received. There's been an equal, if not greater, surprise.

"Oh, I didn't tell you did I, that Sarah of all people called in yesterday."

"Sarah?" Amy looks dumbfounded.

"Yes, Sarah. Actually, I felt quite humble after she'd gone. A bit guilty that I'd maybe been a bit short with her in the past. After all, she doesn't owe me a favour of any sort. It was a genuine hundred percent gesture."

"How is she? I haven't seen her since we caught her in mid-library-round over at Titherley."

"Well, she is just so much different. I suppose that must say something about Warren. Funny, she seemed not only brighter, happier, but physically bigger. All down to having confidence in herself, I suspect. Less of a china-doll, more of a dark-haired gypsy. She told me more about how Clive had behaved before he was discharged to do his dirty work."

"Any startling revelations?"

"No, not really. Not startling if you know Clive! For instance, he'd asked her to obtain a copy of some Ed McBain novel – apparently, he's into detective yarns - and when she went to his ward to deliver it, she inadvertently stumbled across a confrontation between him and Davidson."

"Confrontation?"

"Well a consultation that got of hand, it seems. Anyway, seems like Clive found out that our Scottish friend liked Marlene Dietrich, and he invited him to join in an impromptu sing song of some of her, I presume, better known stuff. But my guess is that Davidson had faked it to keep waters calm, because it turned out that he knew nothing other than the opening words of a few English versions. Clive went positively berserk, and they ended up in a heap on the floor."

"Wow, heavy stuff. No wonder Davidson wanted him out in a hurry. Hey, just thinking for moment, you don't suppose the Ed McBain thing might have been preparatory reading for what he had in mind for you?"

"Now, there's a thought. But no! I mean, if it were to do with escaping detection, he needn't have researched the police mind so thoroughly. Hilda Livermore would never cut the mustard in the eighty-seventh precinct!"

"I guess not, though I've never met her."

"You don't need to have met her. How could any aspiring super-sleuth be called Hilda?"

Amy laughs. My mind goes way back to sitting in the garden at Warren and Sarah's fourth of July party, where she had hinted that I was the most pleasurable company of anyone she had ever met. I think she assumes that no filter is ever activated before I speak to her, that she always hears *me*, and not just words carefully selected for her ears. So perhaps, feeling the need to be equally open with me, she quickly gets rid of her smile and tells me in a matter-of-fact voice about the postcard from Liz.

"Here. It came this morning. She asks for news of you. I guess she thought it wasn't worth her writing directly to someone who might still have been unconscious."

I feel suddenly as if my recovery has been halted or even taken a step backwards. I have lost the laughter that accompanied the recalling of Clive's ill-fated German language duet. I cast a mere glance at the photograph of Rhineland hill country, and then turn the card over to peer nervously at its tightly cramped message. Full of holiday speak, except for the enquiry about me, and the provision of an address at which she would be available for the next ten days. "Did we both ought to write? Separately that is."

"I … don't know. I mean the card is to me. Why don't you let me write to her – I'll do it straight away – letting her know what's happened and then she can contact you directly as she wishes."

"But … it'll be pretty damn obvious that I've now got the address myself and haven't written."

"Which isn't half the insult of her not being here in person in the first instance!"

"Amy?"

"Oh, I'm sorry. Look, forgive the bitchiness a minute and ask yourself whether you wouldn't prefer not to be the one who has to break some very awkward ice."

"I take your point … in a way."

"Come on. There's nothing of consequence you can do at this stage. Just let her make the move. You of all people, Bernard. You don't need me to help you preserve your dignity."

"Dignity, call it what you like, often takes a back seat at times like this."

"Well, put it up front where it belongs. You need a strong will now, if only to get over all this business with Clive. It's no time to pinch out your self-regard."

"Okay, okay. I'll delay writing. But get to your part quickly."

Which she very soon does. But with a lack of enthusiasm that owes everything to two competing loyalties - her allegiance to Liz and her allegiance to herself - one of which is slowly gaining the upper hand and is soon to be presented with a glorious tactical advantage. It comes in the form of a letter from the Reverend and Mrs Keith, which Elspeth and Harold bring with them from the bungalow the morning they come to collect their son from the hospital.

"Oh, a letter for you Bernard dear. I wanted to leave it till we got you back. There's enough to sort out here as it is. But your father insisted we bring it along. You know how he is with mail. Wants to open it before it's through the letterbox."

"Okay. Thanks."

Dear Mr Davies,

My wife and I regret to inform you of our need to terminate your tenancy agreement with us. I have sadly been the subject of rapidly deteriorating health these last few months, and my congregation has kindly agreed to free me from my ministerial duties at short notice to itself. There is, of course, no insistence that we vacate the Manse in unseemly haste, but the very size of the house is a physical burden upon us, and we would therefore, wish to take up residence in our own more manageable bungalow at the earliest possible opportunity. You will recall that our initial dealings with you were of an informal nature in response to a communication which I received from your mother. As a result, we feel we are able to ask you to vacate the bungalow as soon as it is convenient to yourself. It would seem that the customary serving of one month's notice ought not to be necessary in circumstances such as these, when our need is to take possession of our own home and where no written agreement between us ever existed. We are glad to have been of help during your time here in Steynmouth. Perhaps you will contact us as soon as possible over this matter.

Yours sincerely,
Kenneth and Beatrice Keith.

"But Bernard, this is awful. What are we going to do? I mean remember the difficulty you had securing reasonable accommodation in the first instance."

"Oh, don't worry, Mother. I'll not end up on the streets."

"Perhaps, if I rang the Reverend Keith myself and told him of your injuries."

"No Mother, no. They're as good as healed anyway. What's more, it's his house when all said and done."

"Yes, I know that, Bernard, but if he were aware that you were only just leaving hospital, he might see it differently."

"No, no! If you want to contact him, then do so and tell him I'll move out the weekend after next."

"But, Bernard, that's only some ten days away. You'll be in no condition to carry stuff, surely."

"Bill can do most of the donkey work. He needs to lose weight and anyway, there's no furniture to lift. It's all just clothes and personal items. Pickfords wouldn't look at it."

"Bernard, dear – tell him, Harold – this is just silly. Just where will you go? You'll just have to come back to Byschurch for a while."

"On what pretext, Mother? I don't honestly think that even I can fight shy of work via a bogus convalescence. Look, when I first came down here, I knew nobody. Now I do know people. Perhaps someone can put me up temporarily? Either that or some out-of-season bed and breakfast place might be offering silly rates until I can find somewhere more long term."

But Elspeth doesn't like either idea. She likes the first one even less two days later, when she's told of Amy's offer. And even less, again when told of my acceptance.

"Harold, speak to him about it!"

"Bernard, your mother's none too happy at all this. I presume you know that."

"How could I fail not to?"

"There's nothing you could do to settle her mind?"

"How do *you* feel, Dad? I mean, are both of you wielding the stick?"

"Not me, Bernard, you know that. I'm happy enough about it … providing …"

"Providing what?"

"Well, providing you're not getting yourself into deeper water than you can cope with. I mean it's true to say, isn't it, that Amy's been no more than what, to coin a much over-used phrase, might be called a *good-friend*?"

"Basically, yes. Which mum perhaps ought to see as making it a not unreasonable move?"

"Bernard, I think she has some fear or other that you've been stringing Amy along when, against what ought to be your better judgement, you're really keen on Liz."

"I don't really want to talk about it, Dad. At the end of the day, she just doesn't approve of her unmarried son moving in with someone's else's unmarried daughter, whether there's a third party in the mix or not. I don't think I could say anything to reassure her that wouldn't cause her to blush."

"Okay, okay. I'll leave it with you."

But with little hope of me saying anything, dad knows that I'm right, and that all that can be hoped for is that he, as understanding husband, can divert mum's mental attentions to other matters. Reassurance is not on. Come the weekend, she returns to Byschurch in a frame of mind hardly less troubled than that, in which I presume, she had made the journey to Steynmouth.

*

This isn't really a proper moving day. By contrast, when I was eight years old, I experienced the real thing as the Davies household shifted across town to somewhere slightly more up-market. I gazed wide-eyed at the high-sided van into which my whole world was being lifted, pushed, trundled.

"They won't forget my bike, will they, Dad?"

'They' were the men employed by 'BIGGINS OF BYSCHURCH' - whose wordy slogan, proudly boasted in Gothic script along the length of the pantechnicon, was…

"No job too large. No distance too small. No job too tiny. No distance too …"

The ending to the last line was faded beyond recognition, if it was ever there at all. And for years afterwards, I racked my brains trying to find a word which would help convey great distance in an appropriate rhyme. Every Biggins lorry I saw was similarly incomplete in its message. Not until the age of fifteen, did I notice that the same registration number was present on each one which explained why I'd never seen Biggins in convoy. The firm was not the large multi-national that an eight-year-old had imagined.

Vacating the Reverend and Mrs Keith's bungalow is an altogether more-humble affair and fortunately so, with Bill as both foreman and labourer for the day.

"You've got a lot of junk here, Bernard."

"Junk?"

"Well, stuff you hardly ever use, I bet."

"That's a bloody strange definition of junk. I don't suppose Archimedes used his bath very often, but it provided a useful insight when he flopped in it for a scrub."

"Sorry, you've lost me, Bernard."

"Displacement."

"Eh?"

"Oh, sod it. Look what have we done so far?"

Bill looks in along the length of the transit that we've borrowed from Amy. 'Quayside Crafts' has a more cultured air about it than did 'Biggins'. The floor is littered with tiny fragments of wicker. At the far end, tight up against the seats, are the few things that Bill has put in during the hour and a half he's already been at work. So far, mainly books, stationary, records and a few items of crockery, all of which Amy helped pack into cardboard apple boxes yesterday evening.

"You know, it's a bloody shame, Bernard"

"What is?"

"Well, look at these boxes. All these French apples. Even the cider makers in these parts are fetching them in from Normandy nowadays. I mean, talk about giant pandas and all that, but there's no more endangered species than the good old English Cox if you ask me."

"I wasn't!"

"No, but that's just it. Who does? Somebody ought to say something, that's for sure. There's no way apples can speak for themselves."

"Oh, please tell me I'm not in at the birth of one of your campaigns. Bail out the Bramley!"

"No, not really. Just a bit of mental wandering that's all."

"Okay, but at the risk of appearing ungrateful, how about some physical effort around here? I reckon I could make more progress, even with my injured back."

"Look, if you want to jeopardise the well-being of your scar tissue, just go ahead. Otherwise, you'll have to accept my pace of working!"

Our well-humoured dialogue has no effect in accelerating Bill's progress.

"It's like this you see, Bernard. Careful loading and two trips might do it. Throw things in anyhow, and you end up having to drive back and to more often."

By the time he has done his bit, there's hardly a cubic centimetre of unfilled space in the van. One trip will do it. His solid frame has worked up a healthy sweat, despite the leisureliness of his efforts and the cooling effect of his repeatedly walking outdoors from in. His woollen sleeves are rolled up above his elbows, faithful evidence of his contribution to the day's work. Were it not for the fact that I've been hard done by of late, perhaps I might have felt guilty at callously witnessing a one-man operation carried out so cheerfully on my behalf.

"At least, let me drive, Bill."

"No, no. I won't hear of it. If you're not yet fit enough to return to work Monday – merely to lift up a piece of chalk or whatever it is, you do – then you'll not want to be tugging at this steering wheel. Sit back and relax. Let's hope Amy's got the kettle on."

Actually, I'm no longer as physically delicate as I've allowed Bill to imagine. Maybe I've been deceitful, or maybe it's just been a charitable way of letting him enjoy being charitable. But it's not to be a deception to be placed before Amy. So, I lend Bill a hand when we reach her place. Her resulting belief that her new house guest is no more the fragile occupant of a hospital bed will have a very early consequence upon the nature of our relationship. Some three days into my stay, neither of us will feel at all inhibited by whatever legacy has been bequeathed to my constitution by the descent of Clive's malicious bladed hand. Afterwards, my back will ache a little.

*

Bill carries the first of the boxes upstairs. It's as large and as heavy as he can manage. Entering the lounge, he relaxes his grip, simultaneously crouching on one knee, and then capsizes to the floor, along with his load. Books, his shirt and his vest all spill out.

"Where do you want this?"

"I feel it isn't really for me to say. "Umm ... I don't know ... Amy?"

"Oh, I think if we just get everything up here. Stack it neatly for now. Then we can come to some sort of better arrangement later."

"Okay." Bill wheezes a reply which suggests a total lack of enthusiasm for what is left of his carrying duties.

"Don't fret, Bill. Amy and I can fetch up the lighter stuff."

His approach to the re-stationing of my possessions becomes more piecemeal as the time ticks by. Early, red-faced struggles with full boxes, eventually give way to easy handfuls of books and records pirated from their cardboard moving quarters.

I fetch up a light weekend case which I know somewhere, contains the night's toothpaste and pyjamas. "This can't just be put aside for future reference, I'm afraid. Through here?" I wave it towards the spare bedroom. Bill shuffles his feet. Amy nods in confirmation, "I've not made up the bed yet. I presume you've brought your own sheets etc?"

"Ah hah! Yes, but where will they be?"

"Oh well, we'll find them later. Actually, it's interesting watching people unpack their belongings. Material things are a good guide to the person who acquired them. They sort of set out your character before you."

Bill looks a little disconsolate at this, or maybe just plain tired. "They wouldn't tell you much about me. Two or three drawers worth and that would be it."

"Exactly. Perhaps that would be it. Little to display, little to convey!" I toss across a smile to accompany the remark.

"Oh, bugger you, Bernard. Look, there's just one more sodding bag of your stuff down there. Now do you want me to fetch it or not? … Fine … Okay. Well make yourself useful and get the kettle back on or something." His laugh gives him the necessary resolve to complete his task for the day, and he hurries off downstairs.

I sink into the soft sofa, move sideways as a Swiss Cheese plant plays at my right ear. Amy kneels on the centre rug, circular, Indian and faces me.

"Welcome!" She sounds almost triumphant.

"Thanks."

"Look, I can't leave the shop much longer. There've been no customers during this all walking in and out admittedly, but in theory, I'm open for another forty-five minutes yet. When Bill comes back up, help yourselves to tea. Oh, and let's invite him to stay for his dinner this evening. I've prepared enough for three."

"Wow. Heaven!"

She stretches sideways and drags a large green damask-covered floor cushion towards her, hoists it up two handed above her head and lobs it at me. "Listen! Apart from today, until you're back at work, I shop-keep and *you* cook. After that, it'll be fifty-fifty in the kitchen."

I push the cushion away from where it's fallen on to my lap. "What? You mean I do domestic chores *and* pay rent?"

"Sure, I do. And anyway, what's so different between that and what you did back at the bungalow? Except that here, you've someone to share dishcloth duty with you."

"Yeh, it's not a bad deal, I agree."

Bill returns to find us both laughing, and I think feels himself an intruder into a burgeoning private world. The final box seems like his only legitimate passport to entry.

"Tell you what, I'll just dump this, then be off."

"Hey, steady on Bill. What about tea for two?"

"Yeh, you two obviously."

"No. You and me, mate. Amy's about to return to her commercial role downstairs."

"Well, yes, okay."

Amy stands up. "After all, Bill, you've deserved it, and stay on for dinner too."

"True. I reckon I deserve it big-time!" He is swamped by self-congratulation.

*

"That was a great meal, Amy. Too much of this Bernard, and you'll end up my shape." Bill gives his well-satisfied stomach a resounding thump. "Does the hostess have any cheese for us to nibble?"

"By the ounce or by the pound?"

"Well, bring a selection, eh?"

"There is no selection, damn you. You know, I'm sure there's a medical label for your condition. Anorexia at your expense, gluttony at mine."

"What do you mean? I do eat when I'm on my own, you know."

"Eat, yes. Put the world food supply in jeopardy, no."

"Oh come, come. Just the occasional lapse towards a hearty English breakfast. Probably nothing compared with all that sauerkraut and strudel that Liz is having shovelled down her." He bloats his cheeks, hamster-like. With Bill, remarks are often accompanied by a vaguely appropriate and grossly exaggerated physical gesture. "By the way, have you heard from her yet, Amy?"

"You've had too much to drink, Bill. I'll be less generous with the wine in future."

"What do you mean?" He's at a loss to understand her annoyance. If he's here – playing gooseberry to the new flat mates – then why should the mere mention of someone else be so unwelcome? There's really no need to accuse him of over-indulgence or of an inability to think straight. Though knowing, as he does, the extent of Amy's deception at the time of Liz's departure, he might under more sober circumstances be more tactful, simply ask for news when Bernard *is* out of earshot. But Amy's accusation fails to make his error of judgement clear to him. He is drunk.

"C'mon Amy. Not so evasive. It's you who needs *more* wine, not me *less*. To loosen your tongue. C'mon. Has she written to you? Good old Liz."

She looks at me and I raise interested eyebrows.

"I … I … Yes! In fact, I had a letter this morning. I was going to mention it later."

I lean forward. Place both elbows on the table. "Well now's as good a time as any!"

"Not so!" She stares into Bill's glazed eyes. "But since the request's been made! She's still in Germany with her friend Erica. Funny thing, she's been waylaid by old Le Bryce. He's there in his mayoral capacity, on some town twinning jaunt apparently, all at the ratepayers' expense. Needless to say, the old ram is without his wife again. Official business and all that. I gather he regarded Liz as a likely cure for his 'homesickness'. Sleazy or what?"

Bill scratches his head. "She's not obliged?"

"Don't be silly!"

"Well, who knows? All that Rhenish wine, and discretion disappears. Some people just can't handle alcohol."

I tap my dessert spoon against my glass. "Look, at the risk of being boorish and all that … well, does she mention me?"

"Of course. Only …"

"Only what?"

"Well, it would seem my letter to her, about your recovery, has crossed her letter to me on the way. The postmark on hers more or less confirms it."

"So, she asks how I am then? She still thinks I'm lying there like Snow White."

"Yes."

"Anything else about … well, you know?"

"For Christ's sake, Bernard! You can read the damn thing for yourself. Why don't you two just clear off to the pub before closing time? Pour over what she has to say away from me." She pushes back her chair angrily, stands up and leans sideways to grab the envelope off the top of the bookcase, then flings it into the only partly vacated trifle bowl. "Anything else?"

"Yes, the cheese please." Bill opens the palm of his hand across the table and offers me first look at what Liz has had to say to neither of us.

*

"Hey, I'm sorry about yesterday evening. About my tantrum."

"Weak on memory, as well as short on temper?"

"What?"

"You apologised last night, remember? I'm not expecting some sort of daily penance."

"Okay, but well, Bill shouldn't have got my goat up in the first place."

"He didn't mean to be awkward."

"I know, and thanks for not going to the pub!"

"Oh, Bill's not the sort to take offence, let alone act on it."

"And you?"

"Nothing to be offended about really."

"Are you sure?"

"Yeh, I'm sure of that anyway."

"You can be sure of something else too."

"Go on."

"My New Year's resolution."

"Which is? A bit late for me to ask. Something else you say?"

"Perhaps 'resolve' is a better word. Smacks more of determination."

"You want me to stay here?"

"Yes."

"So, we're forgetting that Liz will soon learn that I'm back on my feet?"

"I am. Can you?"

"I don't expect so"

"Bernard. Understand that I'm now on the offensive. To do what Liz has done is incapable of proper explanation. To my mind, it deserves no loyal reward. Well, not your loyalty. Mine is different, she's a friend, past, present and future."

"You're not being very loyal now!"

"I am. To myself. Not disloyal to her. Look, can you honestly accept that she loves you? I mean, to declare her need to compare being with you to a trial period of being without you was bad enough in the first instance but then, to carry it through in the most awful of changed circumstances, that was something altogether more preposterous. At the very least, she could have waited. Was it that important to *immediately* fulfil her intentions?"

"Oh, she thinks she loves me. I'm pretty sure of it. It's just that she's got this thing about entrapment. You know her."

"I know I'd do a better job of it, Bernard. Just as exciting, but without all the anxiety."

"Really? All this is just a bit heavy, Amy."

"Yes." She takes a deep breath. "But I can switch off for now if you can. Maybe you're right. Day two of your being here, we ought to be … oh, carefree or something. I tell you what, let's eat out lunchtime, and go for a stroll afterwards."

"Only if you promise that we'll be back for your famous Sunday afternoon tea. So, a light lunch?"

"We'll be back."

*

"Bernard!" A voice comes up from the shop.

"Uh-huh?"

"Look, can you pop downstairs a minute?"

"What is it?"

"Umm, I've got to disappear on business for about thirty minutes. Could you perhaps look after the shop while I'm gone?"

"What do you normally do when this happens? Allow would-be customers to help themselves?"

"Need I say no! Summers, of course, I have some help in. But this time of year, I just shut up while I'm out. Thought maybe that on this occasion you could hold the fort. Most things have the prices marked on."

"Okay. Just so long as nobody needs advice or technical detail, or whatever."

"You'll manage."

I perch myself on a shaky, high wooden stool behind one of two glass-fronted counters that form a right angle along the rear and left-hand walls of the shop. This proves to be not the most advantageous position in which to continue reading the newspaper which I've brought down with me. Placed on the low countertop, it is too distant to be easily read without an unnatural intensity of visual concentration. Held up closer, it precludes my arms from securing balance against something more substantial than the rickety seat beneath me. The stools are being sold in self-assembly kit form. I'll not recommend them. Amy or no Amy.

I get up and put the paper aside until later. Maybe, I should acquaint myself with the merchandise? I have my back to the door when the customer enters, and I delay turning around until such time as I've replaced a miniature cider barrel on the shelf in front of me. "Just a minute. I'll be with you presently."

"You mean, in time for afternoon classes, Mr Davies?"

I swivel around to face George Pointer. "I … uh … What a surprise! Can I help you?"

It's obvious that George's main expectation is that he be proffered an explanation. The shopping mission, made in obvious ignorance of my presence, he's now relegated to being of secondary importance. Ironically, it has had about it something of the clandestine from the outset. It isn't really done for headmasters to abuse the authority vested in them by plundering part of the working day for their own secular ends. But any guilt he has, is now assuaged by the sight of an apparently healthy me executing someone else's duty at a time when others are presumably executing mine.

"Perhaps. Mr Davies, you feel you have something to say?"

"Only that you've caught me somewhere where I've been for just five minutes and shall be for only a further twenty-five. I'm not into a full day's work yet."

"What, you're a sort of peripatetic counter assistant then? Putting in the odd half hour here and there, until you feel up to that for which you are still being paid."

"Mr Pointer, sir! Putting your clumsy sarcasm to one side, let me point out that your jurisdiction over me is strictly limited. It comes to a grinding halt at the school gates, post four 'o'clock. Now, I have the appropriate medical certificates, fully valid, authenticated by someone more expert than you in appraising my fitness. Copies are, I am sure, with your secretary though I owe you nothing by way of excuses. I live here! You're more likely to find me in the lavatory than in this room. Okay? Or, if you're into voyeurism, upstairs with my woman. Not my wife you understand. Just someone as hedonistic as myself."

"That's quite a mouthful, young Bernard." The sudden change to Christian name, unless an exercise in condescension, is a mystery. My outburst can hardly have been endearing to someone who has never previously faced me on territory neutral enough to allow my antipathy to rise quite so strongly to the surface. The hospital ward maybe, but there I hadn't had the energy, nor had I been sufficiently aggravated.

George continues. "But your eruption is not something I'm surprised by. It merely puts on record what I've always suspected of you. Now, unless you're inquisitive enough to want to delve further into my opinions, then perhaps you might serve me after all."

"Delighted!" There's no cowardice in my rejection of George's implied suggestion that I confess the error of my ways. I really don't give a damn about what he thinks of me.

"In which case, I'm here to ask about your, sorry the shop's, picture framing service."

"In which case, apologies and all that, but I'm such an idiot that all I'm allowed to do is to take items from the shelves, invert them and read off the price tags."

"I see. It seems like you're destined for the bottom of the pile in more than just one avenue of life. See you back at school!"

"I can't wait."

"Not before you're ready of course." He smirks.

"No. Well a few matters to sort out first, Mr Pointer. After all, the demands of the school day are such that one can't abandon ship in mid-course – or mid-morning should I say – to run some trivial personal errand. So, don't let me keep you. I'm sure you *should* be getting back."

"A word of warning Mr Davies. You find me out, and you don't have the clout to do anything about it. I find you out and you're up the creek. Come back, as you say, but you're not going to be paddling anywhere of consequence."

"Well, in a nutshell Amy, he was telling me I might as well stick to shop-keeping."

She laughs. "You've blown your teaching career."

"Oh, I don't suppose so. I could move on. Probably with an immaculate reference."

"Don't, Bernard. Leave it for good. I mean you don't enjoy it."

"No, but I don't hate it either. Money, honey!"

"You've said all this before. But is the money really important?"

"Maybe you can afford to be a bit more casual than me about the money side of things. I think you have plenty."

"Well, enough. But I like running the shop anyway. I wouldn't find money a compensation for boredom. Anyway, you tell me that you're not paid a king's ransom."

"Yes, but looking on the bright side, I'm better off than Bill."

"Very much so. In every way! After all, I'm not offering him what I'm offering you."

"You know what Amy. You're a lot more, bloody precocious than you used to be!"

"Besides, we might make a good commercial partnership as well. I could always dispense with the regular hired help."

"Oh no! I've a poor track record. One customer, no sale."

"True. C'mon, let's go up and have lunch. One less round of toast for my master salesman."

"You mean you pay commission in bread?"

"Oh, I don't know. I can offer other inducements! But I'd have to get some advice on tax liability on that one." Which cools things down a bit. For the fountain of fiscal advice, though not currently at hand, is still casting a shadow over us. Liz might not be available over matters of P.A.Y.E., but she is threateningly present on other more vital scores. We have agreed that her last letter needs no immediate reply, in that the reply has already preceded it. It remains to be seen just what will happen when news of my recovery reaches the Rhineland.

But that evening it becomes clear that Amy has decided not to wait on what Liz might do.

*

"Are you sure you've had enough to eat, Bernard?"

"What's this, an after-after course? I thought we finished almost an hour ago."

"True. Well maybe I'm just trying to get you to drink some more."

"Really? This bottle of wine an evening touch isn't going to become a permanent thing is it? Just a welcome to the fold gesture I'd presumed."

"Yes, you're right."

"And anyway. I don't see that food is a necessary accompaniment. If you want to offer me a drink, then believe me, I can take it in free-standing form."

"Ah, but I want you to acquire both stamina *and* spirit."

"What? For Scrabble? That was the plan, wasn't it? Too cold to go out and all that."

"I've changed my mind. I'm not in an appropriate mood."

"What, not at all?" I feel relieved. The frequency with which my childhood enthusiasms in this direction were stamped upon by the uncooperative two-some of Harold and Uncle Dick had the effect of rendering me inexpert at even the simplest of board games. Besides, Amy possesses a superior vocabulary.

"No, not at all. No Scrabble. Nor anything else out of a box. I couldn't move a counter or shake dice if my life depended on it. But ..." She hesitates.

"But what?"

"I've something else in mind. Something real, not a game."

I look at her. Her hair, longer than of late, still has that cultivated imbalance which flings it across to the left side of her forehead. Now, more of a sweep than a fringe. Soft, shining, still auburn.

She speaks again. "Tell me. You're an aficionado. Is it true that professional footballers insist on wearing the same pair of socks for every game after the one in which they score a hatful? A sort of lucky charm"

"Hat trick! It could be true, I suppose."

She turns around and leaves the room. To return within minutes in the gangster suit she wore to Warren's fourth of July party.

"Amy! What the hell are you doing?"

The suit, borrowed from, but never returned to, an elderly and generous male relative, is far too big.

The trousers balloon around her hips. Held up by a pair of braces beneath the double-breasted jacket, which is unbuttoned, but which she wraps lightly around herself.

I am quickly aware of her intention and feel my pulse quicken. There's no time for any heart-searching about whether or not I want this to happen, no need to ask if this is something that ought to be thought out. Amy is in complete control.

"Remember, Bernard, remember?"

"What?"

"This suit. I wore it on the only previous occasion I ever kissed you, as opposed to putting polite lips to cheek."

"So, previous to now?"

"Yes."

"Hence, the lucky charm bit?"

"Superstition's a funny thing."

"But it seems to be working here, big time."

And her dark green eyes join her lips in a smile born mainly of relief. For this could have been an utterly humiliating venture.

I stand up and face her. She unfolds her arms. The jacket flops loosely open to announce that it, the braces, and the trousers, are all that there is to the Chicago play-acting. I stretch out my hand and pluck gently at the inch-wide elastic crossing her left breast.

"Braces! They look uncomfortable."

"Mmm. They are. They've served their purpose don't you think? Shall we dispose of them?"

I put my hands aside the base of her neck, move them sideways across her shoulders and slowly push the jacket to the floor. One brace now dangles against the outside of her right thigh. She tilts in the other direction and its partner falls away, confirming the excessive size of the trousers, out of which she excitedly steps. She puts her arms around me, hoists herself on to tiptoe and kisses me with a degree of feeling that swamps the memory of its more spur of the moment predecessor way back in Warren's garden. The kiss subsides, revitalises itself and finally finishes. She stands back and looks at me.

"Now it's you that's overdressed! Do something about it while I'm gone." She disappears to her bedroom mysteriously, returning after no great delay with the missing item of her fancy dress. Al Capone's hat on her head.

I stand before her as never before, look at her inquisitively and laugh. "You'll have to take that off."

She looks me up and down. Nervous and eager. She grabs the hat by its brim and casts her eyes to below my waist. "You've given me somewhere to hang it."

*

"Didn't you ought to get up? Your first customer could be knocking on the door in fifteen minutes."

"Yes, I suppose so. Only I'm enjoying lying here. Just talking."

Talking about how much more comfortable this bed is than her own, and how silly to provide greater night-time luxury for house guests rather than for herself and whether she should change rooms, or the beds should change rooms. And nodding in agreement that I must give formal notice of my intention to throw in the teaching towel, whilst suggesting nothing in its place, other than herself.

"But I can't make a *career* out of you, Amy!"

"No. Anyway, I'd resent being thought of as a substitute for work. Or even as a vocation!"

"That's the one problem." I laugh. I'm not in any mood for problems. "I'll *need* to work, and I don't see Steynmouth being the provider." Conversationally, this is also useful as a bogus problem. The real one has not been properly resolved. It was cast out overnight but is likely to find some future way back.

"Oh, forget it, Bernard. Meet that bridge etc. later."

"Yeh, yeh. Look, you though, can't postpone your immediate responsibilities. Now, are you opening up the shop, or am I?"

"Ugh, You're right. Only it's never seemed a chore before today. Kiss me again."

She leaves to dress in her own room. I shout after her.

"Amy!"

"Yes?"

"This room hopping won't do."

"Why not?"

"Stops me from watching you."

"Okay, we'll swap the beds over later."

"What about my back?"

"It seemed robust enough in the night."

"But it's protesting now."

"Malingerer."

"Hey."

"What?"

"It's ten past nine. I'll bring your breakfast down to you on a tray."

*

Coffee, toast, and marmalade delivered; I empty the wire letter basket on the rear of the shop door.

"Oh, thanks, I've forgotten to do that."

I toss her an electricity bill. "That's not for me."

I place the three remaining items of mail on the tray. "I've left my breakfast stuff on the table. I'll take these up and read them there. Be down for a chat in about ten to fifteen minutes. Okay?"

"Okay. Cheers for the coffee."

"My pleasure."

I wink at her and turn for the door through to the stairs. I've already finished breakfast, but to suggest otherwise is the means to excuse myself to read Liz's letter in private. I've tucked it and its German postmark between the two from Byschurch. One is from my mother, disapprovingly addressed to the Quayside Craft Centre. The other, authorship not immediately apparent, has been redirected along with Liz's from the Reverend Keith's bungalow

*

"Dear Bernard,

I've heard from Amy about your recovery. Should you see her sometime (as you're bound to) please tell her of this. I suspect my last pleading for news post-dated the dispatch of her letter to me. I feel strangely nervous in writing to you. I'm conscious of the weakness and inadequacy of a letter as a means of communication. It's as if I shall be unable to quickly remedy any remark which may be unhelpful to what I really want to convey. Which is, of course, my deepest relief and happiness at your return to health (or does 'from injury' sound better?). I felt frightened by the whole episode. It so threatened my ludicrously created pose and equilibrium that I lost the strength of mind, and indeed the loyalty, to give precedence to the unforeseen over the arranged. It was one hell of a bad moment for me to leave. I ask your forgiveness, not for my initial decision but for my inflexibility in carrying it through regardless. Germany isn't so wonderful. Especially with Councillor Le Bryce (yes!) sniffing around. I shall depart for home in a week or so. Except of course, that I permanently vacated my flat (the retention fee was too high). I trust you're still willing to upset your Reverend landlord by having me at the bungalow. Take care of yourself. I'm short on words (deliberately!), but not on sentiment. Feeling the need for you.

  Much love,
  Presumptuously,
  Liz.

*

"Dear Bernard,
Your father and I were pleased to hear you sounding so cheerful on the phone the other evening. We were glad to learn that the move went smoothly, Though I'm sure that you'll soon be able to find

somewhere more long-term (especially with your finances being less stretched than they were when you first went to Steynmouth).

Needless to say, everyone here in Byschurch has been enquiring after your health. Horrified at what happened but delighted that everything is now okay. The telephone has hardly stopped ringing, and a walk to the shops is to risk the Grand Inquisition. Philip rang, of course. He said that if there were any legal services he could offer (any consequences of the affair with Clive) then just to ask. You may, by the way, be interested to hear that one person who seemed less than anxious to enquire after you was Mrs Parry. I guess because her customary report on David's rise to prominence over in Canada couldn't be delivered so enthusiastically when I bumped into her yesterday. I've learned from another quarter that David's marriage has broken up, with custody of the children going to his wife and on top of that, he's defending a medical malpractice suit against him in the courts, with apparently little hope of success. With his much-vaunted career on the decline then, it's nice to reflect on the more settled prospects ahead of you in teaching.

Home news is, as ever, not really news. You father has been doing some late winter tidying up in the garden. 'Dead heading' ready for the Spring burst into life. I've been busy with choir practice for an Easter production at church. Hope you'll visit us as soon as possible. Give me some baking to do.

Do take care, physically until you're fully back to strength. And on other matters, do try to keep on an even a keel as possible,

Love,
Mum and Dad.

*

"Dear Bernard,

It wasn't until the return home of your parents that I learned of the terrible turn of events regarding your 'accident' and hospitalisation. Fortunately, I suffered none of the delay in waiting for you to recover that must have so worried those down there with you. Even so, the extent of my distress was such that I occupied a sort of nightmare world of fear (for you!) for days afterwards, and not until now have I been able to put pen to paper *relatively* dispassionately on this issue. I say 'on this issue' because I need too to talk to you, not at all dispassionately, about how I have been since I last saw you. Indeed, the selfishness of me wanting to do so at a time when your own fortunes were so vitally menaced was another reason why I delayed writing and why, even now, I'll postpone my own self-centredness for a further paragraph or two.

I expect your emotions are still in a mess over what happened to you. Relief at still being alive. Perhaps even a crisis of confidence over 'why me?' Anger. Or maybe just an awful numbness of feeling. I can't imagine what my own reaction would have been. But I know your ability to come through, not unscathed, for that would be to insult your sensitivity (of which I have sometimes been the beneficiary), but not so wounded as a person to lose those qualities which others, myself included, have always found so attractive and endearing.

I suppose it is this latter declaration of mine that forbids me filling further paper before I return to that which I hinted at above. Silly to idly chat about 'nothing' (sorry, wrong word) when what I really want to mention is Philip. And me. But not now at the length I might have done before hearing the terrible recent news about you. It seems almost despicable to elevate my problems alongside yours. At least my life, as such, has never been under threat. Forgive me then. But in a nutshell, things are worse. I can't see me solving them. I could arrange for Aunt Megan to have had a relapse. Could you play her part again, do you think? Or, even if not, please reply in such a manner as to wipe out my guilt at asking it at so inopportune a moment. And not shut the door completely,

Much love, and with apology,
Deb.

*

Amy opens the door.

"Hi. Thought I'd come up for a refill."

She walks across to the coffee jug, tests it for warmth, rejects it. I'm replacing letters into envelopes.

"My my, Bernard. You're popular this morning. We'll have the postman expecting extra recompense at this rate. She senses that her remark has gone unheeded, "Nothing wrong is there? No worrying message or anything?"

"Sorry? Worrying? … no. Nothing … nothing at all really … nothing of importance." I engineer a half-smile, to which she replies more naturally, more generously.

"Amy."

"Yes?"

"You're so deliciously uncomplicated!"

"Is that a compliment? Sounds as if I could become boring". More smiles.

I fix my eyes on her.

"Never. But stay as sweet as you are!"

"Oh, God. I thought for one moment there you were going to burst into song."

Chapter 13

Unexpected Visits

Deborah pulls in to the M5 service station. Her last chance to take advantage of the full range of facilities before the motorway fizzles out beyond Exeter. The windscreen washer reservoir has exhausted itself some twenty miles back, so it's imperative that she refills it before continuing her journey. The thin drizzle and the grubby road spray would be even more of a nuisance in the fading daylight. First though, there is the opposite and greater need to empty herself. She curses the unfairness of nature, which allows men a quick pull of the zip. The rapid turnover at the Gents is in cruel contrast to the queue of women waiting for cubicle doors to open. The lock is broken, and she places her outstretched foot tight up against the door, a contortion which quite takes away the physical pleasure of her relief. At the washbasin, she mutters again. It's impossible to both press down the tap head and simultaneously extract lather from the dried-up tablet of soap, which is on offer as a temporary utility, in lieu of a vandalised dispenser of the same in liquid form. The hot air dryer subsequently scorches the rear of her left hand.

She joins the queue for coffee and yields to the temptation of a jam doughnut.

"You'll need a tray."

"Sorry?"

"A tray. Back at the end there." The young girl at the till points back along the line of twenty sullen-looking customers.

"Surely not."

"Yes, two items or more, and you'll need a tray."

"I'm sure I can manage without."

"You're causing a delay."

"I don't see how. But I would do if I were to unnecessarily walk back and fetch a tray."

"You'd have to join the back of the queue then. Can't keep all these people waiting while you push past and back again."

"Look, I can carry the cup and saucer *and* a small plate, Okay?"

"No … I mean how are you going to put sugar in your coffee with both hands full. You have to do that at the end there, before going to your table."

"So, if I had a tray, I'd have to balance it on one hand while I …"

"I'm just telling you what is expected."

"Anyway, I don't take sugar."

"Well, what about the doughnut then? It's plastered with it."

"Okay. I'll do without the doughnut!"

"You'll have to take it back then, to where you got it from."

"You're joking." Deb pushes both coffee and cake towards the middle of the counter and walks away, ignoring the protests which follow her. She joins a shorter queue at a hot drinks machine which adds sugar to her coffee in open defiance of her press-buttoned instructions. She carries the flimsy cardboard cup to an empty table and looks around her. It's an opportunity to occupy her mind with the antics of other people, irrelevant to her, but a welcome change from the claustrophobic emptiness of the car which for the last three hours, has insisted that she think about the wisdom of what she was doing and just sometimes, on how she was driving.

The cafeteria, despite the efforts of designer and decorators, seems unfinished. Girders and corrugated roof sheeting remain just that, even when painted red and yellow to brighten their exposure. The whole place has a skeletal feel about it almost as if the operators were not confident enough of commercial success to fund anything more elaborate, a sensible assumption if today's level of custom were to be typical of year-round patronage. But the March queue that she had abandoned at its head would, of course, be much longer, come the summer rush to West Country beaches.

She removes her three-quarter length mock fur jacket from her shoulders and drapes it loosely over the rear of the moulded plastic chair in which she is seated. At the next table, is an early middle-aged couple with their two children, tucking heartily and happily into hot pasties and fizzy drinks. Their presence makes her feel uncomfortable, somehow less than clean, a deserter from the wholesomeness of family life. The doubts which have nagged at her since she'd left Byschurch refuse to recede. She ought to have told Philip that this was finally the end, apart from, that is, her inevitable return to extricate her belongings and to insist on sense over the children. Instead, she's faked another visit to Aunt Megan. She ought equally to have forewarned Bernard, but he might have counselled caution and anyway, he'd not hesitated to put out a vague welcome mat in similar circumstances last time. She's tried to convince herself that all she wants is to talk to him, that Steynmouth could be just a stop-over on the way to somewhere. Unless Bernard insists otherwise, or even utters any ambiguous words that she can read as a suggestion that she might linger a while. She sips unenthusiastically at her over-sweetened coffee and doesn't welcome the intrusion of someone joining her at her table.

Neither does the intruder welcome the implication of finding her en route to Bernard.

"Deborah?" Liz's less than instant recognition stems from her lack of anticipation that the other person at the table would be someone she knows, and partly too, from the change in Deborah's appearance since they had last met. Her hair is now cut considerably shorter, and its blackness is now tempered by hazel highlights.

"Liz! I … I … sit down please, I …"

"You're as surprised as I am."

"Yes!"

"What a turn-up for the book." Liz is scared as to the extent of the coincidence. At no time since leaving Germany, has she imagined that something so potentially harmless as a motorway stop could threaten to throw her off course. "I … I'm on my way home. I've been on the continent for a while."

"Oh, I see. You look well."

"Really? Yes, well, I've been mainly in Germany, the Rhineland, but I also spent a week in

Bavaria skiing with some old friends." Thus, the unseasonal tan, complemented as always, by the flowing honey-blonde hair.

"How nice."

"Yes, I'd intended to stay away a lot longer, move around a bit, but … anyway."

It's a staccato conversation. An initial parrying, pending the first thrust towards the subject of Bernard, which doesn't arrive until after unimportant mention of the coffee and the inadequacy of the Ladies toilets.

"I … umm … assume you're on your way to Steynmouth?" Liz is finding it difficult to accept the obvious. When all said and done, the northbound carriageway has its own separate service area.

"Yes." Deb knows she's being asked why. "I thought I'd like to see how Bernard is, now that he's been out of hospital for a few weeks."

"I think you'll find he's okay." Liz feels no option but the deceitful one of implying that she'd seen this for herself before packing her suitcase and picking up her traveller's cheques. She feels some slight relief as Deb shows no sign of knowledge to the contrary. But it's not a confident relaxation. Deb's interest in Bernard's health could have been answered by letter or phone call. Just why is she here now?

The more she thinks about it, piecemeal thoughts within a conversation now veering away from Bernard towards Clive, of whom Deborah wishes to learn more, things are now unwelcomely complicated. The sad truth is that neither she nor Deb have anywhere to stay in Steynmouth other than via begging a roof over their heads. They've clearly both intended the roof to be that on top of the Reverend Keith's bungalow. One of them will have to stay with Amy instead and it will have to be her. This unhappy conclusion is forced upon her by the assumption that Deb has undoubtedly been the more thorough of the two, that she will have already forewarned Bernard of the precise second of her intended arrival. Whereas, Liz has thought it enough to simply turn up on the doorstep which in the past, Bernard has always longed for her to *cross for good*. In the end, she has no choice but to convince herself of the continuing certainty of this longing, so that, however suspicious she is of Deb's motives, she needs only to play a short waiting game. Her hand is the stronger.

"I'm staying with Amy when I get back. I'll tell her I've seen you. Maybe she'll give you a call."

"Yes. Remember me to her. Look, I expect I'll see you down there, but I really must go now. It's been a long drive. I'd almost swap places and take your seat on the coach."

"You might welcome the seat, but not the fellow passengers!"

"True. Have a good trip the rest of the way. I expect you're even more tired than I am."

"Maybe." Liz thinks not. Deb looks bloody tired.

"Ciao."

"Bye."

*

Deb catches the tail end of Steynmouth's mini rush-hour and pulls up outside the bungalow after twenty minutes of stop-start through now dark streets. She turns off the engine and lets out a deep sigh, sits motionless for a moment or so.

She rings again. The Reverend Keith might well have had the foresight to amplify the telephone but had overlooked the equivalent need for the frail doorbell. She knocks loudly at the windowpane to the lounge.

The door opens.

"I ... oh ... I'm sorry, but ..."

"Yes?" The Reverend Keith leans clumsily against the door frame. The ill-health which had occasioned his only slightly premature retirement is well in evidence.

"... Oh ... It's just that I was expecting someone else."

"I'm sorry, my dear. But you'll have to speak up."

"I was expecting someone else!"

"Mr Davies?"

"Mr Davies? ... Oh yes! Mr Davies."

"Beatrice!" The Reverend Keith turns around and shouts along the hallway to his wife. "Someone here for young Bernard Davies." He turns back ponderously to face Deborah. "We've his new address somewhere. I tend to forget these things. Beatrice will know."

"Quayside Crafts, dear. Remember!" Mrs Keith's voice echoes loudly down towards the front door. But there is no personal appearance.

"Oh yes, of course. Do you know it, my dear? He's staying with a friend. I don't know much else beyond that. Sad really that we had to ask him to leave at such short notice. Only, well, there was no other choice really. You're the first person we've had looking for him here."

"I see. So you must be the Reverend Keith? Well, thank you for the information."

"Yes. Now the retired Reverend Keith! Anyway, I hope I've been of help."

The wispy-haired ex-minister shuffles sideways in readiness for some manoeuvre within the outer porch. The loose sole of his slipper catches on the edge of a coir door mat, and he scratches his knee on the brickwork before turning disconcertingly pale. Deborah grabs his elbow.

"Mrs Keith!"

"Yes?"

"Your husband, Mrs Keith, he's taken a slight fall."

"Are you alright, Kenneth?"

And then louder. "Are you alright, Kenneth?"

"Yes, dear. Just a minor trip, thank you."

Deborah looks anxiously at him, and peers in vain for a sighting of his wife. "Are you sure you're alright? Perhaps if Mrs Keith's too busy or something … I could help you back to a chair."

"No, no dear. It's fine. I'm always doing this sort of thing. Bruises and I are the best of friends. Now what about you? Do you know your way from here?"

"Yes, thank you."

"Goodnight then." The colour has come back to his cheeks. They are now grey rather a greenish white."

"Goodnight. I'm sorry to have troubled you."

"No trouble, my dear." He pushes to the outer door behind Deborah. Makes no effort, or forgets, to close the inner one and returns to the lounge where his wife is still knitting in her wheelchair.

*

Liz struggles to get her suitcase into the bus station telephone kiosk. It's raining heavily outside. Even as she fumbles for a five-penny piece, she still hasn't decided whether her first dialling will be to Bernard or to Amy. She picks up the receiver. Nothing. She looks down to see the end of the lead waving uselessly around her knees. She curses and then hails a taxi.

"Yes, Miss?"

"Quayside Crafts, please. You know it?"

"I know the quayside."

"Well, that'll do for a start. My case?"

"Here. On the back seat, alongside you."

The cab pulls out of the bus station forecourt. Across its path a 249 suburban service bus is waiting at traffic lights. Liz glances towards it and thoughtlessly tries in vain to clear the rain-speckled window from the inside. Yet even through this patchy screen, there can be no mistake about the passenger sitting midway along the nearside of the coach. Clive! The coach pulls away. She cranes her neck to confirm what needs no confirmation. Feels her stomach lift and turn. The cab veers left in the opposite direction.

She feels her temper rise, and then recede as a tide of less definable emotions takes over. Her head starts to hum as a kaleidoscope of persons and events swirl orderlessly across her mind. Why is Clive already a member of the public again? Is he under some sort of supervision? And why should he be occupying even a small part of her thoughts right now? Everyone seems to be destroying the hitherto simplicity of her life; Deb with her quite unacceptable but presumably pre-arranged claim to doss down at the bungalow; Amy with what will be her 'nice' way of saying 'welcome back. I told you so'; and above all, Bernard with his campaign of attrition to which she has now unconditionally yielded. She begins to catalogue his appeal. In a way, he's a nobody, but at the same time, very much a somebody. Honest, but not boringly decent. Not bogus like some of his workmates (not like Warren perhaps). Confident enough, without being arrogant. Sensibly self-centred, not insensitive but not consumed by the ultimately hopeless concerns of Bill. Sharply humorous but not destructively sarcastic, not even to Clive, whose disintegration, could never be rationally, nor even partly, attributed to Bernard's irritation with him. Good company, not the twinkling conversationalist whose surface glitter soon dulls, but someone whose words are reliably variable and interesting. Probably for always, which she is now prepared to accept. It's time to lie every night alongside the tall, flaxen-haired man whose insistent presence she's finally found irresistible.

"Where exactly, miss?"

"Pardon?"

"Where do you want setting down? We're at the quay, as you asked."

"Oh, just here will do fine, thanks."

The cab reverses, turns and drives off into the night. The rain has eased slightly but remains unpleasant through being blown from the vertical by a strong wind off the sea. Liz turns up her collar to protect her left cheek. Four yards from Amy's shop is an unoccupied telephone kiosk. She slows her pace and contemplates calling ahead, No, she'll turn up unannounced. A few seconds warning would be no warning at all.

As she approaches the shop door, the window display lights go out. She looks up to see the curtains being drawn in the lounge above. The rain suddenly quickens again, and she scurries into the small open-fronted porchway to press the doorbell. It sounds a triple ding-dong. She peers through the frosted glass of the door to see a figure move towards her through light borrowed from the first floor. Two bolts are slid back noisily, and the door opens.

"Can I help you?"

"Oh, Mrs Barrett!"

"Hello? … Oh, Elizabeth dear. I didn't recognize you for a minute. What a surprise! Come in my dear." Amy's mother moves aside and shuts the door behind her caller. "Are you on your way to somewhere?"

"On my way?"

"With the suitcase."

"Oh no!" Liz manages a half smile. "I've just arrived back from holiday."

"What? Just this minute?"

"Yes."

"Really? Have you been far? It's such a long time since I last saw you. Amy's not mentioned anything."

"Germany. Visiting friends, and just taking a break."

"Well, come on up, Elizabeth dear. You look cold. I'll get you a warm drink."

"Thank you."

"You can leave your case down here. It'll be quite safe."

"Umm … I was wondering …"

But Mrs Barrett has already climbed the first six steps, taking them two at a time. A sprightly, good-looking woman in her late forties. A slightly, toned-down version of Amy, impeccably dressed in expensive trousers and an angora sweater. She has the vitality of a middle-aged woman whose problems have never been financial, who, via the gift of a business to her daughter, has no reason for family worries over the plight of her only offspring.

Liz follows her up in rather less energetic fashion.

"I'm sorry about the mess. Amy certainly hasn't inherited her tidiness from me."

"The mess?"

"You don't think so?"

"Looks fine to me, Mrs Barrett. Just one or two discarded magazines.

"Oh good! You've saved my conscience. Though I'm rather worried about a few of the house plants. Amy ought to have known better than to leave me in charge. She always said that ... "

Sorry? Is Amy not here?"

"No, my dear. Of course, you wouldn't know, would you? What a coincidence! Wouldn't surprise me if your paths haven't crossed on a Channel ferry."

Liz frowns. Puzzlement concealing worry about where she'll now sleep. "You mean she's gone abroad?" It's a query tinged with quite understandable surprise, for Amy has never been one for leaving the shop in anyone else's hands. Least of all, those of her mother whom Liz knows to have acquired wealth through marriage and not through any business acumen.

"Yes. To Paris."

"Oh, I see."

"Not before time. She never relaxes properly. I've told her not to rush back. Even I can cope with the off-season trade. Though she'd never admit it."

"I'm sorry I've missed her." Sorrow bordering on desperation. "You see, I've ..." Liz frowns again ... "I was hoping she might let me stay here for a while. Only, I gave up my last place before going to Germany."

"Well ..." Mrs Barrett smiles.

"Oh, I don't mean to impose. After all, I'd no idea that ..."

"Elizabeth dear, it's not an imposition. While there's a bed to spare you're very welcome, especially on a night like tonight. I'd hardly leave you on a wet pavement. Look, take your coat through to the spare bedroom there. In the meantime, I'll get you a cup of hot tea."

"Thank you so much, though could you make it coffee?"

"Black or white?"

"Black please. No sugar."

"No doubt you're hungry too. Why don't I get you a little something? I was just about to do the same for myself. I'll give you time to hang up a few of your things. You'll find room somewhere I imagine."

"I can see where Amy gets her generosity from! Thanks again." Liz goes down to fetch her case and carries it up and through to the bedroom. She sits down on the French-caned chair and kicks off her shoes, stands back up and flicks loose the catches of the case, picks out one or two less crease-resistant items, folds them over her left forearm and turns to the mirror fronted wardrobe. She slides the door to one side and is assailed by Bernard's clothes. She looks around in sudden panic, now seeing what she hasn't seen on first entering the room, more personal paraphernalia brought over from the Reverend Keith's bungalow.

A voice shouts through from the kitchen. "I hope you're very hungry. Seems like I over-estimated for two, let alone for myself. Super-sized pizza on the way!"

Liz's appetite has gone. She feels nauseous, flinging her dresses on to the bed. She takes a minute or two to only partly compose herself before going to join Amy's mother in the kitchen.

"Hi. That was quick. It'll be half an hour yet." Mrs Barrett hears her arrive, but doesn't look around from the flour and dough covered worktop. "Very much an improvised topping by the way, from what bit of food Amy left behind. I'll have to pay a visit to the supermarket tomorrow. Spend a bit stocking up. My own fault for insisting that they needn't hurry back. Paris for two is not to be rushed."

She answers Liz's anxious question without it being asked.

That second, the doorbell rings.

"Oh, Elizabeth, my hands are rather sticky. Could you?" She still hasn't turned to see the disaster struck face on her visitor.

Liz says nothing, simply spins around and descends the stairs.

Outside stands a hesitant Deborah.

*

Meanwhile … elsewhere … in Paris …